Air & Darkness

(Andras' MoonRiver Series)

By: Angela M Laycock

ISBN: 10: 061577105X

ISBN-13:978-0-615-77105-2

DEDICATION

To My Husband Silas for being my Rock

CONTENTS

ACKNOWLEDGMENTS

First off thank you to all my lovely fans and readers without you this would not be possible. To my husband for all his love and support along the way. To my mom for being my cheerleader. To my Aunt Sandy for being one of my biggest fans.

To my beta readers; Bear & Kay for listening and reading all of my work.

INTRODUCTION

They say the only devil you will ever meet is the one that stares back at you, when you look in the mirror. While I will agree to a point. There are things I have faced that would make you wonder what kind of a boring life the author of such a saying must have lead.

That being said:

There is darkness deeper than the ebony sea itself, there is an evil that exists within a single spark of light that can manifest into a supernova if not snuffed out upon first light. And then there is the darkness that sets into ones bones like an icy chill of an autumn day. It creeps upon you like a shadow, suffocating the air as it blankets the earth.

Like a thief in the night, it destroys what it sinks its teeth into. It is my job to make sure it is destroyed before it ever comes to be. At the crossroads, I sit like a crow on a perch sniffing the air, hunting for my next meal...

Who Am I * laughs softly* I have asked that

question myself a thousand times, my friend. Let us just start with the basics: I am a Fallen, one of the few Angels born of the Gods themselves and their halfbred children the so called Demi- Gods. You heard correctly I said Demi- Gods you know god/half human or god/half demon. That is still up for debate the answers have yet to be given. I am Immortal, ageless, powerful; yet I can bleed. I am among the lost searching for my own truth.

This is my journey: Let us begin.

Let the Darkness in....

Chapter One

~Heir Of Two Thrones~

As I stand in front of the dusty mirror in the make-shift room I call my own, I put on the last of my gear for my hunt tonight. Sighing, I stand to buckle my belt; I shouldn't be getting bored this is what I was made for; what I am meant to do. Yet for some reason I feel these butterflies dancing in my stomach. Knowing that I am searching for something more, I just can't put my finger on it.

My name is Andras' , I'm five foot seven inches tall with long raven blue black hair that comes to my waist, firm and solid piece of art that could pass for human if you didn't look at my eyes, they are a dead giveaway if you know what you are looking for. Solid steel gray orbs surrounded by a black outline. There are other give away signs but they are only seen once in a while. Like the pierce marks on my shoulders were my wings should be, or the scrollwork that comes to life across my face when the moon is full and high in the night's sky.

As I strap my anthem' to my side taking one last look in the mirror, give a slight nod to my reflection, not bad I tell myself. I almost look the part except for this feeling in the pit of my stomach that I just can't seem to shake. Gathering my courage, I gauged my image in the piece of chipped glass; Light stone washed jacket slightly wore, with two patch holes in the elbow from the last hunt I was on. A blood red corset holding my D cup breast firm and snug against my body; leather biker pants that look like a second skin hugging my hips and curves as tightly as a glove, and the bad ass spiked knee high boots that complete my hard-core outfit.

As I feel the tingle of the night air and with it my magic rising from the depths of my soul, I shake the last of the jitters from my skin. Well I say to myself and the moon as it came into view, "I guess it is time to get this party started."

Stepping out into the night air, inhaling sharply the stank of this world still gets to me. How could something so pretty have such awful smells? The moon itself slid across the blanket of the night sky, silver as ever on its Throne so high. As it came to set above my head; and with it the first of the vibration down my body, as the tattoos started to form and take shape molding to me as if I was newly formed myself. From head to toe, I had some symbol or shape etched into my skin with hellfire and silver.

Marking me for what I am, making me stronger as they forge with my magic and brought it all to the focal point in the middle of my forehead.

One of the many perks of being a Fallen.

The heels of my stiletto boots tapped out a beat on the cobble stone street as I rounded the corner. My 69 Shovelhead Motorcycle was waiting for my embrace; I could almost feel it purr to life just thinking about it. What can I say I maybe a girl, but I love the power this thing gave me and the rush of the wind slapping me in the face as I gunned it. It was better than any drug I had ever come across; almost felt like flying.

This place was still new to me, much still laid

in the shadows, lurking in the corners; I still had a lot to discover. There was time for that later; I had a thug to catch. Had to pay the bills, funny how I never thought about any of those things before coming to this place. How much I had taken for granted, was giving to me without a question as to why. A part of me still felt homesick and out of place, the other part craved the adventure and danger that this new world sought to offer. Therefore, with the last vibration of magic and ink piercing my skin like a fresh coat of armor, feeling the beat of the night course threw my veins. I sat there straddling the bike gathering my bearings before the long hunt of the night, exhaling deeply as I grabbed hold of the handlebars, and kicked the old bike into gear; listening to the engine roar as I took off down the alleyway into to the nights' embrace.

The Ghoul I was after would not wait around for me, as great as that would be. There would be bloodshed tonight; it was up to me to make sure it was not that of an Innocent's. The punishment this lowlife was going to get; would be received as soon as I got my silver cord around its scrawny throat. Racing down the cobblestone streets of the mountainside town I lived in, heading south to the city that laid in wait; I wondered to myself what other crimes this Ghoul had concealed. I only knew of the two human girls that it had drained, taking not only their souls but also the last bit of life force they had to. That was enough to make even me be on edge; yet I still wondered and questioned what other secrets were yet to be revealed.

It would all come out when the silver judgment chain wrapped around his specter form. An awesome advantage of being a fallen, the souls of those captured held no secrets from my kind, a nice perquisite to being part of a God. I had a couple leads on where this hooligan hung out, which was great, saved me hours of tracing this bastard down. Which I could do, I could step out of my physical being right into the astral and find him faster than I could if I just drove around looking for him. That would drain me fast, and I needed my energy if I was going to take this brute on. Stepping on to the astral would come as a last resort, one I didn't think I was going to have to use. Always handy to have an Ace in the hole no matter whom you're dealing with. And believe you me there is some of these monsters that even I have trouble dealing with without a helping hand. Speaking of which, were my backup? Probably off chasing, whatever hooker batted her eyes at him, just a typical man. Well If I was going into the belly of the beast, then my back up would at least know where to find me. Dialing the cell number I had, I let it reach voice mail and left a frank but pointed message. With the phone call taken care of and my plan of action laid out before me, things were starting to feel fun; this was going to be a hunt after all I might as well enjoy it. Slowing the speed of the old bike down, I took a moment to sniff the night air to see if it held any traces of the asshole I was chasing; I caught a image of a fairy some kid had spray painted on the side of the building. Oh, this is so not, what I don't need right now, a trip down memory lane when I have a lurker I'm trying to bag.

Chapter Two

As I said before I'm a fallen, I hunt the things that go bump in the night. Granted there are many things that go bumping around in the twilight; yet there are only a few that are stupid enough to break the laws that were set in place when the worlds were divided into the places they now are. It was not always like this, once we all lived together one giant world with no secrets, no fears, without anything to worry about; it was void of even the emotions we have now.

Before I was born, there was an uprising the creations took on the creators; it caused a rift in the veil of the world itself and the magic that held everything together was spread too thin. A hole formed in the heart of everything and everyone; and so like any great magic it back lashed and separated into four pieces, taking with it the world itself. With those four pieces came the four worlds we all now live among.

I grew up in what is called the Otherworld, raised among the Fey and as one of their own by the Unseelie Queen of Air and Darkness herself, and her trustworthy general 'Luke De Murdock.' Luke like the Queen herself was one of the dark Sidhe'; also know as Dark Elves.

There are two courts in Otherworld the Seelie and the Unseelie both are ruled by their own queens, they are the law, which holds the Otherworld together.

My life had been strange from the very first time I ever called the wind to do my bidding at the age of three moons. There were so many strange things and beings that I grew up around that I never thought of any of it as being off. It was just part of what made the Fae what they were. Before I became a Huntress, I played a big part in the laws and orders of the Courts of Otherworld. I was the go to girl, one of the few that traveled freely between both courts. I had power and respect maybe I was even feared a bit I really can't say. That all changed upon my eighteenth moon cycle, when I was summoned to the Throne Room of the Unseelie Queen. Luke had decided that I needed to know my past as well as what my destiny foretold. I on the other hand really was not prepared for the changes that were to come.

-Flashback-

As I climbed the marble steps to enter into the Queen of Air and Darkness' main chambers, my stomach did a flip as if it knew what lay in store for me. I took my place at the Queens feet, sitting upon a footstool made of solid gold claws and a plump crush velvet cushion; waiting for the Murdock and the news that would change my life forever.

I could not help but take in the surroundings, after all its not every day one is summoned to the inner throne room. The floor itself was a checkered board design with white and black crystal squares polished so well that you could see your image within a million different corner cuts of stone. In the center of the room stood a stone angel with broken wings sifting water threw her hands that puddled into a pool at her feet. Next to the angel was a raised dais of gold and black spider silk; sheets of the same fabric hung from gold hooks around the dais to form a curtain.

On the north wall was a glass shelf that held the last of the Sidhe artifacts, and the last of the greatest magic the Queen herself had stored. Two pillars stood guard on either side of a stained glass window of gold, silver, black and blue, the picture its self was a swan on a lake with the moonlight pouring down on her. The Queens' throne was a solid piece of obsidian stone with gold etching that seemed to move and twist as you stared at them. The throne itself was a carved dragon with eyes of red ruby stones that seemed to light up when looked upon. It was beautiful and rather spooky if you had not been accustomed to such. It was said they told the story of the worlds before they were separate, the story of the Gods themselves and the history of the Fae along with all the other sub species in the worlds we now live in today.

When the magic back lashed it caused the four divides; which in turn caused the four worlds to create casting each sub species into a new Portal world, leaving the Gods themselves alone in the heavens with only their angels to keep them company and sing their praises. The Fae were pushed into a portal world, which to those living in it is known as Otherworld, then there is the Underworld were the Undead, Day-men' (demons), Devils and Ghouls, and a few other choice monsters make their home; and last but not least you have earth were the Humans, Were's, Demi-Gods, Fallen and a couple off the radar subs live as long s they keep to the laws no one really cared that they were there or not.

As I sat there taking in the surroundings, thinking about the stories that etched their selves across the Queens' throne as if a living being. I paused; suddenly aware that I knew so little about my own origin, I knew nothing about my own history, never had I know my birth parents for that matter, I was without a past. I had never even worried about the whys and how's of it; it was as if life simply was. I never questioned my difference there were so many different types of Fae I never thought much of it. Now I was wondering. You could not even count the different types Fairy on one hand, hell it would have taken years to count them at all. Growing up among them I never sought an answer to why I looked and felt different from the other children of the court. For that, matter the very magic I had was stronger, wilder, and harder to control if I was pissed off.

Yet nothing seemed out of place.

Otherworld had a tendency to make one forget their woe's; one of the many benefits of Magic. Luke would be here soon, and with his coming would be the story of why I was lead to the inner throne room itself. If I knew now what he wanted to tell me I would have never came to this place at all....

As Luke came into the room it was if the air itself stood still in his presence; I was always fascinated with the way things would stop on a dime for him. "My Lord, what is it you thought I should know of the past and the future?" I meekly asked him from my perch at the Queens feet.

The Queen herself had taken on her statue pose as if this was as painful for her as it would be for me in the end. Luke looked at me and spoke in his voice of silk, "Child of my heart it is not I that want you to know these things, but it was brought about my dear by higher courts.' 'I'm just the messenger in this case if it was up to me; I would never speak of this to you." He began his tell letting the story unfold as if he was a grand speaker in front of a mighty crowd. I still could not believe my ears; my blood boiled so hot I felt as if I would burst threw the seams of my clothing. Never had I felt such utter betrayal! I ran from the courtroom, not able to bear another word.

Chapter Three

There are those that travel freely between all four worlds, as I have already told you; and then there are the ones I hunt. It's my job to seek out the nasty and unruly whomever they shall be, my job to punish, to judge, to deal with. Sweeping my hair back over my shoulder as I slowed the cycle down to gaze into the damp alleyway of Edwards Street, that last know hang out of the Ghoul; I finally caught a scent of the creature I was soon to face.

The Musty tang hit my nose before I was fully ready for it; with it traveled a trail of whispers in the wind. 'This way' the wind itself seemed to call. As I sat there, listening to the wind beat out its message as a shadow stepped forth from the alley as if it appeared from nothing at all. Edam stood against the building lighting a cigar, one leg propped up on the brick wall, and his kneecap exposed to the world threw his ripped denim jeans. His chocolate brown hair was in a tossed messily all over his head.

"Edam, I don't know how you do it, but you do have a way of showing up in the damnedest places." Grinning he replied, "Just a gift I have." I still didn't know enough about my sidekick, as I would have liked. I was told he was a half-breed like me. Yet Edam never really said one way or another if any of it was truth. All I knew is he had magic and power that seem to come from somewhere outside himself. Working with my own gifts that were wild and unchanging I knew what that sort of magic felt like. In the wrong hands, it meant destruction and chaos. Pushing those thoughts a side and trying to focus on what task was at hand. 'Well I know which way the Ghoul is heading; you might as well hop on; times a wasting.' I said. He stood there for a second enjoy his fine smoke, before he finally shrugged his shoulder and climbed aboard. We twisted our way through the narrow streets going about three miles, before the scent of the Ghoul stopped us in the heart of Oak Hill Memorial Park, a well know graveyard where teenagers hung out to see if they could raise a ghost from the graves around them.

Great just what I needed, a whole shit load of teenyboppers to be right in the thick of it all. I slowed the old beast of a machine down by a mausoleum with a half corroded angel standing guard next to the door. With the bike clearly hidden from view, we dismounted and started hashing out a plan of action; this was going to be trickier than first thought.

The moonlight was pouring down on the scene below, the kids were standing around a soldiers' grave, and they had black candles draped around the headstone. Chanting away, they didn't even realize the danger that was hiding in their vary mist. Stupid kids did not even have an ounce of magical blood in them.

Granted there are witches that are born from humans and due to having a forebear being of godly decent or demonic, or fae' depending on the type of magic they held. These young punks held none; they could not even sense my presents, or that of the ghoul I was chasing.

Edam suggested we walk the stone pathway around the tomb and away from the children setting up wards as we went. Not a half bad idea if I said so myself, after the wards were in place we would both go in different directions meeting in a counter clockwise direction until we reach the being point. Grabbing the bag of salt and other magical items needed for the tasks at hand, from the saddlebags, I started to recount the images I had seen in the photographs of the last victims. Most disturbing was the very last girl, as she still seemed to be trying to cling to her body even after the ghoul had finished with her. The photos had been a much needed help as well as constant reminder at just to what the hell; was I up against.

She was laid out in her bed, still in her nightgown; there were a quarter size holes, which went through her chest in a straight line making an exit point in between her shoulder blades. At first glance, it looked like a bullet hole, if it wasn't for her sunk in skin, and the fact there was ectoplasm covering the entry and exit wounds. Her eyes were hung wide in terror. I really pitied her last moments, could not even imagine what personal hell this asshole had put her threw.

The first innocent was found in the same fashion yet her surroundings were the only difference, a dark damp alleyway, it was a short cut from the little local dinner to her subdivision. Poor girls didn't even know they were being stalked.

With the wards set in place, and the salt ring to protect the naive kids from getting hurt, I started making my way back to the crypt were Edam would be waiting. Ready to hunt this foul creature down and put an end to its very existence, I started to get jumpy again; why could I not shake this feeling? It was really getting old.

It was a known fact that Ghouls could make the areas around them enchanted; giving anyone that stumbled upon them a view of something other than what they actually were doing or whom they really were. They could play on fears and create live movie screen images that they used as a trick on the poor saps dumb enough to fall for it; it was one of the ways they hunted their victims. This I knew but I was not prepared for this dirt bag to be able to play on my deep seeded fears or thoughts. I rounded the last little tombstone and ran right into the vary trap I was trying to prevent.

The ground turned to mud, it was littered with soft transparent eggs, and they were cracking, hatching, poking their alien eyes out of the thin membranes of the crust. Thousands upon thousands of snakes slithered out of the broken mess that had once been their homes. Already they were doing the thing my mind's eye had feared, they were gradually pulling back into a striking position.

How many times had this same nightmare entered into my restless sleep? In my dreams, I was always scrambling for purchase as I grabbed for anything to kill these serpents with. Which is exactly what I was doing now without even realizing it was a ploy to get me to lose my control, sending me right into the waiting arms of a monster.

As I scrambled around looking for broken bits of tombstones to crush these nasty forked tongued fiends with, killing two of the snakes before I was able to move backwards, my ankle twisted and I fell on my ass. Crab walking through the mud trying to get some distance between me and the evil worms was all my mind could think of. My back hit the vault door, looking up I saw the feet of the decomposing stone statue of the guardian of the tomb itself.

The very place I was trying to reach to begin with, in a hastened movement I slapped my shoulder into the cement door. It took all my weight to get it to move. Dust flew from the sealed off room in a choke coughing shroud. I dashed into the damp grave, breathing hard, I removed my atheme' from its cover; grabbing my penlight out of my jacket I flicked it on. It was not much use; I needed to find the old oil lamp used in these types of places fast.

The heavens only knew what I might encounter in a place such as this. Finally, I found a small crack in the structure of the room just enough of the moonlight spilled into the room to add to the light of the small flashlight; I saw an outline of an old oil lamp hanging on a hook on the wall. I inched my way toward it using the wall to brace myself as

I moved along. Reaching into the inner pocket of the jean jacket I found the book of matches I had stashed there.

Striking the head on the wall itself I light the fire stick of sulfur letting a eerie glow cast on the walls around me as I slipped the cover off the lamp and light the wick. Turning up the flame and taking it from its resting place, I gathered my courage and looked around the odd room. The coffin of whoever's tomb this was, was against the back wall on either side of it was a stone shelf one held a name marker and the other a single candlestick and a vase of dead roses. There was a small stained glass window with the scene of the Sheppard guarding his flock, yet it was caked with dust and grime so thick that no light shown threw. In the right corner of the room was an odd statue of a Goat with one of its horns broken, it had wings of a bird and the creepiest set of eyes I had ever seen on a statue. Stuck behind it was a loop of old wool and a door carved out of the stonewall itself. At first, I thought it was an escape route, since the front entry way looked as if it would stick from time to time; gingerly walking to it, I noticed that it was actually the inner labyrinth. Meaning someone was buried below the one in this room. Odd why would they bury someone above another? I had never heard of such a thing in all of my reading and history research of this place.

There was no way I was going down into the depths of the earth who the heck knew what foul thing would be hiding there. I turned to the entry way prepared to face the snakes again if I had to. One way or another I was going outside with or without creepy crawlies. As I braced my left hand against the wall, I sat the lamp down and prepared to open the heavy stone encasement.

As I got the door open, I heard a high pitched wail of a teenager, a blood churning sound that pierced threw the night like a knife. Great this is the thing I was dreading, it would be my head on the line if the Ghoul attacked someone while I was present. I ran for it, forgetting all about the snakes and headed straight to where I had last seen the kids performing their phony ritual.

One grave marker left to go I had my head down so I could gain speed, keeping a lookout from the corners of my eyes. I ran into something solid, knocking the air out of my lungs and both myself and the object onto the ground. Looking up I realized it was Edam. "Where the hell did you go?" he gasped. 'Get off me!' "What do you mean where did I go?' 'I was in the tomb, that damn Ghoul used his talents against me." I replied hotly. "Where the hell did you wander off too?' 'The plan was to meet at the crypt!' I snapped.

After all, I had just endured a nightmare while awake and my backup was nowhere to be found. We lay there on top of a crumbling marker, in the dew-wet grass staring at each other as if we were completely lost.

Another scream tore through air. There was no time for pleasantries, we had a monster to catch and punish; enough was enough. We could hash out the, what's and where's later; we needed to save those kids before there was nothing left to save. As we pulled ourselves up, I scented the air, the ghoul was close; to close for my comfort that was for sure. Two steps to the right and we would be right were the little group of hood rats were performing their guise.

The shrieking was getting worse, either the ghoul had decided to grab a quick snack to go; or something else had made its self known. Crouching behind a headstone, we stared forward to where the group was standing with their backs together as if trying to protect each other from an unseen foe.

There was nothing insight, either the ghoul was using a hallucination to scare the shit out of these children or a real ghost had just came out of a grave. I was betting on the former. Okay I can't hide forever someone would get hurt; I stood up and started toward the kids as quietly as possible. The only female in the whole group caught sight of me; her eyes were huge doe like eyes. She started to grab the cloak of the person next to her; I raised my hand in a sign of peace. It didn't matter they were scared and there was nothing that would change that. "Hey did you see a black cat come this way?"

Well shit I had to distract them somehow.

The girl seemed to blink as if she was coming back to herself; finding that she had just been scared by an apparition. 'No, I don't think so." She answered in a mouse like voice. 'Shoot I was sure she came this way." I replied. I had to keep this banter going for just a little while longer, get these kids out of the line of fire. "Well do you mind helping me look for her? She belongs to a friend of mine and if I don't find her, I'm going to be in big trouble." I tried to ask in my most needy voice I could muster.

The rest of the kids seemed to be snapping out of it also, great this was going better than I had hoped. The girl looked at the pale freckled face boy next to her, he gave a slight nod. "Sure I guess we can do that, seems like what we came for wasn't such a great idea after all." She stammered.

The hooded brood started making their way toward me; clomping their feet in the wet earth beneath them, and not caring whether or not they were stomping on a grave. Soon the whole group was insight just a few feet from where we stood.

Edam was still hunkered down behind the grave as if he was waiting for all hell to break loose; which undoubtedly he probably was. I took the time to think of a reason why he would be hiding from sight while the others walked a little closer; 'Let me just grab my boyfriend he should be done tying his shoe." I said. The young girl with the doe eyes just looked at me and nodded. I think they were still in a state of shock. Edam gathered himself up and stood. "Ok, here is the plan we will split in two groups; half of you will stay with me and the other half will go with Edam, hopefully we find the kitty before any big bad ugliest come after us.

The leader of the group finally looked up at me, "what did you say?" He asked. "Well there are things that really do go bump in the night." I told him in a matter of fact voice. "It might be helpful if we knew you names." I told the group of ragtag team of kids. "Oh sure,' the girl said, 'I'm Tracie, and this is

Rusty." She pointed to the boy that was posing as the leader of their group.

The rest of the kids spat out their names as if they were in roll call. 'Ok with that settled then let's get started." I said dusting off my pants. Edam looked at me as if I lost my mind, which at this point was probably closer than he actually knew.

"Can I speak to you a minute, Andras?" Edam said. "Uh, yes I uh guess so." I replied. "What the hell do you think you're doing?' 'We are supposed to be doing a job; not endangering innocents." He raised his voice. "Chill, big guy, I'm just trying to get them away from where the creature is lurking, if we stand around talking we will all be ensnared in its trap for sure." I pointed out. "So here is the plan, we take them to the graveyard side exit; once we convince them it's not safe; we can bag and tag this shit head and be on our merry way,' 'Deal'?

Edam nodded after a moment and then grunted the typical male agreement method. That settled, I turned to the group; it was time to get this over with. "Ok Tracie, you and two others come with me, and Rusty and the rest of you follow Edam; if we don't find her in the next couple minutes of searching we're all going home.' 'It is just not safe for us to be out this late in a graveyard none the less." They all nodded in agreement, Tracie shivered as if the cold was finally settling into her bones.

We took the two groups and started making our way toward the side exit Edam led Rusty and his ragtag gang threw the tombstones; while I gathered Tracie and the few I had to go along the low wall on the north side. After about five minutes of calling kitty kitty and getting no results I gave a dramatic sigh. Looking over at Tracie I said, "I think it is hopeless tonight why don't we head toward the other group and make our way home?" Nodding in agreement she let me lead the way to the others. The cold air swept threw the carpet of flowers and sod that covered the cemetery floor.

I wasn't ready for it to latch on to my skin and press against me as if it was a living being. Tonight was going to be hell on everyone within a fifty mile radius of this place, if we didn't bag that ghoul and do it quick. We had to get the humans to safety. Why did everything seem to get so complicated in a matter of minutes?

Tracie was following back to the others like a lost puppy; for that I was glad; left me one less person to worry about. Her groupies seem to be following suit. Now to just get them out of here and make it look as if we were leaving too. It was a great thing I was raised around the Fae'; having the ability to use the elements as a cloaking device was always handy.

As we moved past the last grave marker a sliver shadow caught my eye from the right. 'Just in time' I thought to myself. I nodded to Edam to keep up the bit for a little while longer. 'Shucks," I said; giving the whole group an exaggerated sigh. " I guess we will have to come back in the morning, its just to dark out here; I'm sure the little kitten will be fine to ruff it one night" The ragtag group of humans grunted and nodded as if they felt the same way.

Edam looked over at Rusty with stern eyes; cocked his head a little to the left and held his gaze on him like a wolf getting ready to eat a rabbit for dinner. Rusty just meekly stood there like a statue, " I suggest you all make your way home, and don't be caught out here trying to perform spells you have no business doing." Edam stated. Rusty lowered his eyes like a beaten puppy, " Uh... Yes sir, I think that is what we will do, we are truly sorry for causing any concern." Rusty's reply seemed to satisfy Edam, whom just grunted in return.

Turning my attention back on Tracie, I looked into her eyes and pulled the veil of magic around me to make sure what I was about to do would stick without raising any questions. "Tracie I think that you need to make sure to call a cab or one of your parents before you leave here. It really is not such a safe place." I put as much kindness into my voice and words as I could. She stood there a little dazed and slowly nodding her head, as her had absent mindlessly reached for her cell phone.

"Yes, I think we will take a cab home." She smiled smugly to her group of teeny bobbers like it was her idea all along. Good whatever it took to get them out of here before they become victims of something that they couldn't even imagine. As soon as Tracie snapped her pink cell phone shut I was ready with the elemental spell that would cloak Edam and I making it look like we faded into the night. All I had to do was wait for the cab to arrive; so they would truly be safer than they were now. The energy of this spell would call the Ghoul to me faster than any other trap I could set. It was a win - win as long as the brat pack was gone.

The cab arrived as if it had been parked around the corner the whole time. As soon as the kids were safely inside; I turned to Edam, "I have a way to finish this night without anymore setbacks we just have to wait until they are on their way down the drive first." Grunting and relaxing one of his shoulders he backed up to the nearest tombstone and leaned against it. It was not long before all we could see of the cab was a taillight; that was good enough for me. I let loose the elemental spell I had been holding like a stick of dynamite; it encased us in total darkness. No one except the big nasty would be able to see us; and like calling in a junkie needing a fix, he came running full hilt.

Edam had his silver blade unsheathed before the ghoul rounded the last crumbling tombstone. My silver chain of justice swinging loosely at my hip as I prepared for impact; knowing full well that it would be drawn to me like a bolt of lighting. It seemed as if for a split second everything slowed down. I had the chain swinging in a full circle; I could hear the wind whistle with the wide arc I was making.

The Ghoul came within arms length as I let it fly out with an audible crack. It wrapped around the ghoul with a loud pop. Edam stood over the struggling form as if he was a knight guarding his king's treasure. Smoke sizzled up from were the chain had embedded itself into the flesh of the nasty gray slug. My eyes rolled back and I was able to see all of the deeds done and those still yet to come; or what would have come if he had been allowed to run muck. It hit me with such a force I almost dropped the silver cord. How so much pain could be brought on by a single action?

I felt as if I was watching a bad movie screen reel. The images were muddled and seem to run together like oil paint on a summer day. There was one image I could not make out, it was as if it was cloaked by magic; the answer to it I would have to beat out of him. I turned to the ghoul, Silver chain in hand, my eyes gleaming red I spoke to the figure before me, "With the judgment chain still wrapped around your neck; you cannot lie to me. I want to know, who this cloaked man is; and why he ordered you to kill these women!' 'You will answer my question, as justice calls forth you will tell me for you have been judged as my duty as a fallen." Edam looked up at me with a puzzled expression he had seen me in action before, but I had never failed to see image before. I could not let him know that it was magically blocked.

To show weakness in front of the ghoul; it would be like feeding an addict their drug of choice. This is something I would have to discuss with my partner later; Right now, I needed to know why this asshole was ordered to kill innocent woman and by whom.

The ghoul stared at me; with hollow eyes, shaking as if trying to resist the command I gave him, slowly raising his head to bark his reply. "The one that hired me has not a name you could ever summon him by; he is not of this realm and sits on high." 'Yet know that he is the one by which all silver light comes, and in the end death is sweeter than his embrace." "I do not know what you are to make of that mumbling fool, or who he is speaking of." Edam stated glaring at the makeshift form of the specter I was holding hostage.

I knew without a doubt who that the creature was speaking of; yet it could not be truth. If it was not for the chain of silver around his neck I would have not believed a word of what it had uttered.

"Open the portal and be done with him; now Edam!" I shook with shock of what it had just foretold. There was a sizzle as the portal came into being. The magic that Edam held still amazed me to no end.

Gathering the supplies and removing all traces of what had just took place; I thought about what the creature had revealed. It just could not be whom he spoke of; it was hard to imagine a light fey being able to control a league of darkness; let alone unleashing it upon innocent beings. Whatever was going on here was much bigger than I first thought. No wonder I got this feeling of unease from the very beginning of this assignment.

"Edam; I think that I know whom the ghoul was talking about, yet what he purposed is not easy to wrap my head around.' 'There has to be more to this all than meets the eye." Grunting and nodding that he heard what I was saying; Edam took another quick look over the graveyard to make sure that all the magic had been cleaned up. "So what is it you are telling me Andras?' 'Are we still on this case, or has it come to an end?" " I think that we are still on the case, we may have dealt with one big nasty but I feel there is more to come if we don't find the one sending them in the first place." I stated grimly. "The only way

I know to get this done is to go to Otherworld in search of the Seer; and to seek clues to the where a bouts of the Lord of Light."

"Do what?" "You can't be serious; do you really believe that is who is behind this?" Edam declared. "No, I don't really know what to believe.' 'But I only know of one so called being that has ever been talked about as the source of Light." I replied in earnest. "I know that the chain of silver wrapped around the ghouls neck would make him tell the truth as he knew it." "So that being said it leads me to believe that someone is using an illusion to look like the Lord of Light or well, the other possibility is just took much too even speak of." "Don't you think?" I replied. "So what now boss?" asked Edam. "Can you open a portal to otherworld?' Get us there so we can start our hunt; this might take a while." He nodded his head as the air sizzled and a blue wall of light formed in the middle of the cobblestone street. It always made me sick to travel threw a portal; the coming apart and back together again always did me in. Yet it was the only way to travel between the worlds. I was willing to feel a little sea sick if it meant solving this case and keeping other innocents from dieing.

On the other side of the portal the field was a deep emerald green as if it had been dipped in paint. The cobble stone street was made of rich purple and blue flat stones that looked as if water had rubbed them to a high sheen. The colors were always so much brighter; the air hung heavy with the magic that was Otherworld its self. The dangers that were present were always more than what meet the eye. Yet this odd place felt like coming home to me.

The snowcapped mountain peaks were raising in the distance, the sky was streaked with an array of colors that would shame any sunset ever seen on Earth itself. I could make out the outline of the castle of the Queen of Air and Darkness, my former employer, and mother figure. Well at least we had arrived in part of Fey that was easiest for me to get answers.

Although, I was not really looking forward to

the reunion if I could help it any. Time moved different here than it did on any other plane; a minute could actually be a day. "Well Edam, are you ready to hike to find the Seer? We have a little journey ahead of us." I had to nudge him to get him to move onto the cobblestone path, as he was staring at everything as if he had never been to Otherworld before. "Edam, you have been to Fey before having you?" I asked. "Not in a very long time" He replied. "Well that makes two of us, come on time is getting away from us; and if I know the Seer we will have to hunt to find her." "She likes to hide in plain sight." I said smiling to myself. We walked onto the street; the blue and purple stones seem to hum with vibrations of magic; as if they recognized us and were spreading the news. On we trucked until we rounded a corner of gold spun wheat; in the middle of the field was a small thatch cottage with a weeping willow tree. I knew as soon as we seen it that the Seer had been waiting on us longer than we had been searching for her.

Prodding Edam with my elbow I pointed to the red smoke coming from the chimney of the little house.

"This is it." I whispered.

Chapter Four

The house itself would remind you of the story book version of the gingerbread house; well at least on the outside it would. The inside was a whole different matter as it would change with the Seer's mood. Magically altered, and colored just as a mood ring. You might find a cozy little cottage setting or it could be as dark as a mid-evil theme. One could never be certain until stepping inside.

Knocking thrice upon the door as is custom in the land of Fey; which I did as I waited patiently for the Seer to appear. It was time to get the truth for which we had come for. Yet, just as asking a question would only get it answered in a truthful manner, you had to ask three fold before you would get the direct Truth. Its also the only way to ask a fey; three times the same way and the same question would causes them great pain, but desperate times call for more dire means. We needed these answers as fast as possible so no more innocents would lose their lives due to the master game that was being played.

Just like in chess we needed to be four steps ahead of our rival or we would fail. That was not an option in my book. Failing was not something I did with grace.

The light from a candle flickered from the cookie cutter window, the curtains drew back just a crack; I had a feeling of being watched from the dark folds of the window were no shape appeared.

"Spooky"... I thought out loud, never having to face the Seer until now; it caught me off guard just a tad. This was not someone I would want to piss off; she had connections to the Fates. If what she could do with the inside of her home was any prediction of what she could do with the magic she possessed then I wanted to stay on her good side.

"Damn Edam, Maybe I should have changed clothing before we came hopping over here." I joked nervously. "Ha, Andras' not even clothing would make me feel comfortable at this moment." He replied matter of fact like; looking down at his own attire which by any standards was not the best.

The door opened; I had to blink twice before what my eyes seen could register with my brain. The Seer stood before us a mere child with gray silver hair sweeping in big curls down her back. The deepest sapphire eyes were set in an olive completion heart shaped face.

I knew that the fey did not age as Humans did but this was not what I was expecting a two thousand year old woman to look like. If only I looked half as good when I came to be that age. Snap out of it Andras, I mentally slapped myself, joking would not save your hide here in this realm; it would more than likely get you killed.

The Seer stood in the doorway blinking her eyes as if the mere sight of me was a shock to her; which I knew was a act of old, but I played along. "Well this is such a pleasant surprise." cooed the Seer. "Excuse us, mama' for not calling ahead, but we are in dire need of your aid." Replied Edam as he bowed at the waist. I on the other hand was shell shocked that he was so formal when he had never produced such behavior before. This man was truly full of mysteries. Smiling to myself I made a mental note to probe a little deeper into Edam's background when we were threw with this investigation.

"May we come in and speak with you in private?" I ask. "We are rather in a hurry and I fear if we dally much we will loose the lead on the suspect we are after." I put that in just so she understands that the tricks she would normally play are not going to get her anywhere today.

"Well by all means; come in my child." The Seer said with a smirk of satisfaction on her face. Apparently she liked the fact that I had done my homework. We step across the threshold of her small cottage and into a world of medieval art work right out of your favor fable about dragons and the like. I mean seriously, snuggled up by the fireplace was a baby dragon in all of its glory with silver and purple scales covering its body and two beautiful silver horn knobs sticking out of its little head. The way the flames played with the colors of its scales was rather hypnotizing.

Next to the dragon was a claw back chair with a crush red velvet cushion footstool. The curtains on the windows were the same velvet that the chair and the footstool were fabricated in with silver cords to hold them in place. There were three chalices sitting on a serving tray with a gold goblet of elderberry wine and a little saucer of finger sandwiches. As if she had truly been waiting on us, or a more formal party of which we were not aware of.

On the other side of the room was an elegant settee; where the Seer motioned us to take a seat, as she made herself comfortable in front of the fireplace. Behind the couch was a painting of the Seer'; sitting under a willow tree alight with yellow butterflies. This dramatic play of space was really pretty if you had time to observe; which we didn't. She picked up the serving tray as if she was having a tea party with old friends and passed it to us. This charade will go one forever if I don't just open my mouth and ask her the question I came to ask. Edam on the other hand is playing right into her hand as if he has somehow forgotten why we had come in the first place. I nudge him after he took his first sip from the flute of wine.

Clearing my throat I look up at the Seer; still a little dumbstruck at the way she looks, I am finding it hard to focus. Maybe she is using some sort of magic to make this seem so much more lucid. "Seer, I have came seeking answers to a puzzle of sorts, I think you maybe one of the only ones to help me with the questions I have."

She sits up straight and stares at me with those eyes that seem to be swimming in the deepest ocean of blue at the moment. "Spit it out child, I haven't all night to dance around the subject." She replies.

Okay so this broad wants to play hardball. Humph; well I guess if that's the way she wants it then so be it. "I want to know who sent the ghoul after innocents and what the Lord of Light has to do with it." 'Just so I know that you have understood my question I will repeat myself,' I say with contempt. "I want to know who sent the ghoul after innocents and what the Lord of Light has to do with it." 'And again I will ask you this so I know that the truth is all I will receive.' "I want to know who sent the ghoul after innocents and what the Lord of Light has to do with it."

The Seer caught her breath and held her frail looking hand over her heart. Gasping, she looks right at me; I swear her features were swimming, as if she is transforming right in front of us. "You may call me Scarlet, which is my name as far as I can remember; I will answer your question with utter honesty as a fey can not lie. Since you used the thrice rule I have no choice but give you the whole truth no matter how it pains me. With that, Scarlet bent down and picked up the baby dragon as if he was a puppy.

Placing him on her lap she begins to pet him as she tells me what I have come to hear. "The Ghoul was sent by an imposter posing as the Lord of Light, the man you seek is a God that has lost his way.' 'The Lord of Light is aware of the poser; and is the one that asked your employer to send you to hunt the criminal down." I'm taking back a bit at that bit of knowledge. Who would have thought that the Lord of Light actually thought me trustworthy to clear his name? Scarlet continues to spill her guts, "This hurts me as much as it will soon hurt you my child; for the God you seek for these crimes is none other than you father."

I can not believe my ears she could not have just said that; yet I know she is speaking the utter truth, for she can not saying anything but. I feel as if the air has just been knocked out of me; I mean come on, how bad does it get. First this S.O.B. abandons me after my mother passes away and now he is hurting the very people I have vowed to protect. What kind of low life scum did I come from?

Edam and Scarlet both seem to be able to read my thoughts; for at the very same time they both speak, "Andras' Do not think of yourself that way, you are not, nor will you be anything but a pure and gentle heart." You are not responsible for the crimes of your father." All over again I'm Sitting in the throne room listening to Luke tell me of my past and what is to become of my future. All over again I am red hot angry at being betrayed.

-Flashback-

"Why can't I stay here?" I ask. The Queen of Air and Darkness and Luke both hang there heads as if in shame. "Child, I wish you could but it's out of our control now." Says the Queen. I remember the crystal tears stained face of my Queen; the way Luke rang his hands and shook as if he was at a funeral of a dearly loved friend.

I guess in a way it was a funeral. The child they had raised as their own was now being taken from them, stripped of all entitlements; and to make matters worse they felt as if they had put the final nail in her coffin. At the time they had been right. I was lost, full of hate and so angry that they had kept not only my father from me but the stories of the mother.

In a way though they did me a favor, for they gave me the tools to stand on my own; and the strength to face the unknown as I stepped out into the world and away from all I had known.

Edam was shaking me so hard my head was snapping back and forth, if I had been human it probably would have came right off my shoulders. "Wake up Andras' doesn't faint on me now!" He screamed. "I don't even know my way out of here!" Scarlet was giggling as if this was the best show she had seen in a very long time; which was probably true as many people stayed clear of the woman unless they had no other options.

"Now if you would like the rest of your question answered I suggest you open your eyes and remove yourself from the dreams you are entangled in." Requested Scarlet with a look of annoyance on her heart shaped face. I sit up straight; wiping my hand across my mouth which feels as if it's been stuffed with cotton balls 'Yuck'.

"Now, the rest of it is quite simple; your father was trying to get your attention if you will, he thinks your place is by his side. Even though he is the one whom sent you among the humans." 'By sending the Ghouls' after the innocents; he has also sealed his fate with the tribunal." Declared Scarlet.

"What the hell do you mean Ghouls'? As more than one?" Edam asked. "And why would Hermes do something so utterly stupid to gain his daughters attention?" 'He will be sent to the Underworld for all eternity!" Edam was hot under the collar about this, much more than he had any right to be; thought Andras'. There was something really strange about Edam; what the heck was his secret?

Scarlet looked up at the dark haired man sitting in the corner of the room, with a look a Cheshire cat would give a mouse right before it ate it. "Why, Edam you know the answer to you questions." 'Why there are rumors that if he can prove that Andras' holds more power than a average fallen; he will be able to persuade the tribunal to allow him to stay in Heaven, in return that she would have to join him so he could train her until time he felt she was capable of holding her own with the gifts she was given.

"Okay lady, I don't know what the hell you stuck in your wine to make you think for a minute that I would do a damn thing to help Hermes! Let alone allow him to teach me to handle these "so called gifts" I am suppose to possess!" I scream out of frustration. How dare she think that I would ever do such things? I have made a vow that I would protect innocents and that if I ever crossed paths with my so called father the only thing that would happen is his head rolling across the floor as I sliced it with the cord of justice. I had more than one day mare of that event taking place. "Edam, why the hell would she think you knew the answer to that question?" 'Do you know my father?' 'Is that what the Seer' means by this?' 'What are you hiding from me?' Edam just looked at me dumbstruck. I knew he was a man of few words but it was as if he had suddenly swallowed his tongue.

Right now was not the time for this; but soon I would get to the bottom of the mystery that was Edam Malcolm. "If you want validation that what I have spoken is truth, you might want to go visit your Queen; she was expecting you yesterday." 'I am afraid time moves a bit odd here in my lovely home." 'Shit, we had only been here a couple minutes how could a whole day have passed?" I think to myself. I don't know if this little expedition is worth facing my past again.

Clearing his throat, Edam stood up dusting his self off as if he had been in a long deep slumber. "I guess we need to get going then.' 'Your help has been interesting to say the least.' 'May the next time we meet be under more pleasant terms?" Edam bowed high as if he was addressing someone of a royal court. In a way he was, she was after all two thousand years old and was one of the longer lived fey. Most did not survive separated from the inner court.

There is no way I can let Andras' know whom I am, not after what she has just found out about her father. Nor, can I allow her to find out from anyone but me why I was assigned as her partner. The Gods' themselves thought she needed protection from the monster her own father had proven to be. I was the only other choice besides; Ares the war god himself. She would have known whom he was the instant he stepped in front of her. I was not as well know, so there for the perfect choice. I had to protect her from everyone, not just her father. There was something about her that I just could not shake. I was mesmerized by her voice, her eyes that seem to dance in the light as if they were a being all of their own.

One day if all turned out right; I would ask her if she would sit by my side on the Mount our kind called home. One day, that is if she didn't kill me for betraying her, and keeping who I am from her. These thoughts and so many more were streaming threw Edam's Mind. He had to get a grip on his emotions before she sensed something was amiss with him. He knew of the special gifts Andras' held, but he had only seen her wield them a few of them. She seemed to be a bit scared of the pure power she held. When angry or hurt they were magnified times ten. With her already feeling betrayed and hurt; she would be able to pick up on him in a heartbeat, if he didn't do something to mask his feelings.

Slowly, he took a deep breath; and gathered his jacket from the couch. Andras' was settling up with Scarlet, a gift was always custom when seeking the advice of the Seer'. "Okay where to now, Andras?" asked Edam. He had to act like nothing was wrong. She could not sense his distress. "

Well, I guess it would be wise to follow Scarlet's advice; and go to the Queen of Air and Darkness to see what she could possibly know about all of this." she said without a ounce of emotion in her voice. If he had to guess, he would say she was preparing herself for her visit with Queen. "Okay, sounds good to me; lead the way my lady." he said at a half bow. Andras' laughed at his formal gesture.

Good that was a start; maybe, just maybe, she would be okay until this trip was complete. He hoped at least she would not question him anymore about his past. So many times he had wanted to tell her who and what he was. So many times he had almost slipped; if it hadn't been for the vow he had made to the Counsel, he would have already told her everything.

Scarlet watched the two visitors depart, oh how she would have like to have kept them for a lifetime. Just to have company again was enough to make her heart ache with need. She had been alone for so long. Scarlet; Keeper of Secrets and Visions of things to come. Yet these things had come with a price, one she sometimes felt the weight of so heavy, it felt as if the air was crushing out of her lungs; with the weight of its burden. If she had just spoke up and told Andras' that she was her Aunt. That her mother was one of the most gifted women she had ever met.

Maybe she would not feel such loneliness; perhaps she would have what others to call family. Seeing the hurt in Andras' eyes was like a thousand daggers slicing through her heart. If it was not for the Tribunal, she would have just opened up and told her everything she knew of the past and what she saw of the future.

Grabbing little dragon at her feet the Seer' began to rock back in forth in front of the fire.

Visions dancing before her eyes, making tears stream down her face. How she wished she could save her niece from the pain she would endure on this journey.

How she wished she could run straight to the Fates themselves and ask them to alter what she saw. She knew in her heart that she had to help ease the pain of her only niece, yet doing so would likely cause more pain for her in the long run. For now she would help her, the most she could without drawling too much attention. She could send little gifts and others to help her along her way. That would still be within the guidelines the Elders set. She would keep her safe from a far; she made a vow to her mother to do just that. I knew some things were not spoken between the three of us when we had sat in the little cottage. I got the feeling that

Edam was not the only one hiding things from me. If she was right the Seer' had secrets of her own that seemed to weigh heavy on her heart. Poor woman, what it must be like to live all alone. To have everyone scared to death of you for what ever reason. All I knew, was I wouldn't have for one instant trade places with her; I would not be able to live like that. I also knew that I really didn't want to face the Queen again after the way I had departed.

Yet it was the only way to get to the bottom of all this. So if facing my past was what I would have to do, then so be it. If the Lord of Lights thought me worthy to clear his name; then that is exactly what I was going to do. Edam and I walked in silence for the last half mile up the cobblestone path. Admiring the beauty around us; both of us trying to think of anything other than where we were going and what questions had been brought to the surface do to the Seers' comments. Soon we would be at the castle; the sooner that happened the faster we could leave.

The Castle was still as it had been when I had left; nothing had changed except me. The black and white checkered pattern floors were the same; love and happiness clung to the fey people as if it was a drug. Drunk on lust for their Queen and happy to just be surrounded by her magic. Nothing about this place would ever be the same for me, the hope and love that this magical place once gave me was long faded.

How I wished, that I could go back into time and erase the last hours that I was here. So much of my being wished those hours had never happened. Deep breathes Andras,' you can do this girl; I coached myself over and over again in my head. Step after step we climbed until we finally came to the door of the inner chambers.

"This is it.' 'You sure you want to come in here with me, Edam?" I asked. "I'm here for you.' 'Besides what kind of partner would I be if I just hung you out to dry?" He smiled a cocky smile that made me laugh. "Okay, then here goes nothing." I said swinging open the doors.

Sable was sitting on her throne daydreaming, remembering the promise she had made to Andras' mother. Her dear half sister wanted her to be raised as any child of the court would have. She wanted her to have strong beliefs and a pure heart; that knew right from wrong. She wanted her to be strong of spirit so she could fight for justice. So she could weigh the deeds of men without her emotions playing to big a role. These things the Queen had promised her as she lay taking her last breath. She promised to raise her until she was eighteen moons old; she promise to guide and protect her after that. She promised to keep Hermes from corrupting her.

Annabelle would be proud of her daughter and her sister alike. She would be pleased with how she had turned out so far. Now to keep the rest of her promises, and make sure that Hermes never got his claws in Andras'. This meant Sable would have to be completely honest with her and tell her everything including who she was to her and why she was raised here. This would prove to be a very hard day; heavy hearts would fall and new wounds would be laid upon old ones.

"Oh please forgive me for what I'm about to do, may it keep her safe and away from all harm." The Queen prayed to whatever spirits were listening. Calling for Luke she waited for the arrival of her niece to return and bring with it her heart. So much had happened in the two years she had been gone, so much that could be corrected if Andras' was willing to help right the wrongs so long ago created. Sable really hoped that the child's heart was not still full of hate and rage. How uncontrollable her powers were when she was mad.

Opening the doors to the inner throne room brought back all the emotions and memories of the last time I was here. It brought back the details of the very room as if it had been yesterday and not two years ago. How I wished a million wishes to take back the way I left that day, yet it was just so hard to fathom what Luke and Sable had told me. I had stormed out of here before hearing all they had to say. For some reason, I knew today I would hear the rest of it no matter how it pained me too. The Angel with broken wings looked more solemn this time; the water still poured threw her fingers into the pool at her feet. There were rose petals floating in it this time though and two fish now swam in the crystal clear waters. The dais was still seated among its curtains of spider silk. The Dragon Throne was alive with more stories etching themselves across the body of it as if it was unfolding this very moment.

The Queen was standing near the stain glass window staring outside as though lost in thought. She didn't even turn as I approached the throne. The Crystal of Otherworld hummed as I entered the room, it seems to be the only being to notice my arrival.

Had I been gone so long that I had been forgotten? No, surely that was not the case; but something was totally different this time, there was a note of sadness that hung to the air that was not present the last time I had sat in this room. This was something I really didn't expect to feel. This new gift of being an empath sure kicked up all kinds of uncharted territory.

"You're Highness, Sorry to barge in like this; but it is rather important that we see you." Stated Edam. The Queen turned from where she was posed in front of the stain glass window; and came face to face with her Niece. The one person she had longed to see for the last two years. Could it really be, or was her heart and eyes both playing tricks on her? How she had longed to just lay eyes on Andras' again.

She was even more beautiful then Sable had remembered. Earth had been good for her; yet it had also been difficult, she knew this as fact. After Andras' had left; Sable had sent guards of the court to check in on her. Never had she thought she would be standing in the same room with her again.

Maybe, the spirits were listening after all. In the corner of the room came a loud humm; it seem to startle the Queen more than anything. Walking over to the Crystal, the Queen noticed that it was singing; as if it had woke from a long slumber. Maybe it had, it had always seem to come alive when it was in Andras' presents.

"My Child, I'm shocked and pleased to see you, never in all my dreams did I think you would actually return." Sable said in the most humbling voice one could have. I just stared at her as if somehow I could hear more than the actual words coming out of the Queens mouth. "Well My Queen, I'm not here to stay, I'm working a case that seems to have led me to your door once more." I finally said with a little heartache of my own, my voice was threatening to crack. I really didn't want to hurt the Queen; that was not my intent. After all, I was still in shock over the latest revelations I had received; and the wounds I had received that last time I was here had yet to heal.

"Forgive me; I didn't come to throw pain around; or to make you feel bad for the things that have happened. "No My love it is I whom needs to ask of your forgiveness." Said Sable with her eyes lowered. She really did not want to cause her niece anymore heartache but there were things that she had to tell her. This may be her only change to tell her everything. "What is it that you have come to ask for my aid?' 'I will help you in whatever way I can." The Queen addressed both Edam and Andras' as she took her place on her throne.

There was a bench that was now across from the throne that had not been there the last time I had stepped inside the inner throne room. If I didn't know any better I would have thought it was a mirror image to the one that was at the Seer's cottage.

Edam had already taken a place on the settee'. I crossed the threshold and took a seat next to him; as I began to explain what we had been told by the Seer and what questions had lead us to the Queen's doorstep. "You see it is hard for me to fathom what Scarlet foretold; I know she can not lie, but you can understand why I'm worried." I said. "Yes dear, I do see.' 'I also fear that what the Seer has said to you is truth.' 'I do have knowledge of the gifts she spoke of; and the deeds of your father that would also help you to understand how dire this situation is." Said the Queen.

"What I have to tell you will come as a shock to you, and will likely open the wounds that have just started to heal; yet if I don't tell you now, I may never get a chance to." Sable told me with heartache clearly written on her face. "I want you to know that what I am about to tell you was not kept from you out of spite.' 'It was kept secret due to a vow I made, and also for your own safety.' 'Everything I have ever done Andras' has been out of duty, and most of all love for you." The Queen went on to say.

"Luke will be joining us in a moment; I feel that in light of everything that is happening you would benefit from his presents." "Would you like me to reveal what I know in front of your guest, or would you like to hear these truths in private?' 'Either can be arranged, but I will leave that up to you, my child."

"I would like Edam to stay, he is my partner on this case, and I trust him enough to keep what is said here between him and me." Shaking as I spoke, the emotions of just being here were so strong. "Very well." Said Sable, with a nod. "We will wait then for Luke to join us." At that she went back into her statue like state.

This was the same way she was the last time I had sit in this room waiting on Luke, the same worried expression on her face. It still bothered me that she could turn herself into a living statue; as if she was hiding from her emotions. Or maybe it was me she was hiding from. Apparently the magic I held was stronger than even I knew. I had never in my entire life thought of them as gifts. Growing up in Otherworld it was normal to wield magic; yet my own had always been wild and uncontrollable. That is why I choose only to use it when I had too.

As we sat waiting for Luke to join us, I could not help but pick up on the underline emotions that were floating around the room. The Queen was worried, anxious, and downright frightened about something. My mysterious partner was swimming in his own current of emotions that seem to be running amuck. He was throwing everything from fear to lust around like a bouncy ball in a shoe box.

Who the hell was he lusting after? It best not be the Queen; that was just a little to morbid for even me to handle. Then again if it was me, I didn't know what the heck I would do; let alone say. The Crystal had picked a new melody one that was a childhood lullaby favorite of mine. I couldn't help myself as I started to rise from my seat and ghost over to where it was displayed. Why was it acting out now? It had always been such a quite piece of

Sidhe history. I was not Fae as far as I knew; so there was no reason for it to be singing a song so close to my heart.

Before I had a chance to ask the Queen about its strange reaction to me. The doors of the inner court opened wide to reveal the only father I had ever know.

Luke stood there looking as if he had seen a ghost of someone he loved very much. His dark black hair swept away from his face giving him a look of someone strong and loyal. Which he was; never had he been anything but. He was still ringing his hands the way he had done; the very day two years ago when all of our lives had changed.

Oh, how I had missed his gentle smiles, and kind praise. I stood, as he came to his senses and slowly started to make his way towards us.

Stopping at the right side of the Queen; he bowed, and kissed her hand. It was a gesture, I had seen him do a million times; yet it struck me different this time. Luke was in love with the Queen, and she with him. Why didn't

I see this before?

Maybe, it was because I was a child; or at least looking threw a child eye the last time I was here. One thing was for sure, what I was seeing was real and had been for a long time. This was not the time to get lost in those thoughts or feelings; I had come here on a quest; now was not the time to get side tracked.

"Good Morrow Luke, You look well." I said in way of greeting. It was custom to be formal when in the inner court. This was about as formal as I was going to allow myself to get. I did not want to remember the way things had been; nor the way they had turned out. I took my seat; as I did the crystal sang out again.

This time with a higher pitch; as if it was really trying to get my attention. "What is up with the Crystal of Otherworld?' 'Is there something I need to know before I start asking my questions?" I asked Sable and Luke with my eyebrow raised, as I tossed another sideways glance at the audible rock in the corner of the room.

"We have noticed that it seems to be more active around hybrids and gods than it has been in the past." stated Luke with a look of caution. Could he be worried about something deeper than just my presents? Something was just off kilter; it was as if they were both walking on egg shells around me. "What do you mean Hybrids?'

'I'm a half-breed not a hybrid, and I'm not full fledged God." 'So why is the thing acting as if it will take off flying if I get to close to it." I asked with a no nonsense voice. I had to be a big girl now, no temper tantrums or burst of anger. I had questions that would be answered if I stayed level headed. Something that was very hard to do when people that were suppose to love you, pussy footed around the subject. Sorry I have trouble controlling myself when justice, truth or the like is being denied; maybe that is why I am so good at my job.

The Queen squeezed Luke's hand, and turned her attention to the young woman before her;

the one she had raised as her own, her beloved niece and the answer to some of the four world's greatest problems. That is if she would take the task the Fates had asked of her. "Andras', the last time you were in this room, we were trying to tell you of your past and what your destiny foretold.' 'You were so angry at the mere thought of us betraying you, that you did not hear all we had to tell you." "If you can spare us the time, and keep your heart and mind open, I will tell you everything, the whole truth." Holding her breath Sable stared at Andras' gauging her reaction. "I'm listening; I will do my best to keep my cool." I said.

The look on Edams' face was enough to make even me crack a smile. Oh how well he knew me, I was like a stick of dynamite lit at both ends. What can I say; I'm a hot head; when I have been wronged.

"Annabelle, your mother, made me promise; when you were a mere child to keep you safe, and to keep you from Hermes, she wanted you to be raised with family until you came of age.' 'She wanted us to tell you of both sides of your heritage." "Two years ago when we tried and failed; I thought I would never get a chance to tell you everything."

'On your mother's death bed, she made me promise to raise you; to tell you nothing of whom or what you were until you were grown. She wanted you to have a normal childhood." "I'm telling you this now because, I want you to know that I didn't lie to you; nor hide things from you without a reason." "I swore a vow to your mother, and I was not able to break that vow until now."

"I understand all about honor; what pains me is by keeping your vow, you kept my mothers' memory from me." I spoke with my head lowered. I was trying really hard to keep my rage under control; yet she was not making it very easy for me. "Can we hurry this along, I have already been here two days and I just found out that I have more than one Ghoul to send to the Underworld. I really don't want innocents dieing on my watch."

Okay, so now I was just being catty; but

truthful none the less. "If I may continue." "It is time you know about your mother and your father, whom I am to you besides your Queen, and why you were raised in otherworld." Sable spoke without catching her breath.

"Your mother was Annabelle of the throne of Air and Darkness, Her parents were my parents." "I was the eldest of three sisters." "Your mother and I were raised her in the court, and Scarlet the seer, was raised by her mother in the outer area."

WTF that was a revelation; The Seer and the Queen were both my Aunts. Was I loosing my mind, or better yet my hearing? For I could not have possibly hear her correctly. "Did you just tell me that my mother was a sibling of yours and the Seers?" I asked utterly confused.

"Why didn't Scarlet tell me that when I was with her?" I asked more to myself than anyone else in the room. "Scarlet is swore to an oath as well, but her vow comes from the Fates' themselves, she was not allowed to reveal herself or what she knows, unless you first brought it up; which didn't happen if you are now standing before me asking these questions." "As for what I am telling you, the rest of this is quite simple." "Annabelle met Hermes at a festival we use to celebrate here, a ball of sorts that was held every October." "The Gods were able to mingle with the Courts of Light, and Air & Darkness.' 'Once we even married between all three." "What came of those marriages were Hybrids, children with the powers of both parents." "The Hybrids power was wilder, stronger, and sometimes more fatal than that of their parents." 'This is the very reason these marriages do not happen today."

"This was the very reason you mother wanted you to stay away from your father while you were a child." The Queen said, as she looked up for the first time since she had started talking. "Your father was always full of tomfoolery; he is after all the God of Mischief.' 'He saw in you a great power that could raise him above all others, and create a divide between the four worlds that would be deeper than it is now.' 'He wanted to have complete control over the worlds, dominating everything and anyone in his way.'

Greed drove him; in return it drove your mother away from him, as soon as she opened her eyes to see him as he was." "She was in love with you the minute she found out she was carrying you; she wanted you to feel, and be loved.' 'To grow into a strong headed woman that would know in her own heart what was right and what was wrong."

"That my dear child, is exactly the woman you have became; you are kind, loving, pure of heart, and stronger than you know." "I feel as if the wishes you mother had for you where kept to the fullest of all our abilities." 'I am dearly sorry that the feeling of betrayal runs so deep, and that is my fault as well as many others." 'I do not hope to have you forgive me; I only wish that you can see the bigger picture."

I sat there trying to soak all of what Sable was telling me in. I was still having trouble processing the fact that I was a so called Hybrid, or that I was a savior of sorts. To top it off I had to swallow the fact that my father was some kind of monster set on taking over all four worlds. Ok think Andras', how do you respond to the fact that everything you have ever know to be true is in fact a twisted perversion of the very reality that has kept you sane.

"Okay, well this was not exactly the type of truth I thought you would tell me, I do know that you're speaking the truth of how things were between my mother and you.' 'How am I to know, what you say about me being a Hybrid is reality, and I know my father is not the best person in the worlds but what truly leads you to believe he is set to dominate the races?" I mean come on I am totally clueless as to the reason they believe that I'm some super hero.

Ya, I admit my job as the Huntress, has its perks and the chain of Justice is a kick ass sidearm. But come on, am I to really believe this crap after all the years they have lied to me.

Sable looked up at Luke, and as if they were speaking telepathically, he nodded his head and walked out of the room. Ten minutes later he reappeared with a scroll so old it looked as if it would blow away into a thousand slivers if the wind blew hard enough. In his other hand he held a journal with a royal blue cover in gold lettering was the name Annabelle. He handed both of these items to Sable and took a seat beside the woman; as if trying to give her extra strength to do what she must.

Sable stared at the items in her hands as if they were alive and could just jump up and start dancing or something. The whole time that these revelations were being told to Andras' Edam had sat in his seat as still as statue. This was the first time he blinked. It was as if he already knew what the articles were, and how much it would change Andras' life and his own. The Queen spoke without taking her hands away from the precious gifts she held.

"This scroll is the prophecy of what is to come, it marks the beginning of the Hybrids and the end of all we had know, it also tells of two possible outcomes in which you play a part in both. The other item is your mothers Journal, something she wanted you to have when you came of age. Your history, past and present are woven between these pages." Sable extended her arms holding both items as if she really did not want to let go. As if they held part of her sisters' soul. "Andras' the questions you have can be answered here."

I got up and took the parcels, placed them both in the side bag I always carried. Returned to my seat I waited for the rest of what would be revealed. "Okay, spill it; Scarlet said you had a task for me." "And the only thing that has not been fully explained is why that crazy crystal has chosen to go hay wire now." I replied in a sarcastic tone. "We have noticed that the veil is becoming more than unstable as of late, it is allowing anyone threw portals, humans have never been able to come to this world and now we are hearing reports of more than one occasion were this exact thing is taking place." 'The Queen of Light has had her guards escort three known humans back across the portals, we both fear that if something is not done soon, it will not just be humans that will be coming across." Spoke Sable.

"What the Queen is telling you is truth. Andras', we need your help. As we told you; your father wishes to control all the races, placing his self as the highest of Gods. The only way he can is threw you." Luke said with a look of sorrow on his face.

"Wait a minute, what do you mean through me?" I must not have been paying as much attention as I thought I was. Luke looked me dead in the eye, something he had not done since I was a small child.

"He can only touch the crystal of Heaven; with you by his side he would be able to touch all four.' 'He has to link with your power to hold more than one at a time.' "Hermes does not wish to close the veil; he wises to make the tear wider, making it impossible to travel without his say so." "Read the journal your mother left, and read what the scroll foretells; you will then be able to make your decision yourself." Stated Sable without taking her eyes off the floor.

"We do have a job for you if you chose to take it.' 'It would be made worth your while as well." "Yet, I must tell you that what we are to ask of you is dire to all four worlds." Sable said. "Okay, so what is this quote unquote job you have for me and will it in any way help me put an end to the madness my father has unleashed?" I asked out of sheer wonder.

"We want you to take the Crystal of the Otherworld to a safe location, and locate and transport the remaining three crystals before Hermes is able to get to them." Luke told me with a twinkle in his eye. It was as if he knew that I was going to jump after this mission like a dog after a rare steak bone.

"Just how do you suppose I locate the other Crystals, Is their some magical map that will lead the way?" I asked with my hand cocked on my hip. "No, there is no Map but the Crystal of Otherworld will lead you to the Crystal of Heaven and so forth" Stated the Queen. "Each crystal has their own songs, and in those songs are clues to the location of the next crystal.

When all four are together they will form anew." "If this happens when Hermes is in possession of them all hell will break loose." Luke said as he held my gaze. Okay so they are not kidding they really thought I can do this, or they would not even ask it of me. "Where is this location you want the Crystals taken too?" It seemed so crazy to even think about the crystals becoming one again. How would these four worlds act if they were suddenly slammed back together again? Better yet what would happen if they went spinning in different directions with out the anchor of the crystals to keep the peace? So many thoughts were streaming threw my mind. What crazy ass dream did I wake up in and why did it seem as if the wool was just now removed from my eyes?

Edam and I sat there a little longer as the Queen of Air & Darkness told us of a cave that was lined with gold. There was a chest there that the four pieces were to be placed in; keeping them separated until the time it would be safe to join them together.

So now I had four different missions, to concern myself with and a shit load of questions yet to be answered. Now was as good a time as any to get this all started. Might as well make the most of it all, no one would be able to say I was going to be bored any time soon. Matter of fact, I had a lot of reading to do and a very short time to do it.

Chapter Five

I gathered up the two gifts that the Queen had gave to me, Slipped the Crystal in the silk lined pouch tying it shut; I gave my Aunt a quick kiss on her head and turned to meet Luke's eyes that seem to be brimming with tears unshed. Reaching to hug him was the hardest thing I had ever done; so many times I had dreamed of this moment.

Now that it was here, I was freezing up inside. Luke seem to get it, cause without a word he swept in close and wrapped me in a bear hug as if I was a mere child again.

Exiting the Throne room was easier this time then it had been the last time I had been to this palace. Closure had been given; and I was finally at peace with who I was. Well at least for now; which was the most anyone could hope for in my shoes. Edam spoke for the first time since coming near the palace; it was as if he was finally aware of whom he was.

"So were to now boss?"

Do we go after Hermes or the Ghouls, or take

the Crystal to its resting place?" "You tell me what to do and we will get to where we need to be." "I really had not thought about it Edam, but now that you mention it we need to get this Crystal to its place.' 'We can worry about the rest of it after that." I said.

Looking down at journal in my hands. "I do have one quick stop before we head off after gods knows what." "Lead the way my lady." Edam said as he gave me a bow. I couldn't help but laugh. He always seemed to be able to lighten the mood no matter what was going on.

Arriving back at Scarlet's cottage I guess, I suspected the new knowledge I had gained would have changed the way her home would seem to me; yet, it still had a medieval touch to it. Edam, knocked on the door as we stood there on the same crumbling steps we had been on earlier that day; but nothing stirred beyond the door.

Odd, were the heck had she ran off to? She must have realized I would come back here after finding out who she was to me. Or, had something happened to make her leave so suddenly? I was just about ready to turn to Edam and suggest continuing on with our journey, when out of the corner of my eye I caught a glimpse of Scarlet. She was standing under the large willow tree facing away from us.

It seemed she was in a trance of some sort. Quietly, I tapped Edam on his arm and pointed in the direction of the willow; what the heck was this crazy woman doing? We started to make our way to willow. Something was really off; she should sense our presence; yet, I got the feeling she was lost somewhere in her own mind.

"Scarlet? Hey you okay?" Okay so this chick had either totally lost it since the last time we were here or something had happened to make her regress this way. Edam snapped his fingers in front of Scarlet's face; after a few seconds of no response he finally just reaches up and shakes her. Scarlet's Oceanic eyes seem to flood with emotion; as if she never thought she would see us again. "Oh child, you have come to seek my help again?" "I take it the Queen did not answer all of your questions?" said the Seer.

This empathy thing was really starting to tick me off; I was feeling the under current of the emotion and words she was not even saying. I really needed to get a handle on this so called Gift.

"No scarlet, we did not come seeking your aid again; and Yes the Queen or should I say your sister did answer my questions. She also left me with more than a mouth full of questions I will have to figure out the answers to on my own." "I came to tell you that I know you were my mother's sister; and you are not bound by your vow any longer." I grabbed her hand, as I spoke these last couple words. Scarlet seem to melt with relief; she held this knowledge to herself for so long.

"Forgive me, Child." 'I never meant you any harm.' The words seem to tumble out of Scarlet's mouth; just as the fat indigo blue tears rolled down her cheeks. It was as if the flood gates to her very soul were wide open; it was at that moment I started to realize just how difficult this all had been on Sable and Scarlet alike. Such a heavy burden to have to carry around within.

I was started to feel like the weigh was lifting off my shoulders; maybe this would be healing for all of us. I would have to make an attempt to visit with both my aunts when all the other craziness was over. "Scarlet, why are you standing out here?' "Did something happen while I was away?" I asked. I just had a vibe that this day had yet to reveal all of its secrets. "No, child nothing happened, I knew I could not interfere in the plans the fates had; and I was trying to call the spirits to help keep you safe was all. It looks like now I will be able to do that myself." Scarlet said with smile lighting up her face.

I was seeing the light at the end of the tunnel; finding strength in the darkest corner of my soul. It did my heart good, to know that I was finally finding out that I had family to lean on. For so long, I had wandered around in a shroud of grey never truly seeing the lining of silver that loomed in the black clouds above my head. Now with the help of Scarlet, I would be able to put an end to the destruction my father had created. Righting wrongs never felt so good.

As we headed out of the meadow and away from Scarlet's home I had a feeling that even though I knew what we had to do, and were we had to go; that not all of the puzzle pieces would fit together as perfectly as we once thought. Too many things to do and so little time to do them. Stopping in at the entrance of the portal we had created; butterflies started fluttering in my stomach. Somehow, I knew that this journey would be packed full of excitement and chaos. Somehow, I got the feeling that it was going to be a very long day.

Arriving back earthside, at the entrance of the cemetery, I removed the magical camouflage from my bike; which had kept it hidden, from anyone that would have tried to take my baby for a joy ride. I stuffed my belongings into the saddle bags, and tied the flap shut again. Sighing, I bowed my head, closed my eyes and just breathed in the scent of wet earth.

I just needed a moment to clear my head

before I could even think of a strategic plan to help us do all the crap we had to do. Edam cleared his throat, something he always did before he spoke. A small grin formed on my face, okay so what did I forget to think of this time. That would be the only reason he would voice his concerns.

"Andras' we all three can not ride on your bike, so I suggest getting a cab for Scarlet and I." ' We can all meet at you're apartment to hash out our plan of action." Edam said. Well shit, why didn't I think of that I laughed in my head? Such a gentleman my sidekick was at times. "Okay sounds good to me; go ahead and call the cab, I follow you over." I said. Good a little alone time will do me a world of good; so much had happened in such a short time that I needed to clear the cobwebs out of the corners of my brain. A bike ride would be the best way to do so.

As we waited for the cab to arrive, I grabbed my mother's journal; leaning against the wall of the cemetery. I might as well get started on this old book, finding that it was giving me solace to learn who my mother was; I dove into the thick tome. I had at least thirty minutes before the cab would get here.

Dearest Andras'

I started writing this book the moment found out I was carrying you. I love you so much; I feel your soul inside me. Such a feeling this is, to finally feel complete. My dear child, I wish for you to have a childhood full of happiness that you grow into a strong and wonderful woman that you let your heart lead you on the journeys life has to offer. I wish a thousand wishes, that you will be ever bit your own person. Never allow someone to make your choices for you. That being said, Hermes is not the man I first thought he to be. I fear that the monster I see looming beneath the surface will try to hurt everyone and everything I love; if he doesn't get his way.

The truth of who he is surfaced so quickly that it sent shards of glass searing threw my heart. I loved him with my whole being, yet, I feel as though it was all a lie. For the person I thought he was, is not the one I see standing before me. I so want to hide away, in a dark cave with you, some place he will never be able to find us. I can not allow him to do with you what he has planned. I'm so, so very sorry my dear girl. Please forgive me for the choices I have made, and the ones I've yet too.

Just as I finished the last sentence of the first page of my mothers' journal I heard the crunch of gravel; looking up I saw that the cab was arriving. I guess I will have to wait until another time to find out more about the plans of Hermes.

For now, I needed to get home, change clothing, and hash out a plan. No way, was I going in to this blind. Nor, would I allow anyone else to get hurt in the cross fire. I damn sure was not going to be used to build someone else's power supply. Cute I maybe, but sucker I am not. No way, was I going in to this blind. Nor, would I allow anyone else to get hurt in the cross fire. I damn sure was not going to be used to build someone else's power supply. Cute I maybe, but sucker I am not. My Mother must have had a touch of the same gifts that Scarlet has, I would have to ask her a little bit more about Annabelle. I knew that some of those trace gifts had been given to me as well; but now I was starting to see that maybe there was more too it.

"Okay, I will meet you both over at my apartment, time to get this started." I said as I stuffed the Book back into the saddle bags. There was no way I was going to allow another member of my family to be stuck in the crossroads of what Hermes had planned. I would not have anyone's blood on my hands except his if I could help it. I kicked the old bike in gear and straddled the top of the magnificent beast as it hummed to life. How I had missed the feel of raw power in my embrace. What was I going to do able the Crystals, and better yet how would I stop the Ghouls my father unleashed and put an end to his plans without becoming a puppet on the end of a string. I was starting to get a headache, why did things always go from bad to worse in a split second. The hum of the bike on the cobblestone soothed my nerves more than first thought; yet, it did little good for the knot that was growing in the pit of my stomach. To much had happened for my being to let go of all of it; or maybe, just maybe it was this ever present empathy gift

I had just learned I possessed. There would be time to figure it all out later, I hoped. For now I needed to just feel the wind slapping me in my face, and the vibration of the motorcycle l was currently holding underneath my body as if it was a lover. I needed the rush of the danger and excitement gunning the engine would bring me. I kicked the gear over and gunned it down the alleyway that lead to my little abode. I knew with in seconds that I was not allow yet I could not for the life of me place what or who was present in the small space by my back door.

Out of the shadows he stepped like a dream. How the hell did he get here so fast, and better yet were was Scarlet. I think I'm loosing my mind. Or maybe its wishful thinking with all this sexual energy I am currently feeling. Was it coming from him, me or both? Damn, this so called gift is killing me, I'm loosing my edge. I slowed the bike to a crawl just as I reached the pool of light from the single bulb that hung on the wall outside my door. There in the half cast light stood my partner and for the first time I was actually feeling heat that was not just coming from the bike.

My breath hitched in my throat, something it had never done before. Wow, what the hell was happening to me? I put the kickstand down and released my thighs from the cycle. Staring at Edam everything felt as if it was in slow motion. "How did you get here so fast, and where is the Seer?" Gosh he was gorgeous; I really had never paid attention to him this way before. "We arrived seconds before you, the Seer, as you put it, is inside. I came out here to make sure that you and your lovely bike both made it in one piece."

Edam stood there with a sly smirk playing on his lips as if he was drinking in my presence; my heart was racing at a beat it had never made before. Why the heck were my hands sweaty? These feeling have been intensifying ever since we were in the cemetery together. All my mind could picture was images of us between silky sheets, legs a tangled mess, bodies meshed together as the heat of the room climbed. What would it feel like to be engulfed by his lush lips, caressed by his callused hands? Why, couldn't I stop thinking about what it would be like to be with him? "Uh um" Edam cleared his throat, and it was as if a rubber band snapped back into place, the fog in my head began to clear just enough to remind me of the reasons we were standing in the ally. Shit, Scarlet was waiting inside; and we had plans to go over. No time like the present to channel my energy into something other, than the well formed body of Edam.

Stepping threw the door to my small studio apartment; I took a deep breath of the air to make sure that there had been no strangers in my home. Satisfied that all was well, I turned to look around the small space; my futon bed was still unmade from the night before. My orchids were still in the sea green vase sitting on a little side table in front of the fridge. Note to self, they needed to be watered soon. The place may not look like much but it was mine, something that I cherished. I let my eyes drift to the chipped mirror were Scarlet now set, facing the mirror as if it were a giant crystal ball. "Okay so, we now have more than one task before us; and the dangers of the outcome could affect everyone in all four worlds if we fuck up.'

Our first priority is making sure the ghouls are stopped so no more innocents loose their lives.' 'We may have to call in back-up to help us with this; Edam, do you think you could call the office and see who is available tonight? He nodded his head as he flipped open his cell phone and waited for me to finish what I had to say. 'Next I have to take the crystal, to its resting place and try to gather the remaining three.'

"Speaking of which, Scarlet, what can you tell me of Hermes plans for them?" Scarlet sat there for a moment her eyes fluttering, as she stared into the broken reflective glass. The look on her face was peaceful almost as if she had stepped out of the vessel of her body. "He wants to dominate, to destroy the balance." She sounded as if she was far away; the words seem to just float on the air. "When a God controls the four elemental crystal pieces, a rip can form with a single thought formed.'

"Dark... Matter... If you have to give it a name; it is the very stuff the gods themselves were created from." 'That is what he wants to create." "He would be able to mold the worlds as he sees fit, taking everyone along for the ride." Her eyes fluttered closed, her head bowed, and the room became as quite as a graveyard.

"Oh Shit, things have went from bad to worse in a single blink of the eye." I thought out loud. "Why did he frame the Lord of Light, what could he possibly have to gain from it?" "And why does Lucas feel I'm best to clear his name?" I asked for adventure, yet I never in a million years thought the rollercoaster would fly completely off the tracks. This really was turning out to be one hell of a day.

"By framing the Lord of Light for the crimes he has committed he can get rid of one of the biggest voices on the Counsel; everyone listens to Lucas.' 'I think Hermes might be trying to remove anyone that apposes what he has planned." What Edam just said made perfect sense, yet for some reason I didn't put the pieces together myself. It's a great thing he is my partner, or I would have thought he had inside information he was hiding from me. "That makes sense.' 'So if he can get enough of the Counsel members removed from their place; he will be able to persuade those remaining to think that what he says is truth." Yes today seemed to be full of all kinds of twists and turns just what a girl needed a Psycho for a father.

"Alright, well make that phone call to see if you can get us any help; I'm going to hop in the shower and clear my head its been a rough two days.' "Then I will figure out how to get the Crystal where it needs to go with out running into dear old dad." Calling that man my dad made my stomach turn like you would not believe. Yet truth could not be denied no matter how it pained me.

As I left the room I placed my hand on Scarlet's shoulder, she was still out of it; as if going into the trance had drained her more than it should have. Maybe, being topside was affecting her on some level. I guess I would deal with it when I got out of the shower, I had to wash away all the grim and muck from the last two days there was just no way around it. Stepping into the bathroom, I took my side bag with me, even though I knew the people in the other room could be trusted; I just did not feel right leaving it with them. It was my job to protect the innocents; and now that task had become ten times harder.

Locking the door. I leaned against it laying my head back, I closed my eyes. Alright so now the worlds were depending on me, and I had no idea how I was going to save everyone, but damn it I was going to give it my all.

Turning on the water, I let the bathroom fill with steam; somehow the heat of the room seemed to help shed away the worry that had been lingering since I started this mission. Stripping out of my clothing, I stood and stared at my reflection; why the hell were images of Edam's hard body still finding a way into my thoughts. I really needed to get a handle on these gifts or something serious would happen.

Grabbing my cherry blossom shampoo I began to scrub away all the mud that had been plastered to my hair. The water was scalding hot, yet it felt wonderful. My mind began to drift to the journal of my mothers, which I now possessed. She really did love me, and she wanted me protected.

It felt like my heart was being slowly being stitched back together. So now I knew I had two aunts; and both of them wanted to protect me. I had a loving uncle that cherished me. Family, wow how strange the word sounded rolling around on my tongue. Never did I think going back to Otherworld would have given me peace, yet, it did.

Rinsing the soap out of my hair, my thoughts turned to the ghouls and how to get them in the same place at the same time, without anyone getting hurt. Damn, this was going to be tricky, but I think I knew a way to do it. Let's just hope that it works. I grabbed the sponge and lathered my vanilla bean body wash on the coral surface. I might be raw from all the scrubbing when I was done but I would smell good again at least.

I guess my shower took longer than I thought

it did, for as soon as I stepped under the steady stream to rinse off, there was a knock on the door. "Yes." "Having Trouble in there Andras'?" Edam sounded concerned. "No I'll be out in just a sec." I turned off the water and grabbed the terry cloth towel and robe from the hook on the back of the door. Gathering up my bag, I opened the door and stepped out in a cloud of steam. God that had felt wonderful.

"You were in there for almost an hour; I thought maybe something had happened to you." Wow, Edam really was worried about me. "An hour, it only felt like a couple of minutes, I guess the time got away from me.' 'I'm running on fumes, but I can not even think of resting until we get this mess taken care of." I replied. "Scarlet?' 'Are you alright, you don't look so hot." It was an understatement she had a grey greenish tint to her olive skin, as if she were sea sick. "I'm just a little drained, I'll be okay." "I think." "No, I really don't think you will be."

"Have you ever been threw the portals before?" "No. This was my first ride threw."

"Andras' I think your aunt's powers are tied directly with Otherworld; I don't think she can stay with us here." "We might have to send her back across, she can send us a message if she hears or sees anything." "I think your right Edam."

"Scarlet, I don't want to risk your life, even though I would love to have you with me; I think it would be best if you go back to your cottage for now." Solemn eyed Scarlet nodded her head. "I can open a portal right in front of her home and be back here in just a bit." "Think you could sit tight until I return." "I have already called the office and we will have a little help in rounded up the monsters Hermes unleashed."

Edam was really taking charge, damn it was sexy. "Yes, I think I can do that." A small smirk playing across my lips, I could have sworn that his eyes just changed color. Wow I needed sleep sometime in the near future. Edam opened a portal right there in my living room. He looped his arm around Scarlet. She really didn't look good, I should have told her to stay behind and we would not have to be going threw this right now. I ran over to my newly found aunt and hugged her as if I would loose her if I didn't. Her Oceanic eyes were brimming with tears as I pulled away. "I won't let you down my dear sweet girl..."

"I'll send some news and help as soon as I can." As soon as the words had left Scarlet's mouth, she laid her head on Edam's chest and wrapped her arms around him. "I'll be back as soon as I can, promise to stay put, please, Andras'." Smiling at Edam, and seeing him in a new light 'I promise, Edam, I'll be right here when you return." With that he shimmered and they were gone.

Sighing, I walked over to my closet reaching for a pair of stone washed jeans, I saw a box wrapped with sea green paper and a little note attached to the bow. My hand lingered on the note, as I grabbed the box; lifting it I walked over to the bed and sat on the edge. What in the world could this be. I lifted the gilded paper from the fold of the envelope and began to read.

My dearest Andras'

I knew I would not be able to stay long with you, and for that I'm sorry. I left this for you in hopes it would help you in some way. This was your mothers; I hope it fits as perfectly as I think it will.

Love,

Scarlet

Placing the note back in the envelope, I tossed it aside. What in the world did Scarlet leave me? Better yet, how did she get it here? This aunt of mine was full of surprises. I stared at the wrapping paper for a moment longer before tearing into. Inside was a royal blue velvet corset that clinched in the front with a satin ribbon. A hooded cape made of the same deep blue fabric lay under it. Lifting out the corset and cape, I discovered a pair of leather pants so black that they had hues of blue in them. Laying the clothing on the bed beside me, I saw something sparkle. Looking down in the box I saw a silver armband with a spiral design. On the last loop of the never ending circle, was a small clasp just big enough for my silver chain to be hooded to.

Was my mother also a Huntress? What an odd piece of jewelry for my mother to own. I guess while Edam was gone I would take the time to read some more of the journal. Drying off with the towel. I slipped into the clothes my aunt had left for me. The corset hugged my large breast better than any bra could have. The cape hit just at my waist

Oh My Goodness the jeans were a perfect fit. Sticking my feet into my favor spiked boots; I stood and stared at my reflection in the mirror. Wow if I say so myself I look hot! I grabbed a pony tail and swept my hair up in a high ponytail. This looked to be awesome outfit. Yet it seemed to be a tad bit fancy to be hunting big nasty monsters in. I grabbed the scroll and the journal and walked back to my bed. Looked like I had a little bit of time before Edam and the back up would be here, I lay back and started to read. Might as well try to figure out where the Crystal of Heaven was and what else my mother had to say. I opened my mother's journal and picked up where I left off.

Dearest Andras',

As you now may know, you are not alone in this cold world. Family will always surround you. One day my dear, you will do great things. This has been foreseen. You are the Heir to two thrones, yet, I know in my heart you will choose the right path for you. You will do what is best for all. You will one day be a strong and powerful leader. Please never forget kindness and justice when you take your rightful place. I hope I'm there to see you when you're grown.

Skipping forward a couple of pages I started to read again, part of me wanted to know ever thought she had ever wrote. The other part just needed the facts of what was going on. I read paragraph after paragraph of my mother's personal thoughts; I know now she went to the fates themselves to ask for their help. She was scared to death of Hermes to the point she had ran and hide from him.

Protecting me was her only thought; yet, no one was there to protect her. Heartache, love, and pain filled my own heart. As I turned to the second chapter her words seem to be more about the future and less about her own feelings. She left me coded messages about the gifts she had possessed. My mother was one of the first Huntresses. I guess I carried on the family tradition.

Closing the journal, I turned my attention to the Scroll sitting in its protective cover inside my bag. I unrolled the edges, the words on the page were written in dragon's blood and gold. It was one of the prettiest scrolls I had ever seen. Carefully I lay it on the bed, grabbed the Crystal of Otherworld, I placed it in my lap as I began to read.

-We have discovered a mutation in the offspring of the fey and God interbreeding. While some of these children are null of magic and resemble humans in almost every sense, others are showing signs of carrying traits of both parents. There is evidence that if not properly trained these hybrids gifts could have dire and destructive consequences' what will come of these junctions is yet to be

seen. -

The air sizzled and a blue haze started to form in the center of my room. A second later Edam stepped threw the portal. "I take it Scarlet is safely home?" "Yes, I got her there without a problem; as soon as she was on the other side of the veil she seemed fine." "I think that it was just too much for her to handle at the moment." After Edam finished telling me about Scarlet, I filled him in on what I had learned from the scroll and the journal.

"So you see we have some issues that we need to address; and I guess, I need to find out more about these gifts I have. "So when is the backup going to get here?" I looked up to find Edam starring with a starry look in his eyes. "Hello, did you hear what I said?" "Ya, where did you get the new outfit; you look, uh, stunning." He gasps as he turned his eyes abruptly away from me. Scarlet left it for me, it was my mother's. "Well it looks nice." "Thanks, I replied."

There was a knock at the door. "I think that is

our backup." Stated Edam. He strolled over to the door and opened it a crack. Two seconds later two men dressed in black stepped threw the threshold. "Andras', this is Kyle, He is a scent tracker werewolf; and this is Domenic, a changeling Vamp that can use his magic to trap anyone in a circle of energy. With them we should be able to round up the last of the Ghouls in one swipe." Edam was smiling as if he had just stuck his hand in the cookie jar.

"Nice to meet you all. I look forward to working with you to accomplish this task." I spoke as I rose from the edge of the bed; stuffing the crystal and parcels back in my bag. "I think we can use an energy trail to bring the rest of the ghouls to the area where we caught the first one.' 'Once we have them trapped, I want you all to stand by, as I use the chain of justice to find and locate the one that unleashed them in the first place.' "Is that agreed?" I looked around the room at the three men standing before me, trying to pick up the undercurrent of emotions as they all nodded in agreement. I did not pick up anything other than what was already present; damn I thought it would be the perfect time to test my newly found ability. I guess, I was wrong. "Okay then follow me to the cemetery, we will meet near the large tome with the Angel standing in front of it. I waited until everyone had exited my apartment before I stepped across the threshold myself.

Cloaking my apartment in a field of magic, I tossed my shoulder bag into the saddle bags, and grabbed my Anthem' to once again strap it to my thigh. Kicking the old bike into gear I lead the way back to Oak Hill Memorial Park. The beat of the cobblestone street against the tires of my motorcycle made me think about the music of the Crystal of O.

Soon enough I would be able to deal with taking it where it needed to be. Right now though, I had to get these monsters back to where they belonged and make sure no one else got hurt in the crossfire.

Crawling to a stop I rolled the old shovelhead behind the tomb. Putting down the kickstand. I dismounted the bike and replaced the cover I had on it previously.

Taking the Chain of Justice and strapping it to the arm band that had been my mothers. I waited on my team to arrive. Looking over the graveyard to make sure we would not have a repeat of the events from the last time we were here. Slowly I scanned the area, seeing and sensing nothing I turned to my newly formed team.

"Okay, guys this is what I would like to happen.' 'We need to pump some magical energy in the air; much more than one person alone can make; at the same time; Kyle, let me know as soon as they are close. Domenic, I want you to be ready to trap all three ghouls in a circle. As soon as all three of them are in one area, set the trap. I'll use the chain of Justice to get the information I need.' 'Edam, as soon as I'm done; opens the portal to the underworld, and sends these bastards back were they belong.' 'I have a feeling that this will be our only chance.' "Are you guys ready?" I asked mainly for my own need, I had to pump myself up for this little stunt. Sooner we took care of this the sooner I could cross this task off my to do list.

"Andras', I think it would be wise to lead them to the soldier's grave that those kids were using the last time we were here." "Good point, Edam that would be a big enough area to do what we need to do." "Alright team, follow me." Taking the lead I wove my way threw the crumbling tombstones. Turning right I looked over the area once more, the coast was clear.

"Alright let's do this!"

We moved in a semicircle around the grave. Together we started to pour as much magic as we could without draining ourselves into the small space. Within seconds the air shifted and grew cold enough to see the mist of our breath in front of us. "Brace yourselves, here they come" I shouted over the roar of the wind to be heard. Slipping the silver chain into my hand, keeping it attached to the clasp on the bracelet I let it swing loose from my fingers. Kyle had his face to the wind tracking the scent of the energy the bastards were putting off.

"They are about five feet from us." "Domenic

now would be a good time to get that circle started; these guys are running some major juice." Kyle screamed in our direction.

Nodding Domenic closed his eyes, bowed his head for just a fraction of a second, when he raised his eyes level with mine all I could see was utter blackness where his eyes had been. Damn that was just plain creepy. Slow smiles played on his lips, the tip of his fangs were visible in the pale moon light. Oh seriously dangerous, I'm so glad he was on our side. Edam widened his stance on my right. "They're here, get ready." barked Kyle. He was starting to shift, his body was rippling. Like another being crawling around just below the surface.

Three grey blobs bounded over the headstone in record speed. Suckers were really after the fix the energy our combined magic would give them. Lucky for us that they were not going to get a chance to taste one drop.

"NOW!" I screamed; Domenic let the circle go from his minds eye, with an audible pop a silver ring formed around the three ghouls trapping them inside. I flipped the cord of justice lightly from my wrist. Within seconds it had wrapped its self around the three specter forms. Sizzling as it made contact, the wind died down as if someone had snuffed out a flame. My eyes rolled back and the images of all there deeds races before my eyes.

Opening them, I let the full force of my fury show threw my eyes. "With the judgment chain still wrapped around you. You are bound to me until I feel justice had been met; no lie will be uttered from your lips." 'You will answer my question, as justice calls forth, you will tell me what I seek to know; for you have been judged as my duty as a fallen." The ghouls shivered under the chains embrace. Fighting against the chain and the circle of energy Domenic had made.

With hollowed eyes they all turned at once to stare at me, sooner I get this dealt with the better we would all be for it. "Are there more of you Earth side?" In unison the ghouls spit out their answer. "No, Huntress we are the only ones." "Where is the one that sent you?" Again they answered together. "That we no not, Huntress, he doesn't think us worth to know his location." The bowed their slime' covered heads, as if they were ashamed that they did not know.

"When was the last time you received orders from him, and where was the location?" The one nearest to the grave shivered trying to fight the command I gave him. The phantoms were doing everything they could to keep from telling me the answer to my last question. "Answer me, now." Shivering the specter looked up and all but moaned the words. "We last spoke to the One; yesterday, he ordered us to do nothing until he said; we were summoned to Highland Park." I knew without a doubt this would be all the information I would receive from these goons. Nodding to Edam, I waited as he opened the portal to underworld; before I gave Domenic the orders to lower the circle. Banishing the three ghouls to the underworld was easier than I had first thought.

As the portal closed, I looked at my newly formed crew and thanked them for their help. We cleaned up the mess and erased any and all traces of what had just taken place. As Domenic and Kyle left the graveyard, I got a feeling that things were going to become a little more unpredictable.

Sighing I rested my hand on the seat of my bike. Edam stood silently in the shadows waiting for me to speak, or maybe he had something on his mind. Either way, I was just too tired to think. "Hop on, I'll give you a ride to my apartment; I need to get a little rest." Starting the bike and straddling the giant beast to keep it steady; I waited for Edam's weight, before, I lifted the kickstand; and took off down the cobbled street.

Chapter Six

Fog rolled in, engulfing the streets in a blanket of mist; the road was only visible were the headlight cut a path threw the thick white haze. My stomach got butterflies again, giving me a warning that things were not yet at rest. Edam was unusually quite on the trip back to my apartment. Chalking it up to the fact we had both used a lot of energy in catching the remaining ghouls I didn't give it much thought. At least not until we arrived at the alley way to my back door.

"Andras, May I come in for a moment?' ' I have things I need to speak with you about; and I fear this may be the only time we get alone to do so." Edam looked at me with doe like eyes. I got a feeling he was having mixed emotions about what he needed to divulge. Shrugging my shoulders, I kicked down the kickstand of the Shovelhead down. "Sure, but make it quick, I need to rest soon; or I will be no use to anyone." Unlocking the door, I pushed it aside and motioned for Edam to go on in. What made me think that I was not going to like what he had to tell me?

Removing the velvet cape, I placed it on the back of kitchen chair. Pulling the chair out, I sat down and motioned for Edam to take the one across from me. As soon as he was at the table, he clasped his hands together and closed his eyes. He looked nervous; it was really not like him to act this way. "When I was assigned as your partner, you were under the assumption that I was a Hybrid / half breed.' "Yet you were mislead to believe such, and I should have corrected you, yet, I could not find the right way to go about it; until now. "I was not only assigned as your partner, but also as a guard to help keep you safe." Edam was staring at me, as if what he was about to say next would cause the whole world to crash down. Maybe, he was right for the filling in the pit of my stomach had went from butterflies too knots, in a matter of seconds. "Go on, if you are not like me; then what exactly are you?" He was clasping his hands together so tightly that his knuckles were actually turning bone white. "Well you see it's much more complicated than who I am, it is also about why I'm here now." "I am a lower God, the God of Force to be exact; I was sent here by the Tribunal to protect you from your father, among other things." "Though I admit, I have truly enjoyed my time here with you, and I have become attracted to you on many levels." "I know that you will not be able to trust me now; that you know that I have kept who I am from you." Bowing his head he pause waiting for me to absorb all that he had told me.

As I sat there trying to ponder all the things Edam had just said to me; my emotions were hitting high on ever scale. First I was in utter disbelief, and then it turned to sorrow, hate, anger, and just confusion. I didn't know how the heck I was supposed to respond to everything he had just laid on the table; let alone deal with it when I had so many other pressing issues to work threw.

Taking a deep breath, I gripped the edges of the table and shoved my chair back; I needed some room to move about. The crap just kept piling on thick; if it did not stop soon then I would need a backhoe to remove myself from underneath it all. "I need sometime to think, and sleep; I suggest you leave now." Turning to the kitchen window, placing my back to the hunk of man sitting at my table, for I just could not bear to look into his eyes at this moment. If I did, its likely things would become very, very complicated, much more so then they already were. Letting out a sigh of defeat Edam crossed the space to the door in a New York heart beat; I felt the breeze of his passing on the back of my neck. I waited just enough time to make sure he was truly gone before; I turned to lock the door and retire to my room. This had turned out to be one hell of a week.

Slipping out of the hand me down outfit my aunt had bestow on me, I slipped into my favorite Hard Rock Café shirt and a pair of plaid boxer shorts. I did not care what I really looked like, I just needed rest and it was the easiest thing to throw on. Gathering my shoulder bag, sat cross legged on the bed; spilling to contents upon my patchwork quilt. I stared at the scroll and hard leather bound book before me. Taking the Crystal of Otherworld from is pouch; I stared into its depths. Uttering out loud as I gazed at its ravishing beauty, "Why, me?" The stone just hummed another passage of the lullaby from my childhood. "Not much help are you?" Stuffing it back into the silk pouch, I placed it under my pillow. There really was no sense in it being left out for anyone to find.

Shoving my feet beneath the thick blanket, I grabbed the two parcels; I began to unravel the scroll. My mother's stories could wait. I needed to know more about my kind. So long I had looked at myself as an outcast, now that image did not fit. I was something much, much more. As to what exactly, I was still seeking the answers too.

The Glint of the calligraphy writing seemed to be shining like that of the Queens Dragon throne. I began to read from where I left off. If I was going to have to take my place among the Gods, in this great scheme of things, then I was going in with as much knowledge as I could.

The Hybrids are showing great possibilities, not only to strength us all as one again, but in their blood they also possess the magical elements in which to destroy us all. They need to be show how to wield their magic, and use their hearts as the judges they will need when the time comes. We fear that in the wrong hands they would be a weapon of like none we have ever witnessed before. In light of our discoveries we, the Tribunal, seek to stop the unions between the Fae and the Gods. We feel it's in the best interested of the four worlds themselves.

Okay, so now I know, that the Tribunal is the reason, more of my kinds do not exist; the same tribunal that thought it necessary that I be placed under protection. Still not finding the answers I was in search of I continued to read. The first four paragraphs were of the dangers we possessed in the wrong hands. It was in very urgent writing that all further unions to create my kind be forbidden. Finish reading about the wild magic some of us hybrids possessed; my eye caught what I had been searching for. Birth records of sorts, well to be exact, they were known unions between gods and fey that had created my race.

Our actual numbers were not written down. It was as if someone wanted that knowledge to be kept hidden for whatever reasons they had. I was beginning to see, that their reasons were not that far off, if Hermes had been the one to raise me instead of the Queen; I would be a walking time bomb ready at his disposal. I was started to put the pieces to this giant jig saw puzzle of a life together.

Finally the ache in my heart was being stitched closed, and with it a fire was replacing the pain. I had to use these Gifts for the greater good; only then would I be more than what my father had become. Only then would my destiny be as it should be, in my own hands. Rolling the scroll back up; I laid the two parcels back in my shoulder bag.

I don't even remember falling asleep, yet, I must have as soon as my head hit the pillow. The clock was going off like a police siren, when I finally cracked my eyelids. Rolling over to smack the damn thing into silence, I realized I had slept until noon. Shit I needed to get up and ready or I would never get to the end of this journey.

Racing to my closet I was stripping out of the

t-shirt and boxers in record speed. I had little time to waste if I was going to take one crystal to its hiding place, search for the remaining three and bag my father in the act. I grabbed a violet halter top and a pair of buckskin patchwork leather pants from the hanger. No time to be picky the day was already half over. Shimming into the snug fit pants, I snagged my matching suede ankle boots with the four inch silver rod heels. Another kick ass pair I had just recently added to my collection.

Gathering my hair back in a messy ponytail, I stuffed the stone back into my shoulder bag; fishing the cell phone from the inner pocket I hit speed dial 4. "Pick up, Pick up!" I was mumbling loudly to myself, finally on the fourth ring, I heard a ruff voice say hello. "Edam, get over to the alley, ASAP, we have work to do." "Oh and if its not to much trouble contact Kyle and Demonic and have them start ferreting any information they can on where Hermes is hiding." "I want to get this case over with as soon as possible." I didn't even give him time to respond, snapping the cell phone shut, I strapped my Atheme to my thigh and hooked the silver chain around the armband.

Slamming the door, and replacing the magical cover; I made my way to the alley behind my apartment. I wanted to get as much of this done today as I possibly could. I was in some desperate need of some R&R. Edam was in the alley before I had a chance to snap the saddle bag on my beautiful bike. I held up my hand before he even had a chance to speak.

"Look I'm not to happy with you keeping secrets from me, lord knows I have had to deal with enough of them in my life; but I understand why you did it." "It doesn't mean you're off the hook, so you can get that look of relief off your face." "All I'm saying is, I get it, but from now on if you hide anything from me, so help me; I will make sure you regret ever doing it." He stared at me in disbelief as if I had just added some wind back to his sails. Nodding his head, he stared at the ground.

Finishing adjusting the compartments on my precious chrome and hard steel baby. I looked up at him; "Did you contact the boys and ask them for me?" "Yes, they said they would call as soon as they found out anything." "Good, then here is the run down on what we are doing today." I ticked off the to do list on my hand as I spoke, first we would take the Crystal of Otherworld were it needed to go, second, we were going to crash the Counsel and the Tribunal little pow wows; for if I was going to be saving the damn worlds, then they were going to level with me. Third, while we were there we would pick up the COH - Crystal of Heaven. Hopping on to the bike, I kicked it into life with an ear shattering roar.

Edam looked as if he was about to turn three shades of green, at what I had just told him. Oh well, he would have to deal with it. If not, then what was the use in him trying to protect me? Besides, I had a right to speak to them all; after all I was heir to two thrones; and I would be damned if I was going to let anyone else decide what I did with my time.

Today was a new day; I was a new woman, well, maybe not new but changed. That was for sure. I didn't think for one minute when I grabbed the case file with those poor young girls in it that it would end this way.

Well, too late, so I fell into the snake pit, at least I was armed to the gills when I did it. As we headed to the Cave, millions of thoughts were racing threw my mind, yet for the first time in a long time, doubt was not among the jumbled mess inside my brain. I actually felt as if I had a purpose, and a chance to become something of my own making. Born to be wild and free, with no chains to bind me, unless I so chose it. That was how I was going to live my life from now on. It was mine to live.

The cobble stone streets didn't seem to be as bumpy as they usually were; maybe, I just didn't pay as close enough attention to the stucco beat they were making under my tires. I had more important things to fill my mind with. I had a path, this journey was mine. So, I let the wind caress my hair, and skin as I rode to my destination; failure and defeat no longer hung to me, as if they were bearing down on my shoulders.

We rode for miles, till we were out of the sleepy little mountain town. At the edge of the city limits we pulled the bike to a slow crawl hiding it behind a billboard, off the beaten path. I placed the kick stand down and started unloading the saddle bags of everything we might need, as we made this journey. One could never tell for certain what creatures you were too met on an adventure such as this. I loaded everything into my shoulder bag; set the magical cloaking spell, to hide my bike from prying eyes. It was no telling when we would return; and I really didn't want to come back to find parts missing. I looked at the blank landscape around us; as peaceful as it seemed, there was a malevolent tang that hung to the air.

The God of Chaos was riding hard on the wind this night; the mere thought set shivers of gooseflesh up my arms. Sighing, I turned and nodded to Edam. He cracked open the void between this world and the next in a single movement of his hands.

The blue portal shimmered into place with a loud pop. Shaking my armband down, I stepped threw the thin film of ether. Otherworld looked odd in the this part of the realm; as if the colors were running like a oil painting that had been doused in kerosene.

"The sooner we are out of here, the better." I said. Grunting as was Edam's fashion of approval, we started our journey on the purple stone path. It would be a long hike to where the moon touched the hanging star above the entrance of the Cave of Gold.

The only thoughts that seem to be running threw my mind were of Hermes and his plan for world domination, I knew I had to stop this madness. Yet, how I was going to do that was beyond me at this time.

First thing first I needed to get the Crystal to its resting place; then I could worry about the rest of it. The Crystal sang its lullaby as if it understood; it was a deep sleep that was in store for it. The lullaby hung in the air; the feeling of hearing it a long time ago was sharper than ever. Bits and pieces of the melody skipped threw the night air.

Oft in dreams I wander

To a spring of spun gold,

I feel her arms a-huggin' me

As wings of an Angels.

Such a soft embrace.

And I hear her voice a -hummin'

To me of days long lost in lore,

When she held me close I can still hear

The Harps a playing

Outside the gardens gate.....

The beat skipped along with our pace, I could feel it in my bones; as if it was trying to wake my very soul. I looked up at Edam with a puzzled expression on my face. "What?" He asked. "Can't you hear the music?" I asked him. "I think my dear Andras' that its music is meant for you alone." Edam answered. He dropped his head to keep from looking me in the eyes I think he was still feeling guilty from what he had told me the night before. Yet, I could not be for sure. On the song sang louder and louder with every step we took toward the Cave of Gold.

Doo-ra-loo-ra-doo-ral, doo-ra-loo-ra-li,

Doo-ra-loo-ra-doo-ral,

Hush now, don't you weep!

Doo-ra-loo-ra-doo-ral, doo-ra-loo-ra-li,

Doo-ra-loo-ra-doo-ral

Many years ago,

This song she sang to me

  In whispers so sweet and low.

Just a simple little tune,

In her good old Irish way,

And I'd give anything in the world to

Hear her sing that song to me this day.

Humm. Hummm, humm....

It was as if it had been a song I had heard when just a small child, yet I could not place the singer. I remembered what Luke had said, about the crystal giving me clues in its own way, yet, I was not sure what the clue meant to me.

On we traveled threw the twilight landscape. I watched the world around me dance and vibrate with every step we took. It was as if the very fabric of what made Otherworld was awaking by us; as if it had sensed our purpose. After going about a mile, Edam finally turned to speak to me; "If you don't mind, can you tell me what song it sang?" "We might be able to figure out what it means, if we work together." I nodded my head, and retold the song, just as the crystal had sang to me. When I was finished, we walked for a while longer, the pieces to the puzzle were in the song; we just had to put them together. "So, what do you think the message means?" Edam had thought of all the words that were in the song.

Of all the words, the Harps, Angels, Wings and the Gate were the ones to stand out the most; he told me so, as we started our long climb up the side of the mountain. The mouth of the cave was not far away now. What we came up with was that the crystals were at one time pairs, and each one sang of its partner's location. Crystal of Otherworld was singing a love song about its partner; who was none other than the Crystal of Heaven.

It was a good thing that was our next stop; now I could kill two birds with one stone. Edam was still nervous about me approaching the counsel, and the tribunal. He was going to have to get over it. They needed to know that I was not going to stand by and look pretty while Hermes destroyed everything that was good in this world. Now that I knew who I was and that I was heir too two thrones. I would do everything in my power to stop this madness.

The path took a sharp turn, the crystal sang louder; letting us know that we were headed the right way. The mouth of the cave opened up like a giant whale, its dark ebony entrance was looming over us as we rounded the curve in the cobble stone path. The sounds of the night were muffled to almost near silence. An eerie quiet started to blanket us in as we inched our way closer to the Cave of Gold. I still had no idea how I was going to stop Hermes from ripping away everything that the four worlds stood for; or how I was going to keep his nasty hands off me. I knew one thing I would go down swinging before he would control how, or what I used my powers for.

Edam was still another concern, how could I trust him? After everything he had shared with me. I vowed that I would never let anyone get close to me again after I left Otherworld; yet somehow he crept into my life and heart. Now I just did not happen between us. Scary how the simple things seem to be the hardest to wrap your head around...

Pausing at the entrance into the cave; the crystal vibrated in my hands, humming softly as if coming home to a long lost love. Lighting the torch that hung in the nook on the cavern wall, I held the flame up high, illuminating the walls of the cave in a splash of red flickering light. The wall was studded with gemstones and diamonds the size of my fist. An arched doorway was to our right; it shimmered with a soft glow. I knew, that the doorway would lead us to the resting place were I would place the crystals one by one into their trunk for safe keeping until it was time to use them.

Slowly we turned to the archway and headed

toward the encased tomb the crystals would call home until who knows when. The room opened up as if by magic. It looked as if it could fit an entire football field in it. There was a marble washed walkway with water on either side in the center of the room, waterfalls cascaded down stone pillars on either side of a gold door that was at the end of the long walk way. On either side of the door were statues of lions with wings. Living gargoyle was common at sites where fey magic was concerned. The Sleeping Guardians didn't stir as I approach with my gift. Slumbering peacefully as if they were just mere stone. Even though I knew Whole heartily it was just a front; and that at any moment they could wake and cause hell of damage if they wanted too.

The sooner we got this over with the better. No sense in sticking around to see if the guardians would stir and cause a butt load of grief. I had enough on my plate and really didn't need to add two very pissed of lions to the mix. I had to pass threw the sleeping statues to place the crystal in is new home. Luke had told me that I must do this part of the journey alone. As the door way was magically sealed and would only allow those with clearance to gain entrance into its golden depths. I motioned for Edam to stay in front of the statues while I journeyed threw the door alone. Walking by the magnificent creatures, I sucked in a deep breath and said a prayer for safe passage.

The wind stirred around the great beast as if to ruffle there fine downy coat. The Guardians eyes glowed an eerie blue light as if they were aware at last of the crystal in my hand.

Yet they never moved from their perch. I placed my hand on the brass knocker. I was told that I need to treat this door as if it was that of a friend. So knocking twice before I pulled the handle seemed the right thing to do. The Brass knocker gave two thundering claps against the solid gold door. The crystal and ruby door knob turned slowly in my hand. I pushed the door open to reveal a room so bright it nearly blinded me. Covering my eyes with my arm I stepped threw the threshold. The Door slammed shut behind me with such force that I nearly lost my cool. I knew it was just a safety spell. But it still scared the be-je-bus out of me. When my eyes finally adjusted to the room's bright wash I saw a silver chest floating in the middle of a manmade pond. With just small stepping stones to the lead the way. Each of the stones was a different color gemstone. Each had its own tone when stepped upon.

Taking my time I gently placed my foot upon one stone to listen to its music, before placing my other foot on the stone in front of it. Six stones, six tones, I wondering to myself at the reason for this; as I continued my journey to the small silver chest. Stepping on the last stone, the lid of the chest lifted up as if some magic hand had yanked it open. I stooped down and placed the Crystal I had been carrying into the velvet folds of the casket, it would call home for a while longer. At least until I got to the bottom of all this chaos. Speaking softly to the crystal I promised I would return the other stones as fast as possible. It felt as if somehow each crystals pair was its soul mate. As crazy as this sounded it made sense to me.

Stepping back from the chest, the lid flew up and realigned itself in its rightful place. The Queen had warned me not to linger to long here. With one finally look around I crossed the threshold of stepping stones; placed my hand upon the door. There was a humming sound and then it softly clicked open revealing Edam on the other side, patiently waiting for my return.

"I'm glad that's over with." Edam said with a frown on his face. "For Now." was the only response I could give him. What was to come next was already making him sweat bullets, not to mention it had my stomach in knots that I don't think would ever come undone... Now to confront the Counsel and retrieve the Crystal of Heaven. After this was all over I was going to take a long vacation on some beach in the middle of no where.

Walking to the portal to head back Earthside, seemed shorter than the trip we had taken to get to the Cave of Gold. I was thankful for that; but we still had a long journey ahead of us. We would have to go across town so I could at least grab some supplies before we headed to the Heavens above. Plus, we needed to check back in with our makeshift crew to see how they were doing gathering up the last of the Ghouls my so called father had unleashed on the world. Missing pieces of my life were starting to fall together, and before this was all over I would have to choose the path I wanted to take. One thing was for sure I would never allow Hermes or anyone else to decide for me. I would go down fighting tooth and nail, but I would never give in. This much I knew in my heart.

Chapter Seven

~Descending From Gods~

The light at the end of the tunnel is emerging; I am starting to see the pieces of the puzzle fit together. So I'm a hybrid, born from a god and a royal fae of the Throne of Air & Darkness. After eighteen moon cycles the truth about who I am, and what I'm able to do are starting to be revealed. My only hope now is to be able to stop my father (Hermes; God of Chaos) from destroying everything that I have ever known. The only way I can prove my worth to the Counsel is to collect and protect the four Crystals of the worlds; while learning how to harness and control my wild and changeable powers. Putting my faith in Edam a lower level God, that has been posing as my friend; to help me awaken these abilities without handing me on a silver plate to dear old dad is a challenge to say the least. How do I trust someone that I barely know? After all I don't have the best track record in having people tell me the truth. Bitterness is starting to creep in; maybe it's the lack of sleep or the unending carnival ride from hell I have been on. One way or another something has to give. Failure is not an option I'm willing to except.

My life had turned upside down so many times, that I felt like I was on a never ending roller coaster ride without brakes. After arriving back from delivering the first of the four crystals; I was already starting to feel the butterflies dancing a jig in my stomach. The coming days would prove to be some of the most challenging I would face. After learning whom my parents were, what my true purpose was; I was still feeling like the rug beneath my feet was being yanked out from under me at each new discovery. Edam had revealed that not only was he in love with me; but that he was also a God. One of the very beings, I had come to despise. My emotions had turned like a corkscrew inside my soul. I no longer knew up from down, where he was concerned. One thing was for sure, I didn't have the time to deal with how I felt or what would become of us; until I was able to make sure Hermes was never able to complete his plan for domination over the worlds. After dropping Edam off at the pub down the street from my little apartment, I was finally alone with my thoughts; not that was providing much comfort. Although, I did welcome the little bit of peace and quiet it provided. Opening the door to my battered studio apartment; I let a sigh escape my lips.

Home, yes that is what this four wall shack had began to be to me. It was nice to have a place that was just mine; a little cubby hole to hide in when I needed to escape the worlds around me. Too many things had come crashing down around me as of late; my head was swimming from all of the revelations I had to process. I really could not wait for this all to be over with; then and only then would I be able to focus on me. Grabbing a glass from the cabinet, I turned on the tap, water slowly started to trickle out of the rusty faucet. My orchids were really starting to look tattered.

After giving them a healthy drink. I grabbed the diary my mother had wrote, dragging the lonely kitchen chair across the floor I sat down at my kitchen table, and began to read where I had left off.

Andras,

I know now that my time here is shorter than I could have ever thought. I have made plans for you to be in the keeping of my sisters, and if the time ever comes or you to face the truth about whom and what you are; I can only pray that you chose from your heart. Never allow anyone to choose your path for you. Each of us walks paths in life that are neither white nor black; but lay somewhere in the gray.

You, my daughter have walked a many gray paths. When the time comes I hope that you are able to see that the truth of all things lies in-between. I can almost see the beautiful woman you are becoming. I only wish I was able to guide you along the way in person. Hopefully the words I have left you will be a guiding light when the darkest of days approaches. Never forget you have family all around you; I am always watching.

Annabelle

Closing the journal, I lay my head on the table. I really needed to get some sleep soon.

Edam should be reporting back soon with news of how our little crew was doing in rounding up the remaining of the Ghouls. Then we would be able to travel to the heavens where the second crystal lay in wait. I still had to face the counsel. Note to self when this chore was through I am taking a vacation; this was all becoming to much. I don't even think I had my eyes closed for more than a minute, when the shimmers of blue started to appear in the small space of my kitchen.

My eyes flew open, Edam and the crew was just emerging from the portals rip; as I gathered my mother's journal and stuffed it back into my shoulder bag. "So, is the mess cleaned up?' 'Or do we still have detail work to do?" I asked the group before they even had a chance to adjust to the surroundings. The faster I knew the answers; the faster I would be able to complete the rest of my to-do list and start planning that wonderful vacation I had been day dreaming about.

Kyle, Domenic, and Edam just looked at me as if I had grown a second head. "Well?" I asked the boys. I really was getting crabby.

Two days of fighting and hunting would do that to a person. Edam spoke for the group, "Kyle and Domenic were able to locate all of the Ghouls, and send them back to the neither; but we do have another problem." "As they were dispatching the last of the big uglies, they found out some vital information." "It seems that the Ghouls were just the beginning of Hermes plans; and we are going to have to get a move on before he unleashes it on all the innocents. If I thought the rollercoaster ride was going to finally slow, I was sadly mistaken.

Looks like things were really starting to accelerate. It was just two days ago that I learned I was more than what I thought. Two days is not a lot of time to adjust to all the crap that had been thrown my way. It was like the file cabinet in my mind was crammed and over flowing. One thing at a time, I kept telling myself. It was the only way I was going to truly be able to keep a handle on everything. My body was humming with so much adrenaline that if I didn't slow down I might actually cause more damage than my father was trying to. The scrolls had made it perfectly clear that the powers I possessed needed to be honed and controlled; or all hell would surely break loose. I turned and grabbed my cape off the back of the kitchen chair.

Time to get this ball rolling.

I was so ready for this all to be over, and soon. We all gathered around as Edam opened up the portal again; this time we were heading to the Realm of the Gods. It was time for me to face my destiny and retrieve the crystal of heaven. I just hoped it would be as easy as that. Holding my breath I stepped threw the either like blue bubble and into the Heavens.

The clouds misted across the bottom of the stone stairway that lead to the Counsels chambers. Right out of a painting the Heavens opened up and before me I saw golden statues of creatures that were long gone. Ivory steps cut into the mountain leading to the very place I would have to present myself. I only prayed that when they heard what I was about to say they would see me as an as a friend. Slowly we began to make our way up the silky smooth looking stone steps; to the silver double doors that were in the shape of two giant angels. Heads bowed, wings out stretched and arms crossed.

The doors almost looked as if they were alive and ready to step away to make room for our passage. I shot a look to my rag tag team, they all nodded. It was now or never kind of moment, here is to hoping for the best.

I gingerly walked up to the silver angels and knocked soundly on the flat stone tablet that was etched between the two figures. The doors swung inward with a soft click; and we stepped threw into an unknown realm, well at least for me it was unknown. Edam lived here apparently.

Even though he really didn't look like he was happy to be home. Taking back by my new surroundings, I took a deep breath. Things were getting ready to get shaking up; I could feel it. There were Gods here that didn't think Hybrids like me were suppose to be alive; and then there were the others that wanted to control and posses the powers we were suppose to have. I knew I had gifts but they were just as normal as most of the other fae.

If what Scarlet had told me though, I had talents that were still asleep inside. Hopefully they chose to stay that way until we were done with saving the worlds. Ares God of War was waiting for us when the doors swung open. Edam's whole body tensed as if this was the last person he wanted to see.

I could only raise an eyebrow at the fine looking statue of a man that was chiseled from what ever rock they had made Ares. 'Yum'. Was all I could say? One of the most famous Gods of Mythology stood in front of me; in all his glory. His eyes were the color of burnt amber, his hair was in long chestnut locks sweeping his shoulders, and my, my his body was a rippled mass of muscle that looked as if oil was hand rubbed into each and every limb. The Greek god was even wearing golden strapped sandals. As if sensing my appraisal Ares, smirked and looked right at Edam; whom I had just noticed was standing lock jawed with his hands clenched into fists so hard his knuckles had turned white from strain.

There was defiantly something major brewing between this two. I made a mental note to do my best to not stir the pot while we were here in their realm. Clearing my throat; I looked at Edam and spoke. "Care to introduce us, and explain our reason for this visit." Edam nodded as if coming back to himself.

"Of course, Ares this is Andras' Hermes Daughter and we have come to seek the advice of the Counsel." "We have news that is of dire importance, I'm sure Zeus would not want to be kept in the dark about what his brother has planned." Now it was Ares turn to look like a deer caught in the headlights. Turning swiftly on his heel he led the way down the winding ivory hall, which was lined with golden scones.

At each turn was a high marble arch; each colored a in a different shade of stone. It was like walking under a rainbow. The winding hall was the center of a honeycomb of other chambers. Some held nothing but books and scrolls in what looked to be glass tubes.

Others were housing rows and rows of dark brown tables. As I snuck a peek at our new surroundings I could only image what it was like to walk amongst these halls freely.

If I had known my heritage sooner would I have really been allowed to study the ancient texts that were so proudly displayed? Or would I have been turned away without another thought. Shaking these thoughts from my head. I stared at the back of Edam's head as he had put his self between me and Ares; as if trying to protect me.

I was gathering it was more possession than protection. I was really getting sick of these male ego trips. I did not have time to think about relationships or love; I had to finish the task ahead of me. Putting a stop to my father's plans forever. I could not allow anything to distract me from that; people in all worlds were depending on me, whether they knew it or not. We came to a stop in front of a bronze cast door that had stories right out of the mythology books on earth. As if they prized the way humans had idolized them.

Ares opened the door, letting a white light wash over the room. In the center of the room was a fire pit, surrounding it in a semi circle sat the Counsel. Edam, our gang, and I were lead to the center of the room. Ares took his spot at the end of the circle. All the Gods were sitting on high back silver chairs. Edam walked toward the fire pit and faced the room. "I have brought Andras' daughter of Hermes and Annabelle to speak to you all, on the dangers I'm sure you are aware of." "I ask you to hear what she has to say and to open your minds and hearts to change."

With that Edam stepped back and waved me forward. Taking a deep breath I swallowed what felt like a mouthful of cotton. "I have just recently found out whom that my parents are this knowledge was kept from me by the Queen of Air and Darkness.' 'Whom I have just found out to be my aunt.'

'The reasons for this knowledge being brought to my attention now, had to do with the case I was working Earth side.' 'Ghouls were being unleashed on innocent women. When I questioned these ghouls; we were lead to believe that the Lord of Light had released them. Yet it was not so.' 'After traveling to see the Seer. We soon discovered that Hermes had released them in an attempt to frame the Lord of Light, and distract me.' 'He is planning something so extreme that none of the worlds are ready for it. He is after the Crystals of the four worlds.' 'I believe that he is trying to destroy everything we know; in order to rule over it.' 'I have been tasked to collect the remaining crystals and store them in a secure location until a time when the worlds are ready for them again." The flames in the fire pit turned an indigo blue signaling that I was speaking the truth.

Zeus stood from his chair and spoke, "Who has given you such a task?" "What would Hermes gain by distracting you?' 'You would not have know your heritage if it was not for this mess." I looked at the white haired god that stood so still in front of me as if he were a mere statue. I knew the answers to these questions; yet how was I to word it with out stirring the preverbal pot. "By distracting me with the Ghouls and trying to lead me onto a false trail; he gained exactly what he had hoped for in a way.' 'I was finally told the truth of my linage, yet the outcome he had hoped for I did not give him." 'I believe he wanted me to become angry about the fact I was kept in the dark like a sheep with wool over its eyes."

'It is my understanding that as a Hybrid I posses certain powers that could be uncontrollable if I'm not properly trained." "I think he was banking on this point, he wants to control me; for his own personal gain." "He thought I would do something rash that would cause you as the Counsel to hand him my leash." 'What Hermes did not count on was my ability of free will, and my love for my Justice." Being a Huntress is in my blood as much as being a child of a God is also." "The Queen of Air and Darkness is the one that asked me to retrieve the Crystals and store them for safety." As I shut my mouth, Zeus looked toward the fire pit as if hoping I was telling a lie. I knew better than come here with any intent of being false.

He turned to the other members of the Counsel as if having a metal conversation with them. Ares was the one to finally break the silence. He cleared his throat, directing the whole room to look in his direction before he even uttered a word. I got the feeling that the God of War really liked to be the center of focus. "Andras' now that we have established that you have come here under no false pretences, what it is exactly, that you wish from us." "As you know we usually don't mettle in the affairs of the other worlds. It causes, how do you put it; oh, yes quite a stir when we do." Now it was my turn to look at him as if he had grown a second head.

"I want the Crystal of Heaven so I can store it with the Crystal of Otherworld, for safe keeping until such a time comes were they can be used properly and for the right reasons.' 'I wanted you all to be aware of what Hermes has done, of the deception he was planning against the Heavens as well as Otherworld.' "I come as the Heir that I am rightfully to let you all see that I'm not in need of being binding; nor do I want to be controlled." "I have come to show you that I can lead; but I will choose my own path it will not be chosen for me." I hope that answers your questions. I was starting to get a tad touchy and I knew showing anger would not get me anywhere. Edam stood from his chair, walking slowly across the room he came to stand next to me. Addressing the Counsel once again, he took my hand. "If you feel the need for Andras' to be trained, I will be the one to do it." "I ask you now to think clearly and not let your own prejudices stand in the way of what is right." "Hand the Crystal of Heaven to Andras', so we may put it away; and keep our world out of harms way."

The room was so silent you could here a pin drop, if I had one to drop that is. I was holding my breath for so long I swear I was turning blue around the gills. Zeus finally stood and turned to the rest of the Counsel; pausing in front of them he nodded his head.

Athena floated into the room as if summons from some unknown source. In her hand she held a golden silk bag. Placing the bag in Zeus's hand she turned and stared right at me. Her eyes were as white as diamonds. I had never seen anything as breathe taking as her eyes. What a beauty she truly was. Zeus waved his hand at the room and with one swift motion the members of this elite group of giants stood and faced me. I was having trouble reading what they were saying through their body language alone. Edam squeezed my hand, trying to help ground me and keep me calm. This was it the moment that would make or break us. Apollo the golden boy himself sang out announcing the Crystals presence and telling all that were in the room that the guardian had come. I was blown away to say the least. They actually saw me as something greater than just a Hybrid freak.

Edam was directed to teach me how to harness my true gifts, I was gifted with the Crystal of Heaven to take to its resting place for safe keeping and the Counsel had grown to have faith that all was not lost again. Now I just had to prove to myself and everyone that I was the right woman for the job. No matter what Hermes would not be able to pull the wool over their eyes again; and I would do my damnedest to make sure that he never got a chance to fulfill his deepest desires.

The life I was given was starting to grow on me and for once I was in complete control of my destiny. I and I alone, were going to pick my path. We left the heavens above and headed back toward the Cave of Gold to deliver the Soul mated Crystal of Heaven to its resting place beside its love. With the Crystals of Otherworld and Heaven both out of harms way; we would be able to focus our sights on finding the Crystal of Earth and removing the Crystal of Underworld from Hermes hands. He had to be stopped. The worlds were counting on us.

Edam thought I should focus on training and unleashing my natural abilities when we arrived back earth side. I, on the other hand was ready for a shower, nap, and food in that order. Standing in my little kitchen; I looked at Kyle and Demonic, they both looked as tired as I felt.

"Guys."

"Why don't you take off and get some R&R?" "We will meet up here in five hours to discuss our plan on getting the remaining crystals to safety." The boys nodded and took off through the back alley; leaving Edam and I alone in my tiny apartment. "Andras' I strongly suggest you start harnessing your abilities you will need them sooner than you think." Edam said in a very passive tone.

If I didn't know any better I would think he was trying to use his oh so wonderful charms on little on me. I raised an eyebrow and stared at him from my perch near the table. "I don't think a couple hours of sleep would possibly delay my training, and if you seriously think I will be much of a student on no sleep; then by all means be my guest, help me unlock these blessed powers." I retorted in a not so nice manner, but right now I was tired; a tad cranky. I could probably eat a grown horse if one was near by; that was how hungry I had become.

Edam looked as if he was mulling over what I had just said, trying to find away to still get what he wanted. Well it wasn't going to work anytime soon. I removed myself from the chair I had been sitting in, and took off through the doorway leading to the shower. I so needed to feel the beat of the water on my skin. Cherry blossom body wash was calling my name. I could almost smell the wonderful scent.

"Where are you going, Andras'?" Edam asked from the kitchen door. "I'm going to take a quick shower, you can make yourself useful and cook us something to eat." "I would be more willing to start training if I have food in my body to help me think." "Ok, but please Andras' hurry; the faster we get to work the faster you can stop Hermes." Edam almost sounded hopeful.

I stripped off and stepped into the hot steam of the shower, letting the water beat down on my head and wash away the fatigue I was feeling. I so needed to clear my head; there was just so much to process. I knew that sleeping even a couple hours was probably going to push Edam's reserve more than I wanted to; I would settle for a decent shower and some grub.

Sleep would come when this was all over. I had a feeling that if we didn't start working harder it would not end well at all. After a nice forty-five minute session in the shower, I emerged rosy red and freshly scrubbed; to the smell of Bacon sizzling in the skillet. My mouth was watering, wrapping the towel around me as tightly as I could.

I walked back toward the kitchen. Drool starting to slowly make its way down my chin; in anticipation. Edam had got my little kitchen table looking like it was holding a feast for the queen herself in the mere time I had been away. Biscuits freshly buttered and golden brown sat on a plate; next to a platter of hash browns. A pitch of orange juice was sitting next to the jam and butter dish. He had really gone over board.

Standing in the doorway in my towel I watched as he flipped the sizzling bacon in the skillet. Clearing my throat I made my way to the table. "Wow, this really looks good." "Thanks." I managed to say without cracking a grin. Edam had turned to see me approaching; and low and behold he was wearing my apron that said, "Save a cook, grab takeout." "It's not problem, I was getting hungry myself." Edam stated as he turned to watch the skillet. I grabbed a glass and poured the orange juice; snatching a buttered biscuit I sat down and began to eat. "I was thinking that after breakfast we could start with the basics on getting these gifts as you call them to wake up." I spoke to his backside. Watching his reaching wasn't as hard as I had thought; it was like I had just lifted a boulder off his shoulders. He had visible relaxed with just the prospect of being able to help me. Getting up I headed to my bedroom to change into some comfortable clothing I was getting tired of heels and tight fitting garments.

If I was going to be training I might as well be comfortable while I did so. Turning to my closet I grabbed the most worn pair of blue jeans still on a hanger; tossing them on to the bed. I went to work on finding a shirt and undergarments. The shirt was easy opening the top drawer in my dresser; I grabbed a Deadheads vintage Tee. A sports bra and cotton panties were next. Laying everything on my bed. I began to change; my mind was racing a mile a minute. Figuring out what these abilities were was a task in its self unlocking their true potential was a totally different issue. I was starting to worry that I would suck big time at what ever task Edam had planned for me.

Strolling back into the kitchen I took a chair next to the little window, Edam had already started to eat. In silence we ate our meal as if it was the last one we would ever have. I have to say he was a damn good cook. "I am not going to push you unless I feel it's necessary." Edam stated as he cleaned his plate. "There will be times were you will want to give up and will have to find the strength within yourself to carry on.' 'I don't want that time to be on the battlefield." He looked at me with the most serious expression I had ever seen him wear. I was starting to feel emotions that were not mine. I had thought before it was just due to the crystals, but I was starting to wonder if it was one of the abilities that were trying to awaken.

"Edam, I need to know what gifts, abilities and powers my mother and father both had." 'Was the ability to pick up on emotions of others a trait of my mothers?" I asked as I helped myself to seconds. "I know more of your father than I do your mother; maybe your aunts can answer these questions for you." 'I was thinking that we would travel to Fae to train; if that was okay with you." Edam said.

In a way he had answered my question without really saying anything. If emotions were not my father's gift then they belonged to my mother's side; or at least I hoped. The scrolls had mentioned that Hybrids had developed gifts that were of neither parent but a combination of the merge. If that was the case then we might have a lot of surprises ahead of us.

"Yes, that would be fine. I would like to check on my aunts and let them know of our progress anyways." I stated as I got up to clear the table. "Just let me gather a few things before we head over." Edam grunted his reply, in his typical fashion.

Leaving the kitchen once more; I headed to my bedroom I was going to see if my mother had wrote about her gifts in the journal she had left me. If so I might have a clue as to what I was going to expect when they finally awoken fully in me. Sitting on my hand stitched patchwork quilt; I sat Indian style on my cover and began pouring over the book wrote in my mothers pen. Flipping threw the crisp pages I got to a creased section of the book.

Inside the crease was a photograph of a woman I could only assume was my mother. Standing facing the camera in a black velvet gown she had a smile budding on her face. In her had she held a silver chain, the same chain I now cared as I dealt with the unjust of these worlds? Removing the photograph from the crease I read what was written on the page.

Andras'

I have included pictures of me at my happiest times. I was just a couple weeks pregnant with you when this was taken. You my darling are going to be the future I just know it. The day this photograph was taken, was the day I found out about my abilities to predict the outcomes of others actions based on their emotional imprint. I had other gifts before I was pregnant and I can only assume the gift I'm now experiencing belongs to you my love. It is said that the child lets the mother know what if any gifts they will carry. This is the strongest one I have felt from you. I know your role as a huntress will be greatly helped by this ability. Remember to let your heart guide you as much as your head. Remain ever the balance in the face of darkness and nothing will ever conquer you. I have the uttermost faith in what you can and will do. I hope that when the time comes you will have a strong teacher, and faithful followers. Good luck my child. May the

Gods watch over you.

Annabelle

After reading the section, I looked closely at the photo before stashing both in my handbag. Adding the Chain of Justice and wrist band that belonged to my mother to the bag. I got up and left the room. Edam was waiting on me next to his famous blue portal. Well here goes nothing,

let the fun begin...

Chapter Eight

Emerging threw the portals rip into Otherworld didn't feel as strange as it did before. I was actually at peace this time coming here. Finding out I had family and wasn't just an outcast had started to help seal the cracks in my heart from the lies I had been told.

Hopefully Scarlet could shed light on these abilities I hold inside of me. I found out from just reading my mother's journal that them empathic gift I have, has been with me since birth. It was strong enough then to project itself onto my mother. Without it she would never have know that Hermes had evil intentions.

The first stop we were making on this trip was to the Seer's home, my lovely Aunt Scarlet. I had not seen nor heard from her since she had to leave earth side.

Hopefully, we can get some answers so we could put a stop to the destruction that Hermes would surely cause. Edam had been quiet since I had agreed to work on unlocking my talents. I couldn't get a read on him at all. It was as if he was shielding his emotions from me. I really was having trouble trusting him after everything. I couldn't help getting the feeling that he had plans of his own for me. Why I felt this way is still beyond me. One step at a time Andras' I coached my self as we walked along the cobble stoned street.

"Alright, spill it; Edam.' "Why are you so quiet?" I could not take the silence any longer. It was starting to way on my nerves. Edam continued to walk, staring up at the Heavens above; like he was seeking advice.

"I'm just worried, Andras'; I have no clue what your father is up to." "Stopping him is not going to be easy." "I just have a bad feeling in my gut is all?" Edam spoke without turning his head in my direction one time. Bull I thought to myself, there is more to it than that. I am not going to stop until I know what. If he wants me to have faith in him, and trust that he has my best intentions at heart; then it has to all be laid out on the table.

"Edam, Stop!"

"I am not going one inch further with you by my side, until I get some straight answers." "You expect me to believe you; when you won't even look at me when you speak." "I have had enough of the lies, half truths and run rounds." "You are going to tell me the complete truth not just what you want me to hear." "Or you can take your Godly ass back upstairs with the rest of them; and I'll do this on my own." Hot under the collar, is a mild way of putting how I was feeling right now. I was sick to death of the crap. Putting my foot down was the only way I was going to get to the bottom of this. Edam stood still; it was as if I knocked the wind out of him. He still wore a blank expression but his eyes were glowing. Every emotion he was feeling could be seen in them. "Truth Andras'; which truths do you want first?" "That I'm scared shitless; that some how I will loose you before I have ever really had a chance to have you." "That your father is hell on wheels, and will stop at nothing to control you like a good little puppet." "That I'm afraid that I won't be able to stop him; if he gets his hands on you." "That your abilities are manifesting and will likely be deadly to everyone including you if I don't train you properly."

"Which Truth is it that you want?" Edam never raised his voice, the tone changed with each statement he made. He was truly feeling like the weight of the world was on his shoulders too.

"Yes Edam, Those truths and any others you have hidden." "I want to know the cold hard truth at all costs." "Walk in my shoes a minute, I have been lied to, abandoned, and controlled." "Now I have to go up against the one person that should love me unconditionally and make sure he pays for his crimes." "So ya, I get where you're coming from, and I understand what you're saying; but if you think for one minute I need shit sugar coated think again." "Do we have an understanding, Edam?" "I need to be able to trust you if your going to train me." I didn't even take a breath as I belted all of this at him.

I got the only answer I needed, a nod and a grunt. Edam's famous trademark agreeing method. Just like a man to go all cavemen when it comes to the heart. We stood there sizing up each other for another minute; until I finally nodded back and continued to walk. The well beaten paths that lead to The Seer's cottage were as I remembered. Fields of spun golden wheat lined it on either side. Taking a look around I noticed that things were a tad different from my first trip here; or maybe I was just noticing the little people that were hiding among the foliage for the first time.

My lovely aunt had people on the look out for us or we were being followed; either way I thought it best to wait till we were safe inside the cottage before speaking of it. Knocking on my aunts' front door we stood and waited for her heart shaped face to appear in the cookie cutter window. It didn't take long for the door to crack open and allow us entrance. "Andras', Edam, what a lovely surprise." "I did not think I would see you again so soon." Scarlet stated. "I don't know if that was meant to be a joke or if you were really not expecting us." I smiled warmly at my aunt. "A little of both my dear child." Scarlet said with a small grin. "Hope we are not intruding, Scarlet." "Andras' and I have some questions; we thought we would start here in our search for the answers." Edam stated at a half bow.

"So my niece knows who you are now I see." My aunt stated as she looked up into Edam's chocolate eyes. Nodding, Edam looked a bit beaten back by the comment my aunt had made; as if he was unsure about how I felt about that revelation.

"Well Come in, you must be tired from your journey." Scarlet stated.

Following Her inside we found the house had changed once again. Gone were the velvet curtains with their heavy folds, the crush velvet couch and footstool. In its place were sky blue lace window covers, and an iron backed picnic bench. The only items that remained the same were the dragon snuggled next to the fire place along side my aunt's rocking chair; and the picture of her under the willow tree.

"Tea?" Scarlet asked picking up the wooden serving tray, which held a teapot and cups along with finger sandwiches. Grabbing a tea cup from her waiting hands, I sat on the bench and sipped the warm honey and jasmine flavored tea.

Waiting for Scarlet to sit down before I started belting questions at her. Edam sat ramrod straight next to be; like he could not wait to be done here. Either he still had things on his mind that he had not shared with me; or he was truly worried about failing. Making a mental note to ask him about it as soon as we were back at my apartment. I thought about the little people I had seen on our trip here.

"Scarlet, are you aware of the little people hiding among the foliage, along your pathway?" "I noticed them on our walk here." I stated. "Yes, my dear I have set up guards to let me know who is coming to and from my home." "In the event that I'm not here; I will still know if anyone has popped in for a visit." "Friend or Foe, you can never be too careful; you know." "I see." I said as I looked in Edam's direction.

"Are you okay, Edam?" Nodding, he just

continued to sit there as if he was waiting for me to ask the questions we both had answers to. Scarlet just sat there sipping her tea; taking us both in as if we were the latest side show act at the carnival. Smirking she raised her eyebrow and waited for me to begin.

"As you know I have been put in charge of the safety and security of the Crystals, I was recently gifted with the Crystal of Heaven. Zeus has seen to it that Edam would be the one to help train me in using my abilities." "The questions we both have; are which are mine and which of them our Hybrid versions of what my parents possessed?" "From reading my mothers journal I found out that the empathic ability I was born with." "So what gifts did my parents have?" I waited for Scarlet to set her teacup down, butterflies dancing in my stomach, like there was no tomorrow.

I had a feeling of dread coming over me and I could not shake it for the life of me. I don't think I have ever been this nervous.

It was as if by mere knowledge of what I was

capable of; was scaring everyone around me; even me. Scarlet folded her linen napkin and places it next to her cup; scooping up the little dragon that had been sleeping soundly at her feet she spoke. "Andras' I know this is all a lot to take in; and even more to carry on your shoulders." "My child you have always been special, your gifts are not just a combination of your parents; they are interchangeable." "Meaning?" I question my aunt. I have to admit I was starting to get impatient; just spill it already, tell me what I can and can't do." Biting my lower lip I rang the napkin in my hands as I waited for her to go on.

"Meaning that you can take the abilities that your parents had and twist them in which ever way you see fit to use them." "You are able to mold them in to new, more powerful, or simpler things.' 'For example your mother could change the weather with a mere thought; where you can do it with your mood, but you can also think it into being." 'Say you wanted it to rain but you were in a bad mood.' 'You abilities allow you to change the weather so that a sunny day becomes a rainy one; but if your pissed off it might flood if you don't think about the amount of rain you want." "Hermes is able to cause dangerous and chaos in others lives, you can actually create and change the type of chaos or danger; yet you also have the ability to remove it completely."

"So; my dear you see it doesn't really matter what your parents were able to do; as you are the one that chooses the fate of the outcome and the events." "What Edam needs to teach you is how to take what is already inside of you and use it to create the life you want." "You Andras'; have to believe in yourself." I sat there digesting everything she had just said to me, trying to get my mind wrapped around the fact that I could create or destroy my world. Is it really possible to stop all this madness that Hermes has created with a mere thought? If so then that explains why he wants to sink his claws in me. With me by his side; he could conquer everything. I knew one thing for sure; I was going to give it everything I had to make sure that never happened.

After sitting and visiting with Scarlet for a little longer; we gathered our belongings, and headed back down the cobblestone path. I still had one more stop before we could even start training. I had to go to the Court of Air & Darkness. I needed to report back to Sable and Luke and let them know that two of the crystals were safe; and what the Counsel had said. I was not dreading seeing the Queen after everything I had learned; this was the first time I was looking forward to go back to my former home. Edam was quite the rest of the journey to the Queen's lovely little kingdom; it seemed as if what the Seer had told us was a lot for him to process. I took the time to notice my surroundings, the colors of this world was as vibrant as ever. Emerald green leaves hung from the trees, blew in the wind. Flowers of every color were blooming along the cobblestone roadside. The winding babbling brook was sparkling with blue green spring water. Thinking back to my childhood spent running threw these fields of golden hay. These were some of my fondest memories. I made a promise to myself that I would come back here; after I was done with the tasks I had at hand.

Chapter Nine

As we rounded the bend to the Court of Air & Darkness; I could sense that Edam had something weighing hard and heavy on his mind. I was bound and determined to get to the bottom of it. After all I was going to have to trust him; to be able to work along side of him. If I couldn't; well, then I would have to go after Hermes beside myself. One way or another I was going to see this to the end. "So, Edam is there anything at all you want to say to me before we go in to see the Queen?" I didn't have to wait for to long before he responded.

"It's just that I have no clue what I am going to be able to do to help you hone your abilities to the point that u could undo a disaster if one were to happen." Edam replied, while shrugging his shoulders and kicking a loose pebble across the roadway. He had a valid concern; hell I didn't even know how I was going to trust him enough to allow him to help me. "One step at a time Edam; we will just take it a step at a time, and see what happens." I told him just as we got to the doors that would lead us to the queen's chambers. Sable was standing at the stain glass window staring out at her kingdom. She was thinking about how much had changed since Luke had told Andras' that she was Annabelle's child.

Now Hermes posed the greatest threat to her beloved niece; more so since the day she was born. She was starting to fear that Annabelle's worst nightmares were unfolding before their very eyes. Sable knew she had to help Andras' put an end to Hermes plans' before he was able to get his hands on her. Andras' was a lot stronger than she knew. It was now that the queen knew she needed to see to it that the bindings were removed so that Andras' could see how powerful she really was. Sable called to the Court Magician to have the bindings that were placed on Andras' as an infant removed. Just as there was a knock on the door.

Standing at the threshold of the inner chambers was her lovely niece. It was a now or never kind of moment. She could only pray that Andras' didn't view the binding of her powers as a betrayal. Andras' step into the room that held her Aunt. The queen turned from the window and greeted her with a large smile. Holding her arms out she waited for Andras' to fall into her embrace.

Andras' ran to her aunt and buried her head in the crook of her neck. It was like coming home, I was so happy to see my Aunt that I didn't even notice the worry etched across her face until after I had untangled myself from her embrace. "My Queen, why are you so worried?" I questioned. My Aunt stared at me in wonder. "Andras' you do not have to address me so formally; I am your aunt after all." Sable smiled why avoiding the question I had just asked her.

"Where is Luke I have news to deliver to the both of you?" "News you will be happy to hear." Sable smiled, grabbing my hand she lead me to her throne. Taking a seat on the foot stool just as I did the day my world changed; I waited for her to speak again. I had butterflies chewing holes in my stomach. I had a feeling that what ever had her worried would directly affect me. I just hoped it wasn't something that would tear my world apart again. "

Before Luke gets back, I have something I must tell you." "I only pray you will not see it as another betrayal." Sable said to me while she rang her free hand on the arm of the throne. "I'm sure whatever you have to say, or have done there was good reason to do it." I replied.

I had come to realize that even if I didn't really understand the why's to my Aunts reasoning, there usually was a good motive for the actions she took. No matter how life changing the may be for me. Holding my breath I urged her to continue, it was like ripping a band-aid off the quicker it was over the less it usually hurt. "Do you remember the first time you called up the wind, Andras'?" Sable asked.

"Yes I do, I don't remember why I did it, but I was three at the time." I replied. Nodding her head she swallowed and began to turn a little green. "You were mad about loosing a game of tag.' 'You called the wind and made it pick up the little boys and girls you were playing with.' 'It tossed them around like rag dolls; you didn't hurt them.' 'They were shaking and scared.' "Luke and I got there just in time to calm you down." Sable continued. "Oh." That was all I could think to say.

"Luke and I made an important decision that day; we called the Court Magician in, and had him bind your powers so that you would be able to have a normal childhood the way your mother wanted." By the time the queen had finished telling me what she had done; she was looking at her feet. I could tell that she was getting physically sick from the mere thought of me being mad about what they had chosen to do. Yet, for the life of me, I could not bring myself to be angry. "Why are you telling me this, now?" I questioned.

"Well you see, I have asked the Court Magician to remove these bindings, for I fear that you will need everything you have to take on Hermes." "You were gifted with the talents of both your parents and the ability to change things with just a mere thought.' 'Now is the time for you to learn what you are truly able to do, my child." "I see." It was all I could do not to visibly shake. I was scared to death of the powers that I was supposing to control. How could I do this without harming others? Yet, I knew I had to try or everything would be destroyed; and I could not allow that to happen. I sat there waiting on the Magician and Luke to stroll into the room.

Edam had taken his place on the bench that was along the wall. Sable was staring out the window from her throne; lost in her own thoughts. I could do this; I kept telling myself in my head. I had to pep myself up after all. I was getting ready to be in control of unspeakable powers. "Sable, I do have one question. Edam was put in charge of my training by the counsel. Do you have a place here at the palace were we can train?" Sable drew herself from her thoughts long enough to nod at me.

"Luke will take you there when the bindings are removed." "Are you sure you are not angry at me Andras'?" She questioned. I just shook my head no and squeezed her hand in reassurance. How could I be mad about something that had gave me a normal enough childhood?

If she had not done the binding I would have hurt someone I loved. How would I have lived with that? The throne room door opened; giving passage to the only father figure I had known. Luke looked as if time did not age him at all. His hair was still peppered with grey at the edges but his face was as youthful as ever. He wore a smile as he gazed upon the queen. The love they shared was timeless. I could only hope to find a love as great as theirs.

Behind the Murdock was a scrawny man in a long velvet lined cloak, a long grey beard hung from his chin like a rope. His face was folded in creases from the wrinkles that told his age. His knobby hands were holding a tattered leather bound book; that was sure to be his book of spells. He walked with a limp, yet he seemed to move with ease of a man years younger than he looked. Luke grabbed my hand and drew me up into his embrace. "My child, Oh how I have missed your with each day." "What news do you bring us?"

I told Luke a Sable all about what the counsel had to say; how we had rounded up the Ghouls that were set loose by Hermes. How that was just the start of his nasty plans. I told them about the Crystals and how I had two now stored in safety. Luke swallowed the large lump that had formed in his throat as I told him that I was there to train and control my gifts; so I could go after Hermes and end this all for good.

He gazed down at Sable, who was still sitting on her throne. They had one of those silent conversations with their eyes; that I had seen them have a million times. She nodded and directed her eyes at the mage that had followed look in. "It is time, Luke." Was all she said?

The mage grabbed my hand and led me to the dais in the center of the throne room. I had always wondered what the gold and black silk cushion was for. The statue of the angel with the broken wings, sifted water threw her hands into the pool at her feet. Her gaze was on the dais. I had never noticed where the statues gaze was, until now. As I sat on the dais; the mage sat down his tattered book on the book stand. He began removing herbs and runes from the inner pockets of his cloak. He began placing the objects around the dais.

Edam was gripping the edge of the bench; his knuckles were turning white from the force he was applying to the benches edge. He looked as if he was ready to run from the room. Sable had locked hands with Luke; they both were staring at me. I had a stomach full of knots.

Taking a deep breath, I tried to get my body to relax. I didn't remember the time when the bindings were placed on my powers; and really didn't know what I would feel when they were giving back. The mage had started to chant from a passage out of his worn book of spells.

The air thickened, my body vibrated and hummed as his chanting grew louder. Over and over again he repeated his words. Wave after wave of magic hit me as if I was being unwrapped layer by layer. I could feel my skin tingle, I could hear the elements of nature their selves.

It was as if for the first time I was truly alive. With each lash of the mage's words I felt myself changing. The tattoos that had only appeared at night when the full moon had risen; were now glowing anew. I could feel them singing along my skin. My shoulder blades felt as if something has attached to them. My eyes were seeing colors I had never seen before. Scents assaulted my nose. I stretched out my arms and legs, shaking my hair; I tried to remove some of the magic that had just poured over me.

That's when I saw it. I had looked into the statues eyes and for the first time I saw my own reflection looking back at me. The photograph of my mother came into my minds eye. I now knew why she said she would always be watching. This is what had become of my dear mother. Turned to stone; a living statue forever. I needed to find out who had done this. Annabelle did not deserve to be trapped like that forever. Angry coursed threw my veins. I felt like a shook up bottle of soda getting ready to explode.

"Breath, Andras'" "Just breath." Edam was by

my side softly speaking in my ear. He had not touched me. Yet, his words had cut threw the fog; and with it had help remove the residue of angry that I was feeling. The Mage had closed his book of spells. Sable and Luke were now standing mere feet away from where I lay. I stood from the dais and took a look around the room. I needed a mirror, something felt different.

I needed to know why. "Sable, I'm trying really hard to control the angry I have coursing threw my veins; but if you don't explain to me why my mother has become a dust bunny catching statue in your throne room; and soon. I'm afraid I will not be able to."

"Edam, find me a mirror I need to look at myself." He grunted as he stood up, leaving the room to hunt down the mirror. Leaving Luke, Sable, the Mage and I alone in the room. Sable turned to the Mage; he bowed to his queen and swiftly left the room. Luke just stared at me in wonder. "When your mother ran from Hermes; he had a curse put on her, we found her this way." "I have had ever mage from near and far; trying to undo this for as long as you have been alive." "None have been able to bring her back." Sable sighed and hung her head.

I clinched my fists at my sides. Hermes would pay for this and everything else, I promised silently. He would pay. Edam returned to the room with the mirror I had requested. I was so caught up in the fact that my mother was standing in front of me; and yet, she could not even tell me, I didn't notice he was there until he placed his hand on mine. Giving him a quick squeeze to reassure him I was okay. I turned and greeted him with an out stretched hand.

"Hand me the mirror, Edam." He paused as if by doing so would change everything. "Now." I said as forceful as I could. Edam cringed, and handed me the mirror. I   got   the impression that I had just commanded him to perform that act. I really didn't care at the moment. I had just been assaulted by unseen magic. Taking the mirror I held it up so I could gaze at my reflection. I stood stock still, gazing into the shinny surface. How could this be?

It was impossible.

My eyes were now glowing bright sky blue. The silver tattoos were now scrolling along my body as if they were alive. My hair was ebony black with bright blue streaks in it. The pierce marks on my shoulders now held powder blue wings that were almost transparent. I looked up at Sable, a look of confusion etched into my face. "How?" Was the only word I was able to form.

Nodding her head Sable, answered my unasked questions. "With the bindings removed; your true form has come through." She said. "I never thought you would have wings of a Fae, as a child you just had the dimples in your shoulders." "The tattoos didn't show their selves until your eighteenth birthday.' 'I guess the rest of the changes are a result of maturity."

"You look so much like your mother." Sable was starring fondly at my new image. Luke had a smile as broad as his face. Edam was the only one that looked like he was worried about everything. I was feeling things on a whole new level; the powers coursing threw my veins was almost as addicting as a drug.

Chapter Ten

Luke led us to the training room the Fae guards used. It was a lead contained padded room. Able to keep magic contained; while still allowing the users to practice and perfect their talents. It was the perfect place to try out my abilities; now that the bindings were stripped away.

Edam had said, he thought it would be the safest place for everyone. I think he meant it was safer for everyone else. Either way it didn't matter to me; my only concern was harnessing these gifts to perfection, so I could free my mother from the fate Hermes had destined her to. We practiced for hours on controlling the weather.

I could bring up a gale force wind just by thinking about it. Yet I was having trouble toning it down. I could form a rain cloud out of thin air; yet, I still had difficulty making it stop. We had to open the doors to the training room twice just to remove the water. "Your trying to hard Andras', trust yourself.' "Feel it humming in your soul and just let it flow out nice and easy." Edam coached from the protective glass cube in the observation room above. I had the feeling Luke was up there silently watching.

That thought was enough to force me to relax. I wasn't alone with just Edam watching the freak show I had become. Why I was having these mixed feelings now was beyond me. Maybe, it was all the pressure I was under. Shaking the thought from my mind; I took a deep breath and shook out my hands. "Good, now let's try to create a cloud.' 'Just a cloud." Edam said. Okay what the hell; I could do this, I coached myself.

Closing my eyes I focused on seeing a nice fluffy white cloud in my minds eye. Slowly, I opened my eyes and there before me floating three inches from the top of the training room ceiling was a little ball of cotton. I jumped up and down, silently celebrating my little victory. Edam cut through my self cheering session with another order. "Now.' 'Make it turn into a rain cloud.' I looked at the fluffy cloud and visualized the outer edges turning grey from the water they held. Slowly it started to change.

Hanging heavy with rain the cloud began to sag and drop. "Now, Andras' focus on releasing a little rain." "A drizzle." Edam suggested from his hidey hole. Nodding to myself as much as Edam; I began to visualize the water that had built up in the cloud coming out in a fine mist.

"Good, Andras'." 'You are doing great." "Now make a lightening bolt; but I want you to visualize it coming to you." Was he flipping crazy? Why the hell would I want Lightening to come at me! "Say what?" I asked starting to panic. "You can hold it in your hand, remember you are not human it will not harm you." Edam sounded as if he was getting frustrated with my questioning.

I closed my eyes to gather my barrens; taking a deep breath I visualized a golden bolt of lightening, small enough to hold. When I opened my eyes, the energy bolt was in the palm of my hand; I gingerly wrapped my hand around its form. "Edam?" "Now what." I asked. There was no answer from the little glass box above the training room. Minutes ticked by; and still I held on to the bolt of lightening. Getting frustrated I flung it at the glass box. A loud crack of thunder sounded from the rain cloud I made. Light lit the room; leaving everything in an eerie glow of unnatural golden light. "That was perfect, Andras'." Luke's voice sounded from the speaker system. "How was that perfect?' 'I lost my temper." I retorted.

Luke opened up the door to the training room and step inside. "You lost your temper, but not your control child." He stated. Sighing I just stood there staring at him as if he was a little nuts. How was that going to help me defeat Hermes? I questioned silently in my head. "Now for some fun." Luke danced on the edge of the mat; I had been standing on. "Picture the cloud drying up and then disappearing." He stated to me. "We will begin your defense lessons next." Luke had a look of pride on his face as he spoke to me. I could not help but smile. I was really doing this. With Luke and Edam helping me hone my abilities; I could take on Hermes and whatever army he threw at me.

Luke used his own magic to create mini disasters; it was my job to dissolve them or change them into something that could be used as a defensive weapon. It was hard at first, but after about twenty minutes I had the hang of things. He made a fire storm sweep across the mat toward me. I redirected it and had it roaring with new life as it sped toward Luke. Jumping out of harms way in the nick of time; he wiped his brow and nodded. I put the flames out with a flick of my hand and a mere thought. The next was wave after wave of water that, I turned into a waterspout that chased him around the room. Laughing my ass off; I changed it into steam. The room felt like a sauna. At least no harm had happened to either of us.

He started throwing insults and hurtful words my way; to see if he could break my control. Nothing he had done; had made me loose my temper or train of thought. That was until. Until he brought up my mother. I was not expecting such an attack.

Completely thrown off guard. I slipped up and almost got crushed by the boulder he had created. Rage coursed through me. I saw red and then all hell broke loose.

It was like someone lit a match in a bundle of fireworks. I assaulted Luke with pelts of Hail, slammed him against the wall with a wall of water. I was getting ready to set his butt on fire when Edam charged into the room. "ENOUGH!" "Stop, Andras'." "Control yourself." Edam had wrapped his arms around me from behind and was trying to physically keep me still. I looked into Luke's eyes and that was all it took.

The room froze. I mean it really froze. Nothing moved except my own heart. I had stopped everything literally. Coming back to my senses I slowly let everything return to its normal state. Luke was clutching his knees and breathing heavy. Edam was still clinging to me for dear life. "That was a low blow, Luke what gives?" "Hermes, will use everything he has against you; Andras'." "Even your mother." Luke stated.

I started to speak then stopped myself; he was right. I had to get a handle on my emotions. Hermes would play dirty; and if I couldn't hang with the big dogs then I had no chance on winning. I had to win. More than my own life was at stake. "Okay; then lets do this again." I said as I stared at Luke.

He held my gaze for a moment longer; nodding to Edam. Edam released his hold on me and went to exit the room. I on the other hand had a different idea. "Stay Edam; you're a lower level god." "It may not be the same as fighting Hermes but I will at least get an idea of what I'm going to be up against. Edam grunted and looked to Luke as if he was taking his cues from him. That really didn't set well with me. "You are my partner and were ordered by the counsel to teach me." "Stop looking at Luke; when I say something it goes!" "Got it?" I had my hand on my hip; shooting daggers at Edam with my eyes. If I was going to learn to trust him; he was going to have to do the same.

"Your right, Andras'; I apologize." "Let's begin." It was all the warning I received as

Edam turned he lifted me off the ground with a gust of wind. I flew across the room. Seconds before I slammed into the wall; grabbed the wall of wind he was forcing at me and converted it into something that would carry me back across the room. It wrapped around me as if a gloved hand. I danced across the mat as it dropped me softly in front of both my opponents. Taking the advantage I had just give myself. I turned the sheet of wind into a rope and wrapped it around their feet. Jerking with only my mind. I knocked their feet out from under them. Edam and Luke slammed into the mat at the same time. I didn't stop there; I formed a lightening bolt and held it like a dagger over their throats.

A smile plastered on all of our faces I knew that I had done the right thing. Clapping Luke laid on the ground; amusement dancing in his eyes. Edam was wearing a tightlipped smile; yet I knew he was proud of me. "You are better than we thought you would be." Edam stated. "Do you think you have had enough training or do we need to continue letting you beat the crap out of us?" He said with humor in his voice. "I think we are done." Luke stated just as Sable Queen of the Throne of Air & Darkness walked into the room. The look she wore was one of pride; yet I could tell that she had come in to tell us something. It had nothing to do with our current training session.

"Andras', Time is running short." "Hermes has unleashed another attack on Earth.' 'You are needed there.' The queen stated.

"I also have a clue that will help you locate the Crystal that is Earth side." "*Look for the place that is named after a Heavenly body.' 'Seven sisters' dwell among the foliage. The Satyrs dance on the hill side. Nothing there is what it seems. Where the water flows backwards, a hut can be found. Seek the old crone that resides inside. Magic she holds; so speak soft and true.' 'Only then will you find what you seek.*" The Queen recited from memory.

"Kind a vague isn't it?" I joked halfheartedly. There were a ton of places on Earth that were named after Heavenly bodies. Edam looked as if a light bulb had gone off in his head. "I know where it is." He stated matter a fact like.

Sable told me that no one would see my wings or scrolling tattoos; unless the were of magical origin. That was reassuring, as we were about to head back to Earth. Where normal folk didn't believe in such things and those that did were either total fanatics or the type that carried torches. I really did not want to deal with either on top of everything else I had going on. After hugging Sable and Luke; I went back to the throne room to say goodbye to my mother. I didn't know if she could hear me or not; but I knew she could see me.

That was enough for now. I wrapped my arms around the statue that I now knew was actually the frozen version of my beloved mother. Whispering into her ear; I made her a promise to undo all the evil Hermes had done. She would be herself again; if it was the last thing I did.

Edam opened the sparkling blue portal that would lead us back into my apartment. I turned back to wave at Sable and Luke; whom were locked in an embrace. This would be over soon I promised silently. Stepping threw the rip; I landed softly in my kitchen. Edam walked threw behind me; and began to hunt franticly for a map.

Our cell phones were buzzing like two angry wasps. Domenic and Kyle had there hands full and were in need of our help. Hermes had unleashed day walking demons; they were currently holed up at the local cemetery. Man, I was really getting tired of going to see dead people just to get rid of bad guys. Hermes was trying to slow me down. I had no idea what game he thought he was playing but I was done dealing with it.

"Do you think we can create a portal to the underworld; and round up all the daywalkers at the same time?" "Force them back into the ether with wind or some other element?" I questioned Edam as we got on the back of my motorcycle. Kick starting it; I let the engine purr to life under us while I waited for his response. "If Kyle and Domenic can run them back to us; it might work." "We will have to work quickly though; if they gain possession of an innocent we might never catch them." Edam stated as he placed his hands on my sides waiting for the bike to coast forward.

Nodding, I pushed forward and roared down the cobblestone street. My bike had missed me as much as I had missed it. Wind streaming threw my hair; I allowed the feeling of the roads vibrations to calm my nerves. I had been wired to the max, like a junky in need of a fix since this day had begun. We rounded the corner of the street and started to head down the mountain side when Domenic's ringtone filled the air. Edam slapped the phone open and placed it to his ear listening and grunting without really saying anything.

"Turn and head for the back entrance; the boys have them cornered." "It is now or never kinda moment; lets put your plan to the test." Edam shouted over the engine. I took a left at the lonely stoplight leading to the graveyard. Spotting Domenic and Kyle and an army of demons I slammed the bike into a half skid stop. Throwing the kickstand down I jumped off; and raced down the pathway to help my team. Edam was hot on my heels as I twisted through the headstones.

"Trap them in a Snare, Domenic!" I shouted

as I climbed over the last grave marker that was in my way. "Kyle makes sure that non get away.' 'Sniff out the air and see if we have them all; we only have a couple seconds to pull this off." I was shouting orders as I stripped off the shoulder bag and dug threw it for the Chain of Justice. Edam was standing ready to open the passage way to the neither. Domenic had the daywalkers trapped in his energy circle; but it was not going to hold them for long.

Kyle sniffed the air and shook his head no. This let me know that we had them all. "Now!" I screamed. Edam opened a giant rip; as we both focused on creating enough wind and rain to drive the demons back to the Underworld. Slipping the Chain of Justice around my hand I snagged one lonely little demon. Just as the rest went flying back into the rip; Edam had created.

Letting go of the wind and the rain. I let my magic pour out of me in waves; the daywalker cringed and tried to free her self from my grip. "You are seen for the true form you really are.' 'A pawn used by Hermes to wreck havoc on this world.' 'Death is the only sentence you will receive." "Tell me where does my father hid." The daywalker eyes turned bloodshot red, her hair crackled in an invisible wind. Her voice was as eerie as her appearance. "He hides in the neither and waits for you, his jewel to arrive.' 'You will not stop him." Jerking the Silver Chain tighter I flung her into the rip Edam was just about to close. "We will see about that!" I screamed at her departing form.

Shaking to the core of my being; I stood there as my crew high-five their selves for a job well done. We had stopped another event from harming these innocent people. They had a right to be filled with pride.

Grabbing my bag from the ground where I had dropped it. I told the boys to meet me back at my apartment. We had to go over our plan of action; in the hunt for the crystal that was here. Then we were going to the neither to capture Hermes; and destroy his plans once and for all. Kicking my bike into gear I headed to my apartment. Leaving Edam with the guys; I needed time to clear the cobwebs in my head.

Things were really starting to get interesting. I felt as if the fog had finally lifted and I was finally whole. With the bindings removed off of my magical abilities; I was feeling things on a whole new level. If Hermes thought I was going to stand by; allowing him to destroy everything he was mistaking. He would not take another thing from me or anyone else. I would not allow him, the counsel, Edam or anyone to choose my fate. My destiny was in my own hands; and there it would stay.

Cloaking my bike in the back alley behind my apartment; I stepped threw the door. Heaving my bag onto the table; I walked into my bedroom. Grabbing the outfit that had at one time belonged to my mother; I slipped out of the tattered jeans and vintage t-shirt. Looking at myself in the full length mirror; I shifted my shoulders to get a better look at the transparent wings that were now attached to my backside. The silver scrolling art that was etched into my body shimmered in the dingy lighting. Beautiful, was all I could think as I stared into my own eyes.

Grabbing the velvet corset and the leather pants I slipped into the outfit. Hooking the matching cloak onto my shoulders. My wings fluttered and snapped closed against my back. Lacing up my knee high leather spiked boots. I stood up and gazed into the mirror once more. It was still hard for me to believe that the form before me was actually me.

Taking the hair tie from the back of the door handle. I wrapped my long locks into a form fitting bun at the base of my skull. Splashes of blue highlights streaked across my crown. My eyes were aglow with a blue fire from within. Walking back into the kitchen I rummaged threw my bag until I had the armband and silver chain of justice in hand. Placing them both on my arm; I waited for the boys to arrive. Sitting down at the table I looked over the pile of maps that Edam had tossed there. He had circled two possible spots both in the same state. Lucky us. We were less than 50 miles from either place. I went over what Sable had said about the site in my head. There were things that stood out. Seven sisters, satyrs. Backwards flowing river, old crone, nothing being what it seemed.

It was as if she was telling us what the name was with out really telling us. She had laid a map out in just a few words. Taking a notebook out of the stack on the table. I wrote down the clues. Who knew, I might have to take them when with us if we found place, wherever it was we were going. Putting on a pot of coffee. I grabbed a mythology book from the stack of local library books I had got when I first came earth side. I had tried to absorb as much as I could about the fae and what humans had thought of the gods. It was interesting to see how they had cherished their myths and folk lore. I turned to the index in the back of the book; taking the list of clues I had. I started to hunt down heavenly bodies that would have dealt with any of the clues. One stood out among them all.

Pleiades also know as the seven sisters; the story told of seven sisters that were titans, how they had gave birth to the myths such as Sirens, harpies, and faun. How they changed forms to hide from Zeus. Taking the map I looked to see if either of the places Edam had circled where even close to the same description. Sure enough, he had circled

Pleiades Wildlife Preserve. The other place he had circled was the Crone's River; which happened to run right threw Pleiades. Pouring a cup of coffee; I started to read the myths about the heavenly body. Apparently these seven sisters were chased and pursued by many. Upon their death they were said to have become the seven stars near the constellation of Taurus. There was also mention of them becoming seven white doves. I was getting so wrapped up in what I was reading; I didn't even hear the boys come in.

Chapter Eleven

"What do you have there?" Edam said. Jumping at the sound of his voice; my coffee cup slipped from my grip. Domenic caught it just as it was going to hit the ground. Gently placing back on the table; he stared down at the text book I was reading. "No way, this is where we are heading?" Domenic exclaimed with sheer excitement seeping from his words.

Nodding my head, I continued to read the passage I was on. "Shit, Kyle we need our camping gear; this is going to be so much fun." Domenic was saying. Snapping my head up from the book; I looked at them as if they were completely crazy.

"What do you mean camping gear?" "I am just going to retrieve the crystal; and that's it." I stated. Kyle just chuckled from the corner of the room. "That maybe so Andras', but I intend on running wild for a day or two, the full moon is approaching; and this would be the perfect place for the bloodsucker and I to hunt." Kyle stated. "Okay, agreed; but can it wait until after we have at least found the crone's hut?" I asked. Both boys beamed from ear to ear; as they shook their heads yes.

It was as if Christmas had come early for them. Edam looked as if he had been caught with his hand in the cookie jar. I had never seen any of them as happy as they were at this moment.

"I have a question." "How are we all getting there?' 'My bike won't hold all four of us; and Edam is drained from opening some many portals in such a short amount of time." I said. "We can take my van." Kyle chimed in. "There is plenty of room and it will give us a chance to regroup our energy before we get there." "Sounds good." I said. Edam and Domenic just smiled.

Here I was thinking this was an in and out mission; and my crew had made it into a camping adventure. Somehow, I had the feeling that we would be meeting with all kinds of interesting things along the way. This journey would be more than a little vacation. Danger was sure to be present in our adventure to the Crone's hut. I only hoped that the challenges that would present their selves would be easier than the ones we had already lived threw.

Loading everything into Kyle's van; we headed down the street to Pleiades. I had grabbed the map and mythology book; figuring both would be a major help in locating the crone and the crystal. Kyle set the GPS, while Domenic slide into the passenger seat; leaving Edam and I alone in the back. I was trying to avoid actually talking to him; sticking my nose in the book I read silently to myself.

There were things in each of the myths that had captivated my attention. I didn't know if it held any truth; but I had a feeling that I would soon find out. Edam was starring out the side window; lost in his own thoughts.

I was trying hard not to notice the frown lines that were forming along his brow. He was worried about more than just camping with a werewolf and a blood sucking vampire. He had my father; the counsel; my self and other things occupying his mind. I didn't have time to get into all of it with him. Things would sort their selves out; sooner or later where he was concerned. I still got the feeling he was hiding something from me. Yet it didn't feel as if it was a betrayal; more like he had hopes and dreams; that he didn't know if they would come true or not. I could tell it was worrying him more than he had let on earlier. Yet, with everything going on; I was not ready to go there.

At this moment I didn't know if I would ever be ready to. I had my own set of worries. I had to prove my worth to the Counsel; I had to stop Hermes, save the worlds, remove the curse that was placed on my mother, and last but not least I had to choose which throne I was going to rule over. It was a lot for a girl to have to worry about. Annabelle had said; to make my choices with my heart. Yet, my heart was torn in a million pieces; I just could not make my choice based on my heart alone.

At this moment; I did not know if I would ever be able to make that choice. Looking up from the book that was in my lap; I realized we were coming to the entrance of the wildlife preserve.

Closing the book, I stuffed it in my shoulder bag; and got ready to get out of the van. Kyle drove down the winding dirt road; I could hear the river running somewhere in the distance, the smell of fish assaulted my nose. Birds were chirping among the trees. The air smelled of magic thickly woven in the tapestry of the place its self. This place was truly beautiful to behold. Coming to a fork in the road; I told Kyle to take a right.

We drove on for another mile or so; a Red deer stood watching us from the meadow. Seagulls danced in the sky. "That's odd." Domenic stated. "Humm?" I mused. "What are seagulls doing this far inland?" He questioned. Sheer wonder was on all of their faces. It was as if we had opened a fairytale book and stepped inside.

Sprites and other fae folk that lived among the foliage in this place were starting to show their selves; as if our presence was drawing them out. We got to a dirt patch that looked as though it had been used as a campsite. Kyle killed the engine; and we took a moment to stretch our legs.

Looking around I noticed the river was just within walking distance from where we had parked. Strolling down the well beaten pathway; I made my way to the waters edge. The colors of everything here were almost as vivid as they were in Otherworld; I was amazed at the way it felt as if time stood still. It was such an odd feeling to have; yet it fit with the surroundings of this beautiful place. As if the outside world had not touched it.

Peeking over the embankment into the water; I noticed that the water ran backwards flowing upstream from where we stood. Pulling out the clues that Sable had said to me I stared at the river. Listening to the sounds of nature and trying to get in tune with my surroundings.

If what she had spoke could be taken word for word; then the crone's hut was near by. Which way; I had no clue, but I would soon find out. Tree limbs behind me snapped; causing me to turn sharply. Kyle, Domenic, and Edam were already in fighting stances. Out of the forest step a bare chest man; or at least I thought it was a man. His bottom half was covered in red fur. When the setting sun finally hit him; shedding enough light for us all to see him fully.

We realized that this was not just a man; but the Satyr, himself. His feet were four black hoofs and the body of a deer; yet the rest of his form was that of a grown man. Naked from the chest up. The only odd account was the antlers protruding from his forehead.

My mouth had dropped open; I do believe. I mean, I grew up with the strangeness of Otherworld. People who had wings, pointy ears, ECT. Yet seeing a creature such as this on Earth was almost too much to believe. He had been here along time; you could tell from the way he walked threw these woods. This was his home; and I didn't think he liked trespassers stomping threw his forest. I waited for him to still; I didn't want to spoke him.

Nor, did I want to fight with a creature such as him; unless I truly had to. "Hello, my name is Andras'." "We have come to see the crone.' 'I was told she could be found around here." Speaking in a soft tone; so that he would know I was not here to harm him or anyone else. I waited for his reply.

"Sister; you travel in search of something do you not?" The satyr as me. "Sister?" I questioned. "Yes, I seek something; I was charged with its protection and I must find it." The satyr chuckled deep in his throat. "You do not know; who I am to you?" "Forgive me for finding that amusing." He laughed as if he had not done so in ages.

I stood there frowning at this odd creature before me. What the heck did he mean by; what he was to me. "You see; we share a common relative." He stated as if that would clear everything up. "Pardon." I was still beyond confused. Edam came and stood beside me; I got the feeling he was worried about how I was going to react. "Hermes is your father; no?" Questioned the satyr. "I do not see why that is your concern." I said getting a little pissed. Smiling; he inclined his head, and stared hard at me. "It's no concern of mine, I was just stating a fact; you see we have the same blood running through our veins."

"Hermes is also my father."

"So; sister, if we are done with twenty questions, I will be on my way." "You're my brother?" I was in shock to say the least. I had not given any thought to the other children my father could have created. "Wait; you can't just leave." I was stalling for time. Trying to keep up with the changing events. My head was swimming; these woods were enchanted, and they were effected me. That had to be it. The satyr inclined his head once more, and pointed to the west. "The old woman can be found around the bend." With that he turned and disappeared back into the forest.

I stood watching after him for some time. Until, Edam finally grabbed my hand. "You will see him again, Andras'." Edam spoke softly.

It was as if he could hear my heart breaking. I

now understood what Annabelle had meant by *family everywhere.* Kyle and Domenic had set up their tent and were starting to gather firewood. Edam and I thought it would be best if they stayed behind. This was my journey; one that I had to see through until the end.

Taking off in the direction my brother had pointed; Edam and I began to walk. The forest was alive with creatures of fairytales. Shimmering lights streamed threw the thickets, the trees whispered of our coming. Was starting to realize that cryptic message Sable had spoke; wasn't as cryptic as I had first thought. If I could put money on it, I would say that I would soon discover more here than I was really ready for. We walked along the clay laid dirt road; Spanish moss and wild grapevines hung down between the think cottonwood trees.

Dark green foliage was littered along the forest floor; sprinkled between were bright pink roses and other wildflowers. The landscape of the forest looked as if it had been hand groomed. Taking a deep breath I let out a sigh. My soul felt as if it was finding comfort in this untouched place.

The fae in me, wanted to run free among the trees. Coming to a clearing on the edge of the forest; stood a moss covered hut tucked into the hillside. A meadow of flowers and mushroom rings lined the ground around the small hut. "I guess this is the place." I spoke mainly to myself even though Edam was standing next to me. We walked up the sandstone pathway that led to the hut. Noticing that the forest around us had become eerily still.

Not a single animal made a sound. I felt as if we were being watched; yet I couldn't tell from what direction, or by whom. Coming to the door; I noticed a crescent moon was etched into the wood planks that served as a door. Marking this place for what it was. The hedge witch resided in this lovely little place.

"The Crone is known by many names, depending on what form you see her in.' 'The maiden, mother, and crone all wrapped in one image.' 'The Crone is the Grandmother, the

Old One, the Earth Mother, the Wise One, we turn to when we need advice. She teaches us that sometimes we must let go in order to move on.' 'She like Scarlet can see into the future and divine events; but only in the near present.' 'She can see into your heart and soul; tell her only the truth." Edam said as we stood staring at the front door of the cottage. "Are you ready for this?" He was concerned that after all the discoveries I had just had thrown my way; that I was not going to be able to handle any thing else.

Nodding my head, I knocked on the door. Seconds later the door opened; yet, no one was there. I didn't know what to do. I didn't want to just walk in; that would be rude. "Hello." I called from the threshold; unable to bring myself to enter. "It's open." Replied a voice from somewhere deep inside.

Looking at Edam for reassurance I grabbed my shoulder bag and hoisted it up onto my shoulder. Stepping into the hut; I let my eyes adjust to the candle lit room. The crone was in the Kitchen with a mortar and bowl in her hand. Grinding herbs up for gods only know what. "I was sent here by the Queen of Air & Darkness." I tell the form standing a few feet away from me. Edam bumped into my back, making me start. Realizing I had been standing in the doorway; I gingerly stepped inside.

"Yes dear, I know this." "The young Satyr told me as he passed by." He had gone in the opposite direction from us; so I didn't know how that was possible. Yet, I didn't question her. For I figured it would be best not to.

Something told me she was not someone I wanted to piss off. Laying her herbs and wares on the counter; she wiped her hands off on the front of her dress. Stepping into the light; I was finally able to see her. Folds of Wrinkles lined her face; almost making her eyes unseen. She had laugh lines and a kind and gentle presence. I felt at easy, just by the sight of her standing in front of me. "You have had a long journey dearie." She cooed. Her voice crackled like fine paper. Her knobby hands were folded over her stomach; as she rocked back on her heels assessing us. "I see you have brought a friend; whom do I owe the pleasure to; for a God to show his self to me after so long." I had no clue what to make of the way she spoke; nor, did I know what she meant by after so long. The puzzle pieces were adding up like parking tickets on a hot summer's day.

"Edam's my name ma'." "I was sent here with Andras' by Zeus." Edam stated; as if that was all he had to say. "Ah." The old woman said. Taking a chair from the little table that served as a dinning area; she scooted it until she was just in front of us. Plopping her butt into the chair; she waited for us to do the same. Edam and I both grabbed chairs, and followed suit.

We were sitting in a semi circle facing the crone. She sat quietly watching us. Minutes passed by and still she did not speak. It was really spooky; sitting here having someone stare at us without saying a word.

I felt like a bug under a microscope. Starting to squirm in my chair, I placed my hands under my thighs to keep still. It was only then that she finally smiled and started to talk. "You heart has many questions.' 'Pray you, what have you come seeking answers too?"

The crone asked. I thought about what she was saying and not saying. Did my heart really hold that many unanswered questions? I knew the main ones I needed answers to. The ones she could help me solve.

The Crystal that was on earth, my mother's cursed form. The last one was in the Underworld; but that was a big place, and it would be helpful to know where it was to be found. I didn't speak my questions but she still heard me. I didn't get a chance to open my mouth to actually voice them before she started to speak again. "You have had some heavy burdens placed upon your head; young one.' 'Such a lot for one such as yourself to deal with." The hag stated from her chair in front of me.

"Nothing I have not been able to handle." I replied honestly. Nodding her head she cracked a smile; revealing her toothless mouth. I don't know if she was comfortable in this form, or if she just wanted to see my reaction to it.

When she realized that I was not taken back

by her form; she frowned. The air thickened to the point it had me coughing. Closing my eyes I tried to get it to stop. When I opened them again a beautiful maiden with long flowing raven hair sat before me. I raised my eyebrow and waited for her to speak. She gestured to me as if it was my turn.

"I do have questions, I have come to ask." I stated to her. "I don't know what name to call you by without offending you." "So I find it hard to ask anything at all." I told her. Smiling at my honesty, she spoke; "You may call me Meriam." "Meriam, I have come to seek the crystal of earth, the Queen of Air & Darkness has charged me with their keep." "I also want to know about the curse laid on my mothers head; and how to undo it."

"The third and final question I have is the location of the Crystal of Underworld." I spoke soft and true just as the Queen had advised. Meriam stared at me a moment longer; searching my soul to see if there was any falsehood to what I just said. When she found none; she turned her eyes on Edam. The black orbs swallowed him. He sat frozen in his chair. I waved my hand in front of his face and got no response.

She had stepped threw the rip of time taking me with her. Edam would not hear a word of what she had to say to me; unless she chose it. "Andras, Heavy questions you have laid on the table." "Are you sure you are ready for the answers I will give?" Meriam asked me. "As ready as I will ever be; for how can one truly be ready for the unknown?" Again I spoke with honesty. She was smiling as if I had passed the biggest test of all. I had a feeling that I had indeed.

"One." She said reaching into the fold of her skirt. "Here lay the crystal of earth; take care of it and see it to safety." She spoke as she placed the bright green crystal in my palm. Reaching back into her skirt she pulled out a black velvet bag; which she also handed to me. I slipped the Crystal into the bag and tied it shut. Placing it in my shoulder bag; I waited for her to go on.

"Two." Meriam said as scyring bowl appeared next to us. She showed me the past events that had lead to my mother being cursed into a living statue. She showed me how Hermes had used a Gorgon to help him carry out his ill act. He had placed me in the gorgon's care knowing my mother would search for me. Leading her right to Medusa's door. The snaked headed woman had toyed with her; using me as bait. She sent my mother on a hunt threw a labyrinth searching for me.

When my mother finally found me, she hid me behind her. I was a mere baby not old enough to defend myself. She shielded me with her body as Medusa came near. Forgetting to keep her eyes closed she looked right into her eyes. Turning to stone and leaving me exposed. The guards from the fae court appeared in the watery bowl. It showed them driving back the snaked headed woman with torches.

The statue of my mother and my self were taken to the castle. "To undo this curse; you must take her head." "Only then will your mother be free." I sat there digesting everything I had just seen. What horrible things my father had done to my mother. Why would you do that to one you loved. It wasn't a question for the crone; just my aching hearts own plea for answers. Those answers could wait. I would choke them out of him if need be.

"Three." Meriam said in a soft tone. "The path that leads you to the crystal of underworld leads you down a many dangerous roads. You will have to travel to the depths of Hel into the abode of Hades his self. You will have to cross the Rivers of Otherworld; be careful of the Harpies as they are friend of none.' 'Take head from the Hell hounds guard the gates that will bring you to the resting place of the final piece.' 'Get there before your father or all as you know it will be no more."

There was a small pop and we were sitting in the room with a confused looking Edam beside me. Meriam got up from her chair and went to the kitchen.

Turning back to me she had a small white bag in her hand. Placing it in my palm she closed my fingers around the bag of herbs. "To protect you along the way." "Fear not, for you have family all around you." With that she faded back into the form of the old woman who had first greeted us. We bid her farewell and left her tiny hut. Heading back down the path to check on the boys I told Edam of how we would find the next crystal.

I told him that as soon as this trip was over we would have to head back to the Cave of Gold so I could return the crystal to its resting place. For now though we were going to have a mini vacation and act as if the worlds around us were not in danger of being destroyed. For now we would be just campers enjoying the little piece of heaven on earth. Tomorrow; well tomorrow it was back to kicking ass and saving the worlds. I just needed one night of nothing.

We spent all night sitting around the campfire; roasting marshmallows and just enjoying our time. The moon was riding high in the night sky; it called to all of us. Some more than other; Kyle had kicked his two legged form for that of his four legged counter part. He was running after rabbits that ventured to close to our campsite. Every now and again he would come back; with his tongue waging and a blood rabbit as an offering. Domenic was flying over the river bed feasting on the things only a bat could enjoy. Edam and I were watching the water sparkle in the moonlight.

From time to time; my brother would peek out of the forest, watching us from a distance. He never came close enough to talk; but I could tell he was enjoying what he saw. At sunrise we loaded up the van and headed back to my apartment. I have to say Domenic had the right idea a camping trip was well needed. I could have stayed there forever. Sad, that it had to end so soon; I promised myself that I would visit again.

Edam had told me on the ride home that the Crone had been a Goddess; in all rights she still was. She had been sought after by Zeus himself. Banished by Hera; the Queen of Heavens and Zeus wife. She had lived on Earth since before the divide of the worlds. Zeus still loved her deeply and visited her from time to time in the secret of the night. It was rather sad really; she was punished for something she had no control over. To be loved by another should not be a thing of evil. I was truly touched to know her name and her story. She had showed me kindness that I was not expecting.

Kyle and Domenic dropped us off; after agreeing to meet us back at sunset so we could Go to the into the Underworld and start what we had to there. Edam and I were heading to the Cave of Gold to deliver the Crystal of Earth with its counterparts. My heart wasn't as heavy as it had been days before. There were still things I had to sort out and deal with.

One thing at a time I kept saying to myself. Just one thing at a time; soon this would end and all would be right again. I just had one promise left to keep and that was to make sure my mother got back her life. It was so unfairly stolen from her. Hermes was in for a world of hurt when I got a hold of him. This I could Promise.

The Jewel as he had called me would be his downfall, just wait and see. He was the one that would be crying sob stories in the end. Holding my head high I stepped threw the portal that would lead me to the Cave of Gold. I was starting to feel the heaviness leaves, I was winning and that was such a great feeling. Edam was still as reserved as ever as we stepped back threw the portal onto the soil of Earth.

He had his secrets and he was not willing to spill them. That was okay I had time to wait. Let's just hope that I can deal with it as well as I have dealt with everything else. Time would tell. Arriving back at my apartment; I noticed a package lying on the doorstep. Walking up to it, I stooped down and picked it up. The note attached to the ribbon around it was fancy. Opening up the golden leafed paper I read the words inside.

Andras'

May this serve you, when the time is right?

You're Brother

Satyr Rye'

Untying the ribbon I removed the paper and looked inside. A flute made from one of his shed antlers was lying on a satin cushion. The mouth piece was pure silver, and it had been polished so that it shone in the sun. What a beautiful gift. I had tears standing in my eyes as I opened the door of my little home. How could someone I had just met; shower me with such love. I would have to find something just as suiting to give back to him; when this was all through. Placing the box on the table; I put the flute into my bag along with everything else I was taking to the Underworld. Grabbing the directions the crone had told me I reread them while we waited on the boys to arrive.

"The path that leads you to the crystal of underworld leads you down a many dangerous roads. You will have to travel to the depths of Hel into the abode of Hades his self. You will have to cross the Rivers of Underworld; be careful of the Harpies as they are friend of none.' Take head from the Hell hounds guard the gates that will bring you to the resting place of the final piece.'

I had added to what she had said; from the notes I had gathered out of the mythology text and from what Edam had told me. Hel was not just a place but the Goddess of otherworld herself; we would have to pass by her to get to Hades home.

Hades was Zeus brother; he may or may not help us depending on his mood. The Rivers of Underworld were not just rivers but gods and goddess that lived in them. They had names; which we would have to address them by if we hoped to have safe passage. The Harpies were the daughter's of the seven sisters. Bird body woman that where said to have been one time Sirens drove mad. Hellhounds were three headed dogs that stood at all gates threw out Underworld. Music put them to sleep.

Rolling up the list of directions I stuffed it into a scroll case; and placed it with the rest of my wares. Walking into the bedroom, I was about to change clothes when I noticed Edam was behind me.

"Don't Change." He said his eyes have cast looking rather smoking. "Why not." I asked him. Who the heck did he think he was to tell me not to change? Smiling, he said; "Your outfit is charmed it will help you, when we are in the mouth of Hel." Nodding, I walked passed him back into the living room, waiting for the boys to get here was starting to get on my nerves. I wanted this over with. I wanted a normal life; what ever that was. Plopping down on the couch I let out a huff of breath.

Blowing my hair out of my eyes. Looking up at the clock on the wall; sunset was only ten minutes away. For some reason it felt like it was dragging its heels getting here.

Edam sat beside me; hands rested on his knees, he to stare at the clock. "When this is all over; do you think we could talk?" He asked me. "I have things I want to ask you to be apart of; but the timing hasn't been right." "I'm not hiding anything from you Andras; its just that, well, it's just complicated." He stammered on. "Yeah, when this is over we can talk." I tried to smile, but was finding it harder to reassure him when I wasn't even sure myself. "For now though, can we not think about anything but stopping Hermes and retrieving the Crystal?" I asked more just to change the subject than to get an answer. Grunting, Edam sat and waited beside me for Kyle and Demonic to arrive.

It was almost time for the hands of fate to be shown to the evil bastard whom had helped create me. I couldn't wait. I planned on taking pleasure in making him pay for his deeds. A knock at the door drug me from my homicidal thoughts. The boys were here. Now we could get going. Edam walked to the door and opened it. In popped Kyle and Demonic a little to chipper for my taste but at least they were energized for this hunt. I would need their help along the way that I knew for sure. "You all ready." Demonic asked. "Ready as I'll ever be. " I replied. Edam opened his portal that would take us to the underworld and into the waiting arms of danger. Something was off the color was blood red, gone was the vivid blue. This eerie feeling started to creep up my spine. Things were getting ready to get bad and fast I could feel it. "What the Hel!" Kyle asked with panic in his voice. "Relax; it's just the aura of otherworld bleeding through." Edam and Demonic stated at the same time.

Flames flickered in the flimsy image the portal created. Heat radiated in waves around us. Things from nightmares danced among the shadows. Swallowing the ball of fear that had formed in my throat, I stepped through the portals rip. It was now or never. Time to meet dear old dad.

Chapter Twelve

~ Even the Devil wears A Mask~

I had just stepped threw the portal into the realm of Underworld. My crew was only a few feet behind me; when all of a sudden there was a loud pop. Turning to look back over my shoulder; I couldn't believe my eyes. The portal had snapped shut without letting the guys through.

The last thing I got to see was Edam's frantic expression. I don't think that was in the plans; or at least I hope it was not.

Whatever had caused the rip to close was not of his doing; that much new for sure. Well I could stand here and wait for a miracle to happen; or I can hunt down Hermes and put an end to this all. Back up would be nice; but I think that someone had a different plan in store for me. I just wish I knew who that someone was; so I could give them a swift kick in the ass.

So, I'm wandering around down here in the belly of Hel by myself searching for a God I have never meet; that happens to be dear old dad; and a crystal that has the power to destroy a entire world. I have a feeling that I won't be seeing my boys again until after this little task is over. I am pretty sure the Fates have had their hands in this. Well I guess its time to begin. Here goes nothing; wish me luck.

Dropping my shoulder bag onto the ground; I took out the notes that would serve as a road map and started to read.

"The path that leads you to the crystal of underworld leads you down a many dangerous roads. You will have to travel to the depths of Hel into the abode of Hades his self. You will have to cross the Rivers of Underworld; be careful of the Harpies as they are friend of none.' 'Take heed from the Hell hounds that guard the gates. They will bring you to the resting place of the final piece.'

Hel was not just a place but the Goddess of Underworld herself. According to the Crone; I would have to pass by her to get to Hades home. From what I had read out of the Human mythology book she was something to see. The description they had wrote of her was that she was two form; seen as both light and dark, or living and dead at the same time. Both beautiful and horrid married together in one form. Let's just hope she is in a kind mood and I get to see her beautiful side. Guess, I would find out soon enough.

Edam had told me that Helheim was her home, one of the nine known cities of Underworld it's self. He was supposed to have opened the portal right out side her front door so to speak. I hope I was in the right place.

Wasn't like they had neon signs hanging from the cavern walls saying "Here lays the home of so and so."

He had went on to tell me that Hel was the judge of souls in her realm; a little like me. Which was kind a spooky. I wasn't looking for similarities yet I kept finding them.

The second clue the Crone had given to me was about Hades. Now Hades was Zeus brother; he may or may not help me depending on his mood. Edam said that he liked pretty woman a little too much for his liking. He warned me to watch myself; not to fall for his tricks. I guess he would be Hels' counter part. I would only gain access to him if Hel saw it fit. This wasn't very reassuring at this point.

The Third clue said I would have to travel threw The Rivers of Underworld which were not just rivers but gods and goddess that lived in them. They had names; which I would have to address them by if I hoped to have safe passage.

Edam had said that no matter what not to drink from the waters. He had given me coins to give to the ferryman for the boat rides to and from. From there the clues had talked about the Harpies that flew over the Rivers themselves in search of lost souls they could gobble up. Or that is what the stories wrote of them had said. The crone said they were not friends of anyone; that let me to think that they were out for number one. They would do anything if it was in their own interest. I was supposed to stay off their radar; let's just hope I could.

The book said that the Harpies were the daughter's of the seven sisters. Bird body woman that where said to have been one time Sirens that had been driven mad. I have seen enough weird things growing up in Otherworld but I have never seen a bird woman. An I really didn't want to see one now.

The last clue the Old Crone had give was about the Hellhounds that were guarding the gate to the where the crystal was being kept. Hellhounds were three headed dogs that stood at all gates threw out Underworld. Music put them to sleep; which was really awesome considering that my brother had given me a flute to take with me on this journey. It wouldn't last long, but I would hopefully be able to slip by them. I also had packed a couple honey cakes as that was said to calm them. I just needed to be able to get in and out of here in one piece.

I already knew that Hermes was hiding with

the crystal down here. I don't think he was down here just hiding; I got the feeling that he was not granted safe passage with the crystal its self and chose to stay here. If what the daywalker had said; had given me any clue; he knew I was going to come for him and it.

My sly father thought he could win by default; he was so sadly mistaking. If he thought he could trap me down here and use my power to gain what he was after; he had another thing coming.

I now knew that I could dismantle and change whatever plans he had just by thinking about a new outcome. He had no idea that I had been trained or that I even knew what I truly could do. I had my ace in the hole. I wasn't planning on letting the cat out of the bag; but believe me; I would if I had to.

Stuffing the directions back in the scroll tube and into my shoulder bag. I stood up and looked around. The flames and flashes of red I had seen before coming through the portal had just been glamour. It was actually cold and damp here.

Freezing mist hung close to the floor and seemed to sigh as it floated threw the cavern. Crystals of ice hung from the damp walls. Eerie blue flames licked the walls from torches that were hung along the cavern walls from iron hooks.

There was a honeycomb of tunnels that led to who knows where. I knew that Hel was only a few steps ahead of me. Edam had said her door was one that was half shadowed. A hexing rune of death was etched into her door; like a giant hook.

Shaking out my hands; trying to remove the jitters I was feeling, I took in a deep breath. I can do this, I told myself over and over again in my head. Walking close to the wall as I possible could I creep forward. Trying to make as little noise as possible. Shadows danced under the blue flames; playing tricks with my eyes. I didn't want to find out if they belonged to anyone. I just wanted to move toward my destination as fast as I could.

The sooner I meet the Queen of Underworld the sooner I could get the Crystal and take down dear old dad. The sooner I did that the sooner I would be back in my apartment; sipping on some nice warm cup of coffee. The corridor split in two directions up ahead. I had to choose which way to go; by pure instinct alone. Hanging a right, I kept walking. Lights flickered up and down the hall; casting strange shadows along them. A doorway came into view; I knew I had found the home of Hel.

Sending up a silent prayer to the Gods above; thanking them for the sheer luck I had just had. I ventured forward. Light was seeping from the crack at the bottom of the door. Someone was home; let's just hope it was the mistress of the night, and not a ghoul waiting on the other side.

Knocking on the wooden frame I waited for someone or something to present itself to me. The hinges creaked as the door swung inward. A woman stood on the other side of the threshold; only half of her profile was visible.

Long black hair hung to her waist, her face was beautiful perfectly heart shaped; from what I could see anyways. Unblemished ivory skin and rose colored lips painted her features. Long thick eyelashes covered her eye; that faced me. She wore a bright red corset with black leather ribbons crisscrossing her mid section, and a crush velvet black skirt that touched the floor hung from her hips. She was truly gorgeous. Swinging her hand, in a gesture for me to enter; she spoke.

"Are you just going to stand there gawking; or are you going to come in? "Uh, sorry." I stammered. "Its just you caught me off guard, I wasn't trying to be rude." I went on saying, as I walked threw her door into her home. The door slammed shut, making me jump. I took a moment to calm myself and look around. Her home was cozy and warm; a dire difference from the cold and damp hallway that lead to it. She was still standing with only half her profile visible to me. I was starting to get a weird feeling.

"Sit." Hel said, pointing to a hardback oak chair that was lined with satin cushions; next to the fireplace. I did as I was told; watching to see what she would do. Grabbing a teapot that was on a serving tray next to her.

She poured two cups; still not giving me a full on look of her face. Matter a fact I had only seen one side of her body this whole time. "If you truly are that concerned on my appearance I can show you what most people see when they come to my door.' 'But I warn you it's not pretty." Hel said, as she sat the teapot back on the tray. "Yet, I would rather you see me as I am now." Nodding, I replied. "You can show me either form but the true form would be best as then I would not be mislead into believing something that was not true."

"My form, dear Andras' Moonriver is always two fold, I am both living and dead." With that the Queen of the Underworld turned and faced me head on.

Nothing about her face had changed; yet, one side of it looked like a holographic image. I could see the bones beneath the skin. Creepy.

"I have come a long way to speak with you; mistress of the night, I came here in search of two things." "The first being the Crystal of

Underworld, for I have been put in charge of the other three for safe keeping.' 'Two is my father Hermes, is down here somewhere; plotting to take over the four worlds themselves." "I must stop him." I spoke with out catching my breath. I just wanted to get out of here before I ended up stuck here for good.

Hel's eyes turned solid black, not a piece of white showed. She looked as if she was going to change forms and gobble me up. I was starting to get nervous. Gripping the edge of the chair I was sitting in; I got ready to bolt. Not that I had a lot of places I could go. "You speak true." She said keeping her void gaze on me. "Yes, I have no reason to lie." I replied holding her gaze.

"Giving up the Crystal of Underworld is not something I'm fond of doing; you must understand." Nodding my head I didn't speak I just waited for her to continue with her line of thought. "As for your father; I have no use for a God that doesn't know his place." "Hades is not going to be happy about this."

"Speaking of Hades; I was told by the Queen of Air and Darkness to seek him out; after speaking with you of course." I told her as I sipped on the tea she had handed me. Hel's eyes flashed at the mention of Hade's name; something shadowed moved across her expression. If I was a betting person; I would have thought her to be jealous or in love.

Keeping that thought to myself; I bid my time. I didn't want to make her angry. Hel stood up, and crossed the room in two swift strides; leaving me sitting by the fireplace. I lowered the teacup and rested it on my knee. I had no clue how to respond to a being such as her.

`This realm was so different than the other three. It was as if the rules here didn't apply. "Death comes in many forms, child." "Do you know what you ask?" "Hades has not seen the likes of a living, breathing woman in many, many years." "I don't think it is wise for you to go alone." Hel responded from the opposite end of her home. Her chest was heaving as she spoke. As if the mere thought alone was causing her pain. I knew that this was more an act to get what she wanted; than it was a concern for my safety. I would play along for now at least. If it got me safely to the door of Hades; and a step closer in catching Hermes; then who was I to decline. Sitting the teacup back on the tray I spoke. "I'm not afraid of dying, yet that doesn't mean I am ready to do so." "I agree that having company along this journey would be soothing to my nerves."

A smile lit Hel's face causing it too take the form of a mask. I was starting to get a huge knot in my stomach. There was something this woman was not telling me; and I feared that when the time came I would be up shit creek without a paddle. Holding my breath, I stood letting her know I was ready to leave. "Well then, I guess I could join you; if company is what you seek." Hel said with that eerie smile still glued to her face. I was starting to get the jest that I had just made a deal with the devil herself. Crossing my fingers; I prayed for the best. I hope I hadn't just sealed my own fate.

One second we were standing facing each other in Hel's living room; the next we were back out in the corridor. She had popped us out of her home without even opening the door. I blinked a couple of times and looked around; we were standing outside her door again. As if I had never entered to begin with. We started walking away from her door toward the hallway that leads to the left. The torches lining the cavern walls were licking the walls with bright yellow flames.

I noted the color change in case I had to find my way back without an escort. Walking in silence, we ventured further into the city of Helheim. Creatures were emerging from the little cubby holes; that were starting to look a lot like an outside market of some sort. Daywalkers were hanging out rugs made of some kind of silk, or maybe it was hair. I wasn't going to examine it that closely to find out for sure. Jars and bowls of odds and ends lined one of the tables, necklaces of bones and other jewelry lined another.

Each table had something that was of use to the people that lived in this realm. Noting the oddities; I continued to walk along side the Queen of the Underworld. I noticed how the residence seemed to quake in fear of the very sight of her. Hel seemed to swell with pride at the fear she inflicted on the patrons here. I kept my mouth shut and just watched as we went along the pathway that leads to Hade's home.

I was really starting to wish Edam and the boys were with me. Something was off down here. I knew Edam would have been able to tell me if I was walking into a trap. Right now I had no one to rely on but myself. That thought wasn't providing much comfort. We walked for miles it seemed. The hallway snaked along side a canal of water. I felt like bugs were crawling up and down my spine. Shivering, I wrapped my arms around myself. Hel looked over at me; with that goofy smile still plastered on her face.

"We can always go back; and enjoy our tea." She said as we walked forward. Shaking my head, I replied. "Thank you for the offer, but I must see this through." Hel's smile disappeared; her eyes flashed again, a tight line formed against her mouth. Okay. I got it she wanted to be the one in control; I was to strong will. That alone was starting to be a problem for her.

I needed to watch my step or I could end up down here for good. Choosing my words carefully I spoke again. "Have you met Hermes before?" I asked the mistress of the night. "Yes I have met him; not much to look upon; if you ask me." Her response was short and sweet. Apparently Hermes was not on the top of her things to do list. Not that I can blame her; I mean, I had never meet the man but he had already left a sour taste in my mouth.

Hel stopped so fast that I almost ran into the door that was standing in front of us. An iron door with strange symbols etched on it stood in front of us. "We are here." The Queen said.

Tapping on the door; she stood and waited for the metal peek hole to slide open. Green light poured from the slot; as shadow with red eyes peeked from behind the door. "We come to see Hade's." The Queen said to the red eyed form. The peek whole slide closed with a loud smack.

Making me jump at the sound as it echoed off

the cavern walls. Taking a deep breath; I gathered my composer. The door flew open; a gust of warm air hit me making my hair fly up and into my face. Standing in the doorway; stood a tall and dark figure. Shadows danced across his muscled chest.

Long locks of black hair covered his head. Dark Amber eyes stared at me from the perfectly formed face. A well trimmed beard peppered his lower jaw. Black leather pants hung tight from his hips, well oiled boots were upon his feet.

He looked as if he had stepped out of a modeling magazine. The man was gorgeous to say the least. I knew for sure that my mouth was hanging open. I could feel the drool pooling on my lower lip. Hel had a look of pure lust etched into her ivory face. I took the moment to calm myself. I couldn't risk making her mad after she had so kindly showed me the way here.

"Hade's, I take it?" I questioned as I raised my eyebrow at the lovely looking man that stood before me.

"Correct." He said with a voice that sounded like velvet. "My aren't you a lovely sight." He smirked as he looked me up and down. Cold shivers ran up and down my spine again. Causing me to wrap my arms around myself tighter. "Do come in." Hade's said as he bowed at the waist sweeping his arms in a wide arch, to bid us passage. Hel held her head high, nose pointed toward the sky as she strolled passed us; and into Hade's home.

I followed her in; keeping a close eye on both of them as I turned to take in the room. High backed red leather chairs were placed around a polished mahogany table. Black furs were scattered across the stone floors. Books lined the walls from shelves of polished ivory bones. A fireplace stood along one wall. It was big enough to walk threw. Doors lead to other rooms within his home that I could only assume were bedrooms and the like.

Red crystal goblets sat on a silver tray on the table; filled with dark liquor. Next to them was an assortment of fine foods. He had prepared a feast; for whom was the question. Surely he had not been waiting on me. Then again he was Zeus brother and a God. Anything was possible at this point. So much had already happened; I wouldn't dismiss anything. "Meet Andras' Moonriver; Hermes long lost daughter." Hel told Hades from her perch on one of his leather chairs.

"Oh, is that whom has coming calling upon me?" Hade's asked as he swept his eyes across my body once more. He was starting to creep me out big time. I was starting to feel as if I was a meal on wheels, I really didn't want to become anyone's lunch.

"Yes, I have come to ask for your assistance, in tracking down my father; whom is holed up somewhere down here." "He has the crystal of Underworld in his keep." "Zeus and the Queen of Air and Darkness have tasked me with protecting the four crystals; and bring Hermes in for questioning." I stated as I leveled my gaze so we were looking eye to eye.

"Ah, I see." "So my dear brother thinks I will just willing help him again." Hade's asked. He walked over to the table and picked up a goblet; taking a drink he sat down at the head of the table.

"I am not sure what Zeus thought, nor do I really care." "I'm here because my aunt asked this of me." "The Gods have paid me no mind until now." I stated as honestly as I could with out getting angry. If these two thought that toying with me was going to be fun; they would soon find out that games were not my forte.

Placing my hands on my hips; I waited for one of them to speak. Hel and Hade's gave each other a look. After a long pause Hel got up and left the room; leaving me alone with a God I had no trust in. Taking a deep breath I waited a moment longer before speaking again.

"Look, I am trying to save the four worlds and keep Hermes from doing what he thinks fit to do." "What ever squabbles are going on between Zeus, Hel, you or anyone else is not my concern. I have other issues I have to attain to." "I came here out of respect to tell you first hand what I was doing in your realm and why." "Now, it would be easier if you choose to help me, but if not, I can just as easily go about my way."

"Well put; so you truly are the daughter of a God." "It's a shame really; about what happened to your mother." Hade's stated as he took another drink of his liquor. I wasn't going to allow his off the wall comment to distract me. Training with Luke and Edam, had paid off in that way. Comments about my mother's current state didn't affect me like they once had.

"Yes, it is." I replied coldly. Hade's raised an eyebrow at me; pausing to place his goblet back on the table he sat up straight in his chair.

"Oh." He replied. I guess he wasn't expecting me to rely that way. "What if I told you I could help break her curse?" He asked me. "I would have to tell you; no thank you." "I will figure out a way to help my mother; without selling my soul to do it." I answered. Smiling Hade's laughed; filling the room with his booming voice. "Very well." "I can take a hint." "You are all business, loosen up my dear." Hade's tried his best to joke with me.

I was not going to fall for it. I knew enough about him to know that he would try and strike a deal if he thought he could. "Follow me." Was all he said; as he stood, and began to walk to a door at the back of the room. I followed not really knowing where we were headed. The door opened leading to another passageway of tunnels within the cavern. "You will have to pass threw the rivers of underworld; into Tartarus.' 'From there you will have to seek out Minos who will escort you to the gates were the crystal is kept.' 'Your father doesn't have possession of the crystal as he leads you to believe." "So be careful my dear, and don't say I didn't warn you." With that he vanished into thin air; before I had a chance to even thank him.

Chapter Thirteen

I knew I would see Hades and Hel again; something told me that they had a bet going on. I had become a pawn in their chess game. The sooner I was out of here the better. I really hoped Edam found a way to get a portal open again before Check mate was called. I walked along the passageway toward the Rivers of Underworld. Taking a moment to retrieve the coins Edam had given me, I stuffed them in the pocket of my pants.

Taking the silver tipped flute the Satyr had gifted to me; and hooking it to the clasp on the silver armband that also held my chain of justice. Strapping my atheme onto my thigh, I stood. Like it or not I had a job to do and now was not the time to get cold feet.

 So, now I had to travel threw the rivers of the underworld, into another city in search of some guy named Minos. This was turning out to be a very draining task to say the least. The torches flickered along the path; providing just enough light to see a foot in front of me.

I kept looking all around me waiting for something to jump out and say boo. I guess you could say I was on edge. I had been down here; to long for my own liking. Things were starting to play tricks with my mind.

Inching forward, hugging the wall when the cavern narrowed in spots. I felt eyes on me; yet I couldn't see anything. Coming to the end of the long passage, I could hear water lapping against stone. The sound was almost deafening. A wooden bridge hung from ropes leading down to the waters edge. Lit by the same torches that had hung from the cavern walls. Eerie Red flames were shooting a foot off of them.

I stepped up to the bridge and gently placed my foot on one wooden slat. Testing it to make sure it would hold my weight. The bridge creaked and moaned; but didn't give. Holding my breath I stepped on to it. It swayed under my weight; causing me to grab the ropes that served as handrails. I took small steps; inching my way to the boat I could just barely make out the object in front of me.

A man in a cloak stood in the boat as if he had been waiting a long time. I inched closer, not really trusting the bridge to support my weight. "Hello there!" I called out from half way across the wooden platform. The cloaked man didn't seem to hear me; he just kept standing there. Coming closer to him I tried to get his attention again. Nothing; not even a nod to let me know he had heard me.

It wasn't until I had stepped on to the boat that he even registered my presence. "Where to?" He asked as he held out his hand for payment. "Tartarus, I'm in search of Minos." I replied as I handed him one of the gold coins. Gripping the coin tightly, the Ferryman moaned. "Tartarus, it is then." The boat lurched forward; causing me to wobble and loose my footing a little. Stumbling forward I put my arms out to steady myself. Mist rolled across the inky water; torches lined the river as it snaked out into the distance.

Eerie ghostly images kept sweeping through the mist covered water. I looked up making sure that no harpies were flying over head. Unsheathing my atheme from my leg I held it loose in my palm. Wailing and moans echoed off the walls. This would be the best haunted ride to take on Halloween if it was a ride. I was trying to add a tad bit of humor to my thoughts, to keep my wits about me.

From the river I could see caverns on either side with more honeycombed tunnels. They must lead to some of the other cities. I didn't have time to find out. Yet I got the feeling I would see this place again. Facing forward again; I almost jumped out of my skin to see a female staring back at me with inky wells for eyes.

Chalky skin pulled tight with high cheekbones and blood red lips painted on her face. She wasn't blinking just staring at me as if she had never seen another being before. "You are not dead." The woman stated. "Why are you on my river?" She questioned without blinking.

Swallowing my lunch back down, I found my voice again. "You must be Lethe (forgetfulness)." I stated. "No, I am very much alive; and I am on your river do to the directions Hade's gave to me. I am on my way to Tartarus in search for Minos." I tell Lethe, as she stares at me without moving a muscle.

"Ah, I see." She sighed in a low voice. Sitting on the bench seat the boat provided she stared up at me. "You must be parched." "Please have a drink." Lethe says, as she took a flask and filled it with the inky water we are crossing. "No thank you, I am in no need of refreshment." I tell her. "Suit yourself." She shrugs her shoulder as she tips back the flask and pours the contents down her throat. Moaning in pleasure; she replaced the cap and stared out into the distance.

Lethe is one of the Goddess of the Rivers of Underworld; the very one Edam had warned me about when he said not to drink from the river. If I had I would have forgotten everything I had even known. It was a good think I had been paying attention; or I would have been very sorry. Lethe seemed to be getting bored with me as we sat staring at each other in silence as we crossed the dark river. The Ferryman paid us no mind. It was as if he was void of emotion.

"Well; this has been quite lovely." Lethe stated rising from her seat causing the boat to quake. I widened my stance to keep my balance as I met her gaze head on. "Yes, it has." "Thank you for accompanying me." I replied politely. I knew I would see her again before this trip was over. Her dark unblinking eyes stared at my face a moment longer before she nodded her head and blinked out of sight as if she had never been there.

I have Goosebumps rising on my flesh and knots in my stomach from all of the things I had witnessed since coming here. I so wanted to go home and be done with all of this. I longed for a hot shower, and a good book. To pretend I was just a normal human and to forget about the craziness my life had become.

The boat slammed into the side of the bank; causing me to fall forward a step. "Tartarus." The ferryman exclaimed, as the boat stopped at another wooden bridge. "Thanks." I stammered, as I disembarked from the vessel. He gave no reply; just kept standing there in his boat. I was glad I didn't have his job, or I would have been driven mad by now.

Tartarus was a nasty looking city. Crumbling buildings that looked as if they were going to topple over at any moment rose from the ground. I didn't know much about this city; other than it was where the truly bad souls went when they died. I had put a couple of the residence here myself. Hopefully, I didn't run into any of them. If I did, I would be ready. Oil lanterns hung from sign posts on each of the establishments; not that you could really call them that.

One sign had the word PUB wrote in what appeared to be blood. I wasn't going to examine it close to find out for sure. Thinking it would be a good place to start my search for Minos; I walked inside. The barkeep, a nasty looking zombie look a like, was wiping down the bar. Several men were sitting at tables scattered through out the pub. They all swung their heads in my direction as soon as I walked through the doors. Hollow void eyes starred at me from the patrons of the local pub.

I avoided eye contact with them all; as I strolled up to the bar. Keeping my thoughts on the task I had before me and not the way their creepy stares were making me feel. The barkeep continued to wipe down the bar, not really paying me any attention. Clearing my throat, I asked in a strong voice where Minos could be found. It was then that the whole room silenced; as if by invoking Minos name had caused them all a great deal of fear.

"The center of town in the old square would be a good place to look." The barkeep suggested without meeting my gaze; as he continued to wipe the bar with the dirt covered rag in his hands. Taking the hint I turned to walk out of the bar. The men at the table closest to the entrance; rose to there feet. "Your kind isn't welcome here." They told me as they shuffled closer.

"Oh, and what would be my kind?" I questioned. They froze; as if someone had them on an invisible leash. I stood there starring at them for a few seconds longer; not knowing what to make of them. Void expressions and lifeless bodies were all they appeared to be. Deciding not to waste more time than I had already had on the goons here. I walked out and back into the street.

Following the broken concrete slabs that severed as sidewalks; I walked toward what I hoped was the center of the city. Rubble from the decaying buildings fell off in chunks; rolling across the street like giant tumble weeds. The wind kicked up dirt from the barren fields; forming a wall of thick mud like goo that caked the near by buildings.

Broken benches, and stumps of trees were scattered along one whole lot; I assumed it was a park of some sort. More oil lamps hung from iron hooks lighting the buildings in a spooky glow. Nothing about this place was inviting.

I was starting to doubt that I would even run into Minos here; when I rounded the corner, and came face to face with the end of a snake's tail. It lashed out like a bullwhip before I even had time to arm myself. Coiling around me it dragged me forward to the fountain in the middle of the courtyard. Trying to wiggle free from the hold I was in; I found myself unable to breath. The more I struggled the tighter it wrapped around my body.

Giving up for fear of being strangled to death; I went limp in it's' grip. I figured it would be better if I conserved the energy I had; and used it to fight the creature that had a hold of me, as soon as I was able to see its' face.

The snake like tail had a grip around my body, lifting me up and over the broken benches and stumps along the path. I focused on the sounds around me. The scales of the snake skinned tail snapped and crackled like old paper. The stench of scorched skin and sulfur filled the air.

Taking a look around, I could see charred statues that look like the remains of people. All in various agonizing poses. Torches like the ones that had lead to Hades door were placed in giant circles that enter loped each other. The snake stopped two feet from the center; and hovering my body over a torch as if it was going to cook me. I tapped my nails against its body; trying to remain as calm as I could.

A voice from below spoke to what I could only assume was me. "What are you doing in Tartarus; when I can tell you are very much alive?"

The voice asked. "I was sent here to seek the help of Minos." I answered. The coils tightened once more; then relaxing so fast that my arms were flaying about me as I tumbled down from its grip. "What do you want with him?" The voice asked as the snake moved away and out of sight. Getting up from the crouch I had landed in, I looked around trying to find my questioner. Stars danced in the edges of my vision; coughing and sputtering I tried to regain my breath.

"I was told by Hades; that Minos would escort me to the gates of the crystals holding." I said, into the dark space from where I thought the voice had come from. I was met by silence; the torches shot a foot high causing me to cover my eyes. When the flames had died down enough for me to remove my hand, I was standing face to face with a man. Glowing green eyes stared at me from a face that could have only have come from a god or the offspring of one. Who he was exactly, I had no clue.

"Why would Minos escort the likes of you anywhere?" The man questioned me. "Look, I didn't realize I would be playing twenty questions. The Gods have sent me here to recover two things." "One being the crystal of Underworld, and the other being my father Hermes." Ticking them off with my fingers I told the noisy man with the flaming green eyes. The man smiled, and started to laugh as if that was the funniest thing he had heard in years.

"Oh, so you must be someone quiet important, if the Gods have such faith in you." He taunted me. "Important to them I care not; I just want to get what I have come for and be on my way." "Now if you're done with the interrogation I would love to find Minos; and get the Hell out of here." "No pun intended." I told him, as hoisted my shoulder bag back into place. Extending his hand, he spoke again. "Names Minos and you would be?"

I stared at him as if it had to be a joke; what the hell was this guy's problem. If he was Minos, what was with the game of questions? "You got to be kidding me." I said more to myself, than to the man in front of me. Again, he laughed like a barrel of monkeys. Slapping his knee and wiping a fake tear; he straightened back up again. "Sorry; I find the living to be quite amusing, usually the cast of folks I deal with are quite dead you see."

Laughing he looked up at me as if that was going to make everything better. Sighing I struggled to regain my composure. "So, you're Minos?" "What was the deal with the serpent tail choking the life out of me, right before you popped out of where ever it was you were hiding?" I asked him.

"That old thing." He answered, waving away my question as if it wasn't important. I raised my eyebrow; placing my hand on my hip I tapped my foot in return for his flipped response.

"Oh okay, if you must know." Minos answered as he rolled his eyes and looked over his shoulder. The tail of the serpent came back into view as if it had never left. "Look Down." Minos said with a grin plastered on his face. His glowing green eyes danced with delight. I took the moment to do as he said, and when I looked back up again he was laughing so hard tears were rolling down both his cheeks. "You looked shocked, haven't you seen strange things before?" "Yes, I have." "I just wasn't expecting you to be the thing that had attacked me."

"Attacked you, now my dear; I'm offended, I did no such thing." He stated as he narrowed his eyes at me. "Well, then what do you call squeezing me to the point I had trouble breathing, or dropping me from ten feet from the ground?" I throw back at me. "Point made." Minos said still smiling like a Cheshire cat. "I could have sworn you had two legs not a tail just a bit ago." I said to him. "You would have been correct; I can take both forms." "A perk of being a judge of the dead." He shot back without even batting an eye.

"So, about the escort to the gates?" "Are you going to take me?" I asked. I was having a little trouble reading him. Hopefully, I didn't piss him off to bad by being so forward. His blonde hair was standing up in a million different directions, his green eyes were glowing and that smile was still chizz led across his face. He sure was a sight. "Awe, but we are having so much fun." "Why rush." He joked. I got a feeling that he was either half crazy; or was really bored. Both way; I needed his help, and I would play along for a little while if it got me were I needed to go. "Lovely place you got here, but I don't see a couch." I joked back. Laughing in a fit of hysterics, he slapped his knee over, and over again. "Good one." He told me. "Awe, I guess your right; I guess my décor is a little out of date. I don't usually get guests; well, the type that can stay and chat that is."

"Alright. I guess we can get a move on then." "Hope you like big doggies." Minos said, as he took off walking threw the torches so fast that I had to run to catch him. "I can manage." I said, as I hoisted the bag back onto my shoulder.

I hoped what I read about the Hellhounds was enough to get me past them. If not I would have to think fast or become doggy chow. That wasn't a very pleasant image to picture in my head. Shaking the thought away; I fought threw the crush of decaying branches, scattered bones, and what knots that lay across the ground as I tried to keep up with Minos. His head was bobbing to its own beat as if he was listening to music in his head; as I finally caught up with him. He truly was a strange man. I would have to keep an eye on him.

"So tell me, what is it like on earth now?" "It's been many years since I have seen it." Minos stated. His eyebrows were rising into his hairline giving him a comical expression. I was trying hard not to laugh at the cartoon image of him that was dancing through my mind. Maybe, I had been here to long and was becoming delusional. "Uh, well it's different; I haven't been there long myself." I told him as we rounded a boulder that ran along the river.

We were headed into what looked like a dark forest. I hoped there were more torches because seeing in the dark was not one of my abilities. "Oh." Minos said prompting me to go one without really saying much of anything. "Well ya, I have only been there about three years; before that I lived in Otherworld." I told him. Minos stopped dead in his tracks and turned on his heal to face me. "You're the fae's daughter." "I can't believe it." "I'm walking and talking with a legend." Minos went on chattering like an old hen.

Laughing at the thought of myself being a legend. I raised my hand to my mouth to cover it up. "Sorry, come again?" I said. Minos looked me up and down walking circles around me as if I was a piece of artwork. "Humm, interesting." "You have the markings of a God, with the wings of a Fae." 'Come to think of it your eyes are glowing a rather odd color of blue.'

"What a marvelous sight you are." He beamed up at me. I started to blush, and feel foolish for no reason at all. "I take it; you haven't seen many Hybrids?" I asked him; as I tried to stand still as he continued to circle around me. "Erm, well none as beautiful as you; my dear." Minos went on as if he was talking to his prized pet.

"I think we need to keep moving." I tell him; not able to take the comments any longer. "Aye, not so comfortable in your own skin; I could help you out with that if you want?" Minos said, wagging his bushy eyebrows at me again. I guess the look on my face was enough to set him into another fit of laughter. "I don't find it funny." "Can we please drop it?" I urged.

Throwing his hands up in fake defeat he backed up a step. "So Andras' I guess we have more in common then our fathers being Gods." Minos said as he continued on the path. "How did you know my name?" "I didn't give it to you." I asked his back. "I told you, you're a legend. "Oh." I said, puzzled by the way he kept bring up the whole legend thing.

"You see we both are in roles that we would not have picked for ourselves.' 'Yet the fates chose for us." Minos says as if it was mere fact. "That may be your case buddy, but no one chooses for me." I tell him as I struggle with my bag again. It was starting to get heavier by the minute.

What the heck did I have in this thing? Something moved inside my bag, causing me to start. I jumped and tossed the bag onto the ground. Minos raised his eyebrow and looked from me to the bag and back again. "Something wrong?" He questioned. I reach down and opened the flap on the top of my purse. Peeking inside; I jumped back a few feet. There was a flipping winged, red eyed creature sleeping inside it. "What the hell is that?" I said, pointing to the bag. Minos walked over and looked at the fussy little being; laughing at me as if I had said yet, again something funny.

"Gargoyle would be my guess." He shrugged his shoulders, as if it was common knowledge. "Is he yours?" "Awful cute little bugger, wouldn't you say." Minos said cheerfully, as he scratched the gargoyles head causing it to gurgle.

"No it's not mine." 'I wouldn't have flipped out if it was mine." I tell him as I stare at the sleeping fur ball. "Well, he is yours now." Minos tells me matter of fact like. "See." He says as he scoops the creature out of my bag and flopped him into my arms. The little Gargoyle opened his sleepy eyes enough to look up at me and then snuggled into my arms. "What the heck do I do with him?" I asked as I stared down at the little being.

"Um, I would suggest putting him back so he can continue his nap." "Be gentle would ya." "They sound awful when they are upset." Minos said as he continues to laugh at my distraught form. Placing the fuss ball back where I found him. I picked up the bag and placed it on my shoulder. Where the heck did I pick up a hitch hiker was beyond me; but it looked like I was stuck with him, for now at least. We would see what would happen once it was awake.

"If you're done fussing with the bag and your

pet; we might want to continue." Minos informs me as he starts walking again. If Edam was here, these things would not be happening. I really missed his company. "Are you taking me all the way to the crystals holding place; or just to the gates?" I asked. I needed to find out what else was in store for me and a little heads up would be nice. "To the gates." "I can not go any further than that, at the moment." Minos said as he frowned.

I think it really bugged him that his journey with me was going to end so soon. "Well I do appreciate you escorting me." I tell him trying to lighten the mood. Minos shot me a small smile from over his shoulder; as he continued to walk. "So, about my little tag along." "What can you tell me about Gargoyles?" I ask him as we get to the edge of the forest. "Well, that is a very good question." Minos said as he stopped; and looked around, as if he was trying to figure out which way we needed to go.

"They tend to be too needy for my taste in pets." He said jokingly. "Truth be told you are one lucky girl that it picked you." "They choose someone to guard for as long as they live." "Looks like your food bill just went up." He said laughing at his own joke. "They pick?" "You mean; I got no say in this at all." I look at my purse again; as if it becomes a foreign object I had stuck to my shoe. I sent Minos into another fit of laugher.

"Yep, Afraid so."

"You will come to appreciate him in time." 'You'll see." Minos tells me as he grabbed a torch from the path and held it in front of him. "Okay, not trying to alarm you here; but the forest is not a nice place to be.' 'I'm afraid we have to go threw it to get to where you need to go." "You know how to kill birds' right?" Minos asked, as he started to creep forward a step into the tree line. "Erm, I take it you're talking about Harpies; and not real birds." I stated, as I followed closely behind him.

"You would be correct again." Minos says. "Two points for you." He boomed with another fit of laughter. "Well I'll be there with ya; so no worries, love." Minos tells me. I unbuckled the atheme from my thigh and held it loose in my hands. I guess my sleeping fuzzy bucket would have to wake up if we came across the birdies. I would need both hands to fight if I had to.

Minos waved the torch in front of him like a giant flaming sword; as we inched forward into the tree line. No sounds came out of the woods, except that of our own feet crunching on the leaves underfoot. Pulling my shoulder bag up higher, the little fuzzy creature sleeping inside was weighing it down. The eerie still quiet of this forest was enough to have the hair rising on the back of my neck. I was still getting the feeling that I was being watched.

Looking around to make sure it was just a feeling. I caught the glimpse of feathers streaming threw the tree line. "Heads up!" I tell Minos; as I lower my shoulder bag to the ground, and unwrap the chain of justice so it can swing freely at my side.

Pointing the tip of my atheme in the direction where I saw the wings; I waited to see what would happen. Minos took a baseball players stance with his torch. It was a sight I tell you. If it wasn't such a serious matter, I would have laughed. Screeches filled the air, the wind kicked up; sending us back a step.

Two women with silver hair and black wings landed in front of us. Their eyes were blood red, there hair was unkempt, and the feathers from their wings covered their upper body leaving only a silhouette of heavy breast visible. Razor sharp inky black claws hung from their hands. Their feet were normal except for the dew claws protruding out the heels. The bird women stood still in front of us, chests heaving from the flight they had just taken.

"What are you doing in our forest?" They ask Minos as if I am not even there. Which suits me fine at the moment. I was still blown away by what I was seeing. "Your forest, your forest, when did it become yours?" Minos replies still holding his torch like a bat. "Since we kicked your sorry butt out of it." The one to the right of me said. Minos laughed and for the first time it didn't sound cheerful; there was a wicked undertone that was sending shivers up and down my spine.

There was history between these three that much I could tell. The bird women looked at each other, then back to Minos, and finally their gaze landed upon me. "Why are you here?" They questioned me with a puzzled expression glued on their faces. It was as if they knew me but how could that be. I had never seen such a sight as them before. I would have remembered seeing a woman covered in bird feathers I do believe.

"Well its really quiet simple I was sent here to collect my father and the Crystal of Underworld." I tell the woman. They looked at me with their heads cocked to one side as if what I had just said had puzzled them.

The one to the left of me studied me for just a moment longer before she seems to realize that I was not the person she thought I was. "Your father would be?" She asked with her head still cocked to the side. "Hermes." I replied. Light seem to register in her eyes, a smile lit her face.

"Forgive me, you reminded me of your mother for a moment." She tells me. "I take it you would like to cross through the forest with the likes of him." She stated as she pointed one inky claw in Minos direction. "Yes, I would." I tell her. "I See." She says.

"Minos do you have anything to say for yourself?" The woman questions him. Minos was about to open his mouth to spout what I was sure would be a nasty comment, instead he just snapped his jaw shut as he looked over at me.

"Well then, I guess I can allow you to pass, but remember I was kind to you this time." She tells him. Turning her attention back to me she raised her clawed hand holding it out for me to shake; she spoke in a kinder tone. "I'm Silkie, the Queen of the Harpies.' "Your mother was a friend of mine and I'm pleased to have known her."

I was blown away. Shaking her hand I just stared at her. Here I thought I was going to have to fight my way threw.

The other bird woman stood silent just

watching as the Queen and I shook hands; not bothering to introduce her self to me. There was something off about her. I made a mental note of it as I continued to process what I had just been told. "You knew my mother?" I questioned Silkie. "Yes, I knew her." "Then you know what has become of her." I stated. Nodding her head she lowered her gaze.

"I do, and I hope dear one that you can one day fix what we were unable to stop." Silkie said as she gazed up at me again. Her eyes were misted over for just a mere second. Just as quickly as she had shown the emotion it was gone. "Behave yourself, Minos." The Queen warned. With that she turned and took flight, her sidekick at her side. Leaving Minos and I alone once again. Coughing to gain my attention Minos spoke.

"Guess we need to get moving." He said as he took the lead once again. "Mind telling me why they seem to have a problem with you?" I asked him as I picked up the bag that held the sleepy creature and started after him. "Oh, that it's nothing." Minos stated as he waved his hand as if it was not a big deal at all.

"Nothing? I wouldn't have called that nothing." I stated. "They looked as if they were ready to fight us.' 'An I take it; it was because of something you had done." "Well if you most know, I refused to marry one of the harpies." "Silkie took it as a direct insult." "So we have been fighting for a decade or so now.

"A decade!' 'Wow you all really do hold a grudge don't you?" I say in a semi sarcastic tone, as we continue deeper into the heart of the forest. "Well, I guess; we have nothing better to do down here." Minos said with a shrug.

We walked on chatting a little here and there. I kept glimpsing winged woman watching us from their perches in the trees, yet none took action against us. I kept a close eye on them just in case; as we ventured forward. The little creature that had been sleeping in my bag was starting to wake.

Catching Minos attention, we came to a stop near a big dead oak tree. I placed the bag on the ground and slowly opened the flap. The fuzzy little guy stretched and opened his eyes to stare up at me. Blinking a couple times, he looked around. Gurgling, he climbed out of my purse and snuggled against my leg. "Well look at that he likes you." Minos tells me. "Really how can you tell he isn't thinking about biting me?" I question.

Minos started laughing, as if that was the funniest thing he ever heard. Yet I was quite serious; for all I knew this little guy was just trying to get me to warm up to him so he could make a meal out of me. I arched my eyebrow and looked at him, causing him to go silent. We stood near the dead oak for a while longer letting the gargoyle wake up. I squatted down and started to talk to him as I patted his head. I didn't know if the creature would be able to understand me; but I needed for him to walk beside us. I had carried him long enough. If something decided to fight us I would need both my hands.

"Okay little one, I need you to walk now. It won't be for to long." I tell the cream colored fuzz bucket as he continues to rub against my leg. He gurgles some more as if he understood what I was tell him. I stand up and place the bag back on my shoulder. Minos is scratching his back on the dead oak tree. "Ah that feels good." He tells the tree. "Have you named your pet yet?" Minos asks me as he continues to scratch his back on the tree. "No, I haven't a clue what I should call him." I reply as I look down at the wobbly little fuzz bucket.

"Well he looks like a 'Fred' to me." Minos says as he finally removes his backside from the bark of the tree. "Fred?" "What do you think about that?" I ask the gargoyle as he wobbles around stretching out his little leather wings. Gurgles emerge from his mouth as if he likes the name that's been chosen for him. "Okay then Fred it is." I tell him.

"Okay now that your back has been scratched; and the pet has a name, can we get going?" I ask Minos as I gather my belongings from the ground. "Always in such hurry." Minos teases me. "What is your rush to leave for anyways?" He goes on chattering as he starts to lead the way again. I was starting to feel like I was babysitting. Minos had the attention span on a toddler. Why in the world Hades told me to seek him out was beyond me. Maybe I was the ass end of some Underworld joke.

If that was the case, then you could rest assured I would pay them back when I got a chance. Right now I needed to get to the gates, past the Hellhounds and to the crystal so I could get out of here. I really wanted to be top side again. Not that it wasn't interesting down here; but I missed my apartment and all of its comforts. Hopefully Edam and the gang found a way in to get to me soon.

Chapter Fourteen

We inched our way threw the forest; down a little path of broken decayed stones. An inky stream ran alongside the path. Black moss hung from the tree limps like giant spider webs waiting for prey. Eerie sounds were filling the air. I could hear the breath of Fred and Minos coming out in gasps. Everything had my nerves on high alert. I really didn't like the forest here, with the red overcast of the sky here, it seemed alien and void of life.

Yet, it was full of things that would scare the crap out of most people. "How much further do we have to go?" I asked Minos as I looked up into the trees to see more harpies perched above us. "Twenty yards or so to the cave that will take us to the gates." Minos tells me as he catches a glimpse of a tall, gangly harpy perched above him. "What the heck?" He states as the armed bird like women descend on us. Fred starts to hiss and spit at the sight of the women.

They were not here by their Queens order I knew that. Yet, here they were armed and ready to fight us. The foot soldiers of harpies circled us, letting their wings stretch out from their back, hissing they faced us.

The one that had been by the Queens' side was standing out in front, crouched low with a dagger in her hands. "Silkie is weak, and stupid; if she thought we would just let you threw without a price." She spits at us.

"Minos, tell me you have a plan to get us out of here in one piece." I say as I grab my atheme and chain of justice. "Working on it, Love." He states as he takes aim at one of the harpies that had closed in on him. Setting the side of her body afire with his torch as he swung it out like a baseball player. "Take that!' 'You fowl beast of a woman!' Minos screamed as he swung his torch for the second time at the woman in front of him.

Fred's eyes had started to glow and little lightening bolts of electricity were shooting out of the ground around him as he hopped back and forth between my self and the harpies closest to us. I gave the silver chain of justice a wide swing, letting it fly; it landed around the arm of the Queens' sidekick. Drawing her closer to me and my atheme; the little electric bolts that Fred had created in cased her feet in a bubble; causing her to stumble, and land at my feet.

The other harpies seem to catch on that their leader was in trouble; yet, none of them came to her aid. Instead they stood still waiting to see what would become of her. The chain of Justice sang causing the air around me to warm. My eyes turned white as the images of what this woman had done filled my minds eye. She was in bed with Hermes so to speak; he promised that she could rule over all the harpies if she helped to capture me. Oh, how sad it was that she had fallen for his tricks.

"You go against your Queen, and believe lies from a god that is known for his trickery." "Shame on you." I tell her. Minos just stares at me as if I have grown a second head. Clapping his hands, Minos finally finds his voice. "Bravo O' Andras'. 'Now will one of you feathered beauties fly off and grab your Queen; I think she needs to see this." He tells the harpies as he continues to clap his hands like he is watching the greatest show in the world.

Two of the harpies that were at the back of the line take flight; I only hoped they were seeking out their Queen and not just fleeing from the scene. The Silver Chain of Justice started to smoke; burning threw a layer of the Harpies arm.

She hissed out in pain. Pure hate was etched into her face. I looked down at her; my eyes were glowing from the images I was receiving "You really thought he would just hand you everything?"

"So, Hel has her own part in all this; somehow that doesn't surprise me." I tell her as I jerk her forward and onto her knees. The wind kicked up just as I touched my atheme to the harpy's neck. Sounds of huge wings filled the air. The two harpies that had flown off; returned with their Queen in tow.

"What is the meaning of this?" She questioned me as if I was the one in the wrong. "I will let her tell you." I respond with venom in my tone. "Speak and tell your

Queen the truth at once." I tell the wretched woman at my feet.

"You don't deserve to be Queen!" The harpy spit out. "You see Silkie, this one has made a deal with Hermes and Hel to capture me in return for your throne." I tell the Harpy Queen as I push the point of the atheme closer to the woman's neck.

"An these lovely birdies aren't as loyal as you would have thought they would be.' 'Seems they would have sold you out to follow her.' Minos says as he points at the withering form in front of me. "I see." Silkie replies as she takes a moment to look at her subjects that had formed a circle around us.

"Andras' thank you for bringing this to my attention; I will take over from here." Silkie tells me as she lifts the harpy off the ground by her hair. "Let this be a lesson to you all." She states as she takes her inky claws to the young harpies throat. In one quick motion she swipes threw leaving the body to fall to the ground. Holding up the severed head of the woman; she tossed it into the crowd of her subjects. They all bow their heads in shame.

Knowing they will receive the same fate; if they are found plotting to take over her throne again. Silkie turned her attention back to us; speaking in the most humbled of voices. "When the time comes that you should need my aid, I will be there."

With that she and her court of bird women take to the air. Leaving us once again alone in the forest. "Well, love I do have to say things are interesting around here since you arrived." Minos tells me as he brushes imaginary dust off his sleeve. "It has been a very enlightening trip; I do have to say." I respond as I gather my belongings and pick up the Gargoyle that is circling my leg. Seems the little guy has some magic of his own. I will have to thank the person whom gave him to me as soon as I found out who that was.

At least now I know that I have a couple allies myself down here. If Hermes and Hel had their way I would need all the help I could get. Hades and Hel had made a wager it seemed the prize was little oh me. Hermes had thrown his own dice into the mix striking a deal with Hel behind Hades back. Funny how I became a player in a game and wasn't even asked if I wanted to play. Good thing I had brought the Chain of Justice with me; or I would have walked into a trap with my eyes closed.

"I appreciate you escorting me threw the forest and to the gates, Minos." "Seems like everyone has a plan to get what they want and are willing to use me as bait if need be." "Nice to know I have you to count on." I tell him as we continue to walk toward the cave. Minos lowered his gaze, and kept silent. It seemed like he was blushing but in dark of the forest it was hard to tell. I hoped that he wasn't entangled in this web to.

That's all I needed was to be completely alone down here with no one to count on. I was really missing the guys. I hoped that Edam would find a way in before all Hell broke loose.

Blue crystals sparkled off the entrance of the cave. It looked rather out of place in this dark place. Like a beacon of hope it sparkled against the inky darkness of the woods around it. "Take it this is the cave you were talking about?" I ask Minos as I let my eyes light with wonder.

Smiling, Minos nodded, and entered into the cave. The walls were lit with blue crystal cones along the cavern halls. There were paintings all over the walls.

History of Underworld was written in pictures for all to see. It was a lot like the throne my aunt sat upon. "Thought you would like this place." "The big doggies will be up ahead, I hope you're ready for them. I forgot to bring doggy treats." Minos says, back to his joking self.

"I can wait here for you; but I can't cross throw the gates." Minos tells me. I nodded and kept walking looking at the stories that were painted all around me. I was amazed at the story I was reading. Seemed that there had been several struggles of power that had played out over the years.

Hades seems to always come out on top. But Hel had tried to take over several times; only to lose time and again. No wonders she seemed so moody.

We walked on for what seemed like miles. All through out the cave were stories of the lives of every subspecies that had ever lived here. Daywalkers had thrived off the sale of their hand made rugs, Vampires and other creatures all had their own stories told about them.

The one that caught my attention was of Hel; she had been the sole ruler of Underworld until Zeus tricked Hades into coming here. She had fell in love with him and tried to win his favor; only to be turned down time and again. Not only had he refused her love he stole her kingdom. Leaving her to rule over just one city; while he ruled over the rest of Underworld.

"Love, you need to stop taking in the sights and start to prepare.' 'We are nearing the gates." Minos tells me as we round the last boulder that served as a path marker. "Fred; I hope your energy bolts work on big doggies." I tell the fuzzy little gargoyle that has been tagging along behind us.

Opening the shoulder bag I removed the Silver tipped flute that the Satyr had gifted me, adding it to the clasp on the end of the arm band that was also holding the chain of justice. I removed a honey cake from the depths of my bag. I had to move quickly to get a chance to use anything I had brought with me. A chance was all I needed to be able to get threw the gates and to the crystals holding place.

The old crone said that the Hellhounds would lead me to the resting place; I hoped it would be that easy.

It would be nice for something to be as easy as it sounded for once. We would see. "Thank you again Minos, I would not have made it this far without your aid." I tell him as we come to a sudden stop. "Don't mention it love." "Was my pleasure." Minos replies in a kind yet dry tone. I could tell something was bothering him; yet now was not the time to probe into it deeper. Minos picked up a giant turtle shell and gave it a quick thump. "If those big doggies are in a bad mood we might need this."

He tells me as we duck under some rock formations hanging from the ceiling. I was hoping that we wouldn't need to find out what the shell was for. Praying to who ever was listening I sent out a silent plea for everything to run smoothly. The ground quaked under us; causing several small rocks to fall around us. I put my hands out to brace my self; just as a loud rumble echoed off the cavern walls.

"That didn't sound like thunder." I tell Minos as we duck to keep from getting flattened from a giant rock that went flying over our heads. "That was the doggies I was telling you about, Love." Minos replies from his hiding spot under the turtle shell. He looked rather ridiculous with his hair standing on end and a giant shell over him.

Here he was a son of a God and he was hiding underneath a shell, shaking in his boots because of a dog growling. Just as I sat there casting judgment on poor Minos; as a flame shot out from the back entrance of the cavern causing me to dive for cover right along with him. Snapping of giant jaws and more ear shattering growls pierced the air. I looked over at Minos to find the fuzzy little gargoyle with a death grip around Minos' neck. "Mind getting your pet off me love, before he chokes me to death." Minos manages to ask me as he turned three shades of purple from the grip my winged pet had on him.

Grabbing the gargoyles chubby little hands I removed them from Minos neck; tossing him into the shoulder bag. "So what do we do now?" I asked Minos as I latched the shoulder bag close. "We wait until they stop spitting fire then we run toward them.' 'We can duck behind this,' he points to the turtle shell; 'to keep from getting cooked, but I warn you it will get mighty warm.' 'When we get close enough you will have to play the flute."

'I hope you have practiced." Minos says as he catches his breath. "Run Now." He tells me as the room suddenly fills with silence. We take off running toward the back of the cave; right toward the hellhounds and gods only know what else. We had only gotten about twenty yards when a loud crack, followed by a hellstorm of fire that flew over our heads. Minos and I ducked under the turtle shell again; hugging the floor as closely as possible. We waited until the dogs were done with their death defying flame show. Minos nodded at me and we bolted again toward the guardians of the gates. We were finally close enough to them that I could see that the humans that had wrote the mythology book I had read had never actually seen one of these creatures up close and personal.

Three dog heads were welded to one huge body. Red glowing eyes and razor sharp teeth lined their mouths. Venom was leaking from the folds of skin that hung from their lower jaws. Sharp black claws grew from their feet. Sniffing the air, they sat in front of giant iron gates. "Now would be a good time to use your flute, Love." Minos whispers as we peek from under the giant shell. "Ya Okay." I tell him, my mouth still hanging open from the image before me.

Nudging me with his elbow to gain my attention Minos repeated himself. Just incase

I didn't hear him the first time. I took the flute from the clasp and placed it to my lips. I blew out the first three notes of the song I had been practicing.

The hellhound's ears perked up; then before I could get the fourth and final note out they started spitting fire balls at us again. Ducking back under the shell I waited for the fire to stop. "Not so forceful this time.' 'Just let it flow." Minos coached me from under the turtle shell.

Taking a deep breath I gathered my bearings and started the song again. This time they didn't seem to mind the sound coming from the flute. Swaying to the tune, I provided for them; they stretched out and lay at the base of the iron gates. Taking that as a sign, I left the safety of the shell; and slowly made my way toward the huge monster of a dog in front of me.

"Easy boys." I cooed, as I unwrapped the honey cake and broke it into pieces. Tossing the sticky bite size pieces at the two giant dog heads in front of me; I waited for them to take my offering.

"I just need to get past you guys; to the holding place of the crystal." "Easy boys." I tell the Hellhound, as I reach out my hand to scratch one of the heads behind its ear. The other dog head turned sharply in my direction; its red eyes were glowing as it stared at me. I was frozen from fright. I was to far away from Minos to run for cover; and I was not looking forward into becoming a burnt dog snack. What happened next amazed me beyond belief. The Hellhound spoke, "Well all you had to do was ask." it said. At that he went back to licking his chops. "You mean you can talk?" I said purely out of stupidity. I mean come on, how many times in your life have you had a giant two headed dog talk to you; after it spit fire balls at you from over twenty feet away.

"If you will pardon me I will be right back; I have to go gather my bag." I tell the hellhound. A sigh left one of the heads as the other nodded. I turned and walked swiftly back toward Minos. Who was still cowering under the shell. Tapping on it twice I wait for him to lift it up. "I need my bag.' 'Are you going to be alright till I get back?" I ask him. Minos head just bobbed up and down; his hair was still sticking up all over the place like a static charge was going threw it. He truly was a comical character.

Taking it that he was going to be just fine here under the turtle shell, I gathered my belongings. Returning to the front of the gates I stood in front of the Hellhounds.

Grabbing the last honey cake from my bag; I divided it into, and tossed it to the two dog heads. Chopping the sweet cake in mid air, they both mumbled their thanks. "So May I pass by you to get to the holding place of the crystal?" I asked the giant dog in front of me. "No." they both responded at once. "What do you mean no?" I questioned with my hand resting on my hip. Here I thought we had an understanding only to be told NO!

"You may not pass us, but we will lead you to where it rests." "We can not allow you to go alone. " The head to the left of me replied. Feeling rather foolish I looked at the ground.

"Oh, okay well thank you." I told the hellhound. With that the giant dog stood and turned. I had to duck to keep from getting smacked with its huge tail as it went swishing through the air. The iron gates hummed and creaked open revealing a cobble stone path lit by more blue crystal cones.

"Follow us." The hellhound told me as it headed through the gates. Walking behind the enormous creature made me feel rather small. If I hadn't known I was born with unspeakable powers I would have been scared senseless. I followed the Hellhounds through the gates, down the cobblestone path that was lit by the blue crystal cones. The walls were painted with images of the history of Underworld. More images of Hel and Hades mini wars played out along the passage way.

There were corridors off to the sides of the passageway; making it takes on the shape of a labyrinth maze. I was glad I had an escort or I would not have known where to go. The hellhound didn't speak as we walked along the path. It just kept moving forward; I followed behind closely while I took in everything around me. There was a humming coming from one of the rooms ahead of us. The closer we got the louder it sounded. The humming noise turned into tones. Like something you would hear in a warning broadcast on a television. It was starting to hurt my ears; I could only image what it was doing to the hellhounds'.

I looked up to see if the noise was having any effect on the giant beast in front of me. Only to discover that the hellhound had vanished. As if it was never there to begin with. Covering my ears with my hands I kept walking toward the noise. The vein in my temple was starting to throb. I didn't know how much more I would be able to take. One of those times when I really wished I had a ton of cotton to stick in my ears just to help muffle the sound.

The fuzzy little gargoyle was starting to make a fuss. I had to keep reassuring him that it was okay. I guess I was not the only one that found the sound unbearable. The pitch in the tone changed causing it to vibrate the floors beneath my feet. Little pebbles started to rain down from the cavern ceiling.

As I came to the doorway of the room where the noise was emerging from; it stopped all together. I shook my head and tried to get my ears to pop. Closing and opening eyes to try to adjust to the difference. I opened them to discover a black crystal sitting on a stand made of silver. It was pulsing a purple light. Causing the room to take on a weird glow. I felt like I was at a rave party.

High pitched tones and pulsing lights all that was missing was sweaty bodies crammed into a tiny space trying to dance. Laughing in my head at the image I had conjured up; I looked around the room. There was nothing else in the room except the black crystal and the silver stand. "I guess this is what I came after." I spoke to the emptiness around me. I was sure Hermes was down here close by.

Hades had already told me that he didn't have the crystal. I got the feeling that he was waiting to ambush me as soon as I left here. I hoped the feeling was wrong.

Walking across the room I looked around for

anything that might come jumping out of the shadows. When nothing came out to get me like I thought it would; I exhaled a deep breath that I had been holding. It was a now or never kind of moment. I did not have a clue how I was going to leave the Underworld; yet, I knew that if I didn't pick up the crystal then this trip would have been a total waste.

I still had to hunt down and capture Hermes before I could leave here. Somehow I did not think finding him would be as difficult as I first thought it would be. As bad as I wanted to hand out his punishment myself; I had to take him to the counsel. My mother was a statue because of this man; and one way or another he would pay for that. I picked up the crystal; the high pitched noise stopped as soon as it was in my hands. That was a relief as it felt like the blood was already pooling in my inner ear.

Turning I left the room and ventured back the way I had come with the Hellhounds. I took time to take in the pictures on the walls around me. So many wars had played out here; much more than there had been in

Otherworld or on Earth for that matter. Somehow I didn't think the fighting was going to stop any time soon. One day I would be able to delve into the history of before the rip. Right now I had to get back to Minos and threw the forest again. I knew that Edam and the gang were working non stop to find a way in to get to me. I couldn't help but wish they were here now.

Somehow that made everything I had already gone through better. I walked down the winding passage way, feeling a lot better knowing that I had at least got the crystal in my possession. As I neared the Iron gates I could see the Hellhound sitting on the other side like a giant statue. Its tail was thumping up and down as if it was waiting for another honey cake; of which I didn't have. Both heads were looking at me and I could not help but feel guilty that I didn't pack more treats. They were not as scary as I would have thought them to be; well at least since they had stopped spitting fireballs at me.

Coming to a stop at the gates I waited for them to creak open; I had to get back to

Minos and out of this forest. Time was ticking away and I still had to find Hermes. "Thank you for your escort." I told the big beast in front of me. The hell hound nodded its heads. I passed through the gates and passed them just as they spoke. "Call upon us if your in need, but do so only if necessary." With that it vanished leaving me alone at the entrance of the holding place. "Minos, you can come out now." "The big doggie is gone." I said as I saw the turtle shell quivering from Minos body shaking beneath it. He peeked from under the turtle shell and looked around as if I was just joking with him. Unable to suppress the laughter any longer; I doubled over. When I was finally done; I looked up to see a not so amused Minos standing in front of me. "Well if you're done; then I guess we need to get out of here." Minos tells me trying to get back some of his dignity. I snapped my mouth closed and tried to stop laughing. He was starting to fume. I had to admit it was very cute. His wild blond hair sticking up in every directions, flaming green eyes, and steam rolling out of his ears from being the butt end of a joke.

Chapter Fifteen

We started to walking back the way we came; through the inky black forest. We kept a look out for the harpies that had been with the queens' second when we had been ambushed. The forest was deathly quiet, not even the crickets were making a noise. The hair on the back of my neck was starting to rise. Fred was making a lot of grumbling noises from the depth of my purse. We stopped near an old knotted tree; so I could let him out.

Figuring that would help calm him a bit. It only made it worse; he hopped around spitting and causing a fuss. Minos raised his eyebrow and shot the little fuzz bucket a look. "I don't like how quiet the forest is; and I think Fred has a problem with it too." I said as I looked around to see if anything had changed. Minos had a worried expression on his face; something was bothering him. He kept looking over his shoulder as if he was waiting on someone to come. "Are you expecting company?" I asked him after the third time he peeked back down the path we had just been on.

"I uh, well." He said as he kicked the dirt with the toe of his boot. Something was up and I really didn't like the feeling I was getting in the pit of my stomach. I was hoping my gut was wrong and it was just fear. Yet, I couldn't help but notice the look on his face as I stared back at him. He had sold me out; it was written all over his face. Why I had not seen it until now was beyond me. "How could you?" It was all I was able to ask before all hell broke loose. It was as if they had been waiting the whole time to just make their appearance.

Hermes appeared next to a huge oak tree with sweeping branches; a grin plaster on his face. Flanking his right was the Queen of the Underworld herself, along with several Harpies that did not seem to get the message the queen had provided earlier.

Minos backed up and away from me as if at any moment I would explode. I just stared at the people in front of me. How could a father be so cruel and cold to their own child; how could my mother have ever loved a person without any integrity was beyond me.

Oh how I wished the boys were here then at least I would have someone on my side. I would then at least stand a fighting chance of winning this battle. The only ally it seemed I had was a fuzzy little energy bolt shooting gargoyle; that only provided a little comfort.

Hel spoke as if she had been preparing for this moment her whole life. "Andras Moonriver, may I present your father Hermes God of Chaos." As she said this, the mask she had been wearing earlier when I had been in her company gave way. Revealing the bones on one side of her body. She truly was the embodiment of life and death. I would have much rather looked at the mask she had worn than see the empty shell of a person that now stared at me.

How could I have ever thought her beautiful was beyond me? I pitied her; for she had all this power and yet she was not whole. My eyes searched my fathers looking for any sign of regret; he still had the smirk etched across his face. There was not any sign of love that should have been there only greed.

His own wants and desires to rule everything had clouded his heart leaving it in a dire state. I could not even feel anger at him just bleak sadness; for I remembered my mothers words. She had loved him or at least the person she thought him to have been. Now though; well, now he would have to pay for what he had already done and what he had planned on doing. I would have to make sure of it. "Hermes may have been the one to help create me; Hel." "But you were mis informed he is not my father." I stated as cold as I could; while I stared into dear old dads eyes. Something changed in his eyes; there for a mere second was a glimmer of hurt. He didn't like that I rejected him. Well, good I didn't like the things he had done.

"Now Andras' that is no way to speak to your father." He said; his words as smooth as silk. His grey hair flowed down his back; his bright sky blue eyes looked like ice as he stared at me. He smirk remained on his face. I new what he was doing he was using his magic to control the situation. The bleakness I had been feeling before returned with it was a thread of hopelessness. As if something was urging me to give up. I knew what he was trying to do.

He was trying to make me feel defeated, and alone. If I thought I was already beaten then he would be able to get me to do his bidding.

Well, I had news for him I was not putty to be molded. I had tricks of my own.

Opening my minds eye; I was able to see the black smudges of his magic thick in the air. Purple hues ran through it like a ribbon dancing in the wind. He was using Hel's power to amplify the feelings of doubt and failure. The thick smog like cloud hugged his form stretching out from him and touching everything around him. I thanked the Gods above that Luke and Edam had shown me how to see past magic's and directly to the heart of the matter; or, I would have been screwed. Minos was still near by but he was making no move to help my wretched father. I think he regretted telling him where I was. I gathered up my strength and focused on the purple ribbon I saw dancing threw the black cloud that hung think in the air. I slowly unwrapped it, and sent it back to its owner.

Removing Hel's magic from Hermes helped but it didn't stop the feelings of dread; or the voice in my head telling me to give up. I knew it was Hermes that was the cause of it; yet it was hard not to give in. I was holding my head trying to shake the voice of doubt out. Fred was still kicking up a fuss near my feet.

When to my left I saw Minos rise and morph into his snake like appearance. Standing next to me in all of his glory as his giant snakes' tail snapped back and forth like an angry wipe. The voice of doubt was still there; like a bad cough it was tickling the back of my brain. Trying to persuade me to bend to the will of the man before me. A loud claps of thunder; followed by the brightest lighting bolt I had ever seen pierced the sky above.

Just when I was about to buckle to my knees a portal ripped open in front of us. Edam stepped through. Flanking his side in all of his glory was none other than the Master of Hell. Hades stood with his arms crossed as if he was just observing a boring movie. Next to him was the goddess of the river forgetfulness; the same one that had sat with me as I crossed the river of the underworld in search of Minos.

Here I was thinking I was all alone and the reality was I had more help than I had ever needed before. Gods praise whatever forces had brought Edam through the portal. I was not sure the rest of the people standing with him were actually on our side. I guess I would soon find out.

"Nice of you to join us." Hel hissed as she looked toward Hades. A sly smile lit her face as if she had been waiting on him to appear. He returned her smile with a wink that spoke volumes of what he really thought. This was all a mere game to them.

For me it was more than; I was fighting for my life and the life of every living being in the four worlds. I would not be stopped. "Are you okay?" Edam asked me as he came to my side. I squeezed his hand and nodded; afraid if I tried to speak that all that would come out would be sobs. I stood there with Edam beside me waiting to see what the rest of them would do. I still didn't know where they all stood.

"Andras' you are well I hope?" The River Goddess Lethe asked me. I stared into her dark eyes; puzzled by her appearance here and not really able to answer. "I see my gift has served you well?" She stated as she stared at the fuzzy little fur ball that was darting between my legs. Blinking back the tears that had started to form in my eyes from the force of Hermes magic. I found my voice; "Yes, and thank you. " I told Lethe. If I had known she was the one who had given me the little gargoyle I would have gave more thought to his name.

"Well it looks like you are having a party Hel; and we were the last to be invited." "Do tell, what is the pleasure of this little get together." Hades asked the Queen of the Underworld as if he finally noticed he had been summons to the dark forest. I was starting to see that this was more of Hermes doing and that he was not here just because of the bet he had with Hel. "Yes I would like to know that to; among other things." I said as I looked into the dark eyes of the Lord of the Nether.

Hades blinked as if this was the first time he had noticed me; among the crowd of beings that were gathered around. "Well Andras' fancy meeting you here." Hades joked as if he had not been plotting against me this whole time.

Putting up my hand and giving him my palm; I let the look of disgust register across my face. It was enough to snap his mouth shut without a further word. I had seen the plans he had in store for me; when I had used the Chain of Justice on the Harpy. Hel and Hades had a wager placed on who would be able to get me to strike a deal first. Who ever won would get my soul.

Well I had news for them both I would not be signing any dotted lines with my blood any time soon. Hel had double crossed him; striking a deal with Hermes behind his back. Looked like Hades was just starting to put the pieces together. Hermes had no love for me; he was willing to trade my life for the crystal.

Or so he had lead Hel to believe. In reality he wanted to be able to control me; what better way to do so than to have me in safe keeping in the Underworld.

Well, I was no ones slave, nor pawn; I would not be kept as a prized pet by anyone. Lethe; wasn't here because of a bet or deal. She had her own reasons what ever they were; she was not sharing. Edam I knew would have my back; but Minos he was stills a wild card. I didn't know if I could truly trust him; not after learning he had been telling Hermes my every move. One way or another I would get out of here; and with the crystal even if I had to fight tooth and nail to do it.

Hermes magic was still over powering me; bringing me to my knees. Edam squeezed my hand; getting my attention. "Andras' you can fight this." "Remember what you have learned." Edam reminded me that I had been trained for this moment.

I could change the outcome; I could untwist Hermes magic and use it against him. I took a deep breath and nodded to Edam that I was in control. He let go of my hand; we both started fighting the assault of magic that Hel and Hermes had conjured up.

The purple ribbon of Hel's Magic was dancing through the air as if it had a mind of its own. Striking the air like a giant serpent; it lashed out at everything around us. Uncontrolled by Hel or Hermes it spun erratically around us. I closed my eyes as I began picturing it becoming a knotted rope. Every few feet I imaged a knot forming. After I had the whole thing knotted; I pictured it wrapping around Hel's body and tying its self together by the ends.

When I opened my eyes; there was a loud scream. Hel lay flat out on the ground. The purple ribbon was now visibly tied around her body. Her own magic was now her enemy; the more she tried to free herself, the tighter it became. Hermes had a look of total disbelief on his face. Hades stood there just appraising the situation. "Does someone mind telling me the reason for all this?" Hades said while waving his hand about at the crowd in front of him. "Its quiet simple; you should not have to ask." I stated as I shot him daggers with my eyes.

"Enlighten me if you would." Hades retorted. He must have been brought here do to the magic that had been conjured after all this was his domain. "You made a wager with Hel; did you not?" "One about me; and who would get to keep me." I stated. Hades eyebrow shot up; he didn't like the fact that I knew what he had been up to. "Well hate to disappoint; but Hel here she double crossed you making a deal with my father."

"Guess she wants to rule over the Underworld again; and he apparently offered a sweeter deal." "Oh, and then you have my dad here." "Hermes, he is not just here to gain access to the Crystal of Underworld but wants to control the power I have." "Then you have Minos; who just wants to be earthside again; even though he betrayed me by telling Hermes my whereabouts he didn't try to capture me." "Lethe is here for the entertainment." "Edam is the only one here just to help me." "Now that I have given you the run down on everything can I get back to what I am trying to do?" I yelled at Hades. He stood there shocked as if he didn't know what to say. I had to stop focusing on him.

I had to find a way to stop Hermes so I can take him to Mount Olympia for trail. Turning to face my father; I was shocked to see Edam fist slam into the side of Hades head. I did not know what that was about but I was sure that Edam and Hades alike could fend for their selves. Hermes was inching away back into the tree line; hoping no one would notice his escape. I grabbed the Chain of Justice and flung it out.

The end of the chain wrapped around his arm. Hermes hissed in pain; smoke rose up from the flesh of his wrist. I could see all his plans, deeds, and the Truth. I think the truth is what started me the most. He truly had loved my mother; and he did love me. He just didn't know how to show it; the thirst of power controlled him more than anything else.

"I have to take you in to see Zeus." I told him as I ushered back the tears that were forming in my eyes. "You have caused too much trouble this time." Just as I was about to lock my hand around his arm; something struck my legs. Fred had followed me. Little lightening bolts were shooting all over the ground. He must have thought I was in danger.

Cute little bugger; was the greatest ally I had. Hermes jerked under the weight of the chain; trying hard to free himself. I held on to the chain; there was no way I was letting him get away again. After everything I had been through I would finish this task. "Give it up; I'm not letting you go." I tell him as I lock eyes with the God that created me. Hermes didn't plead; he didn't speak at all. He just stood there looking at me as if I was a ghost that had haunted him for a long time. He walked forward and thrust his other arm in my direction. I wrapped the chain around both his hands; like a makeshift pair of handcuffs.

Slowly we walked back to were Hades and Edam were rolling around on the ground; fighting about who knows what. Minos stood against a tree; slow smile was creeping across his face. He seemed to really be enjoying the show the boys were putting on. Lethe was standing a few paces off; a void expression still locked on her face. Hel lay at her feet. Pain was shooting across her face as it morphed from bone to flesh and back again. Her own power was attacking her; she was getting all the punishment she would ever need.

"So looks like you caught him." Minos said as he thumbed his finger at Hermes. Nodding I just looked from him to the two guys rolling around on the forest floor. "I knew you would win." Minos said as he looked at me and then to the ground.

"Did you?" I question still watching Hades and Edam fight. Nodding; Minos smiled and lay against the tree. "Why?" I asked finally looking him in the eyes. Minos smiled, 'Because you were true of heart, you had no other thought." He stated in a matter of fact tone. It was my turn to smile. Minos may have told Hel and Hermes were to find me; but he had never left my side and that counted for something.

"UHUm!" I cleared my throat. "If you too would mind telling me what the hell you're doing I would appreciate it." I would love to get out of here and back to my life." I tell the two boneheads that are still rolling around in the dirt. It was as if they had just been waiting on me to say something. Both men shot from the ground; and began dusting their selves off.

"He wanted to keep you." Edam said as he finished removing the dirt from his shirt. "I thought I had already stated that." I shot back. Hades smirked as if he found the whole thing funny. I raised my eyebrow and shot him a look that said don't push your luck. "That still doesn't explain why you two were rolling around in the dirt; like to crazed dogs." I retorted.

"Allow me to explain." Lethe finally spoke as she kicked Hel's withering form. "The boy there is in love with you." "He was fighting for your honor." Lethe stated as if it was just common knowledge. "Hades; meant to make you his." she finished saying. I looked at the two men in front of me as if they had both lost their ever loving minds. Minos cracked up laughing like he had been sprinkled with tickle powder.

Edam blushed and shot Hades a look that said I kill you if you try. Hades just raised his eyebrow and smirked as if he was amused by the threat. I was growing tired of the banter; I had been through HELL and Back to find an end to this madness my father had created. Now I finally captured him and all I wanted to do was go home; get into my nice comfy sweatpants and sleep in my soft bed.

"Well I'm not an item that you can just have." I tell Hades as I shoot my own eye daggers at him. The smirk left his face; he looked as if he was just dumbfounded that I didn't find his offer appealing. "That being said; if you don't help us get out of here I will unleash Hel and give her back all of her power.' 'When that happens, she will regain her throne." "I really don't think you want that to happen now do you." I told Hades as I stepped forward with Hermes in tow. Edam and my lovely gargoyle were in step behind me.

Hades had a look of fury on his face. He knew he had been bested at his own game; and he didn't like it one bit. Yet, there was nothing he could do about it at the moment. "Well then." Hades stated. "I guess I have no choice other than to do as you say." "I would ask you to think about what I would give to you. A remember that if you ever change your mind you know where to find me."

Edam balled up his fist and went to jump at him again. I put up my hand stopping him from hitting the one person that would help us leave. Restraining his self he grabbed on to Hermes and stood silently beside me. I nodded to Hades that I would think about it and waited for him to do what ever he was going to do.

"I'm going to." Minos stated as he jumped up and away from the tree. "Been a while since I seen everyone." "I'll be back; I don't have a choice about that part now do I." Minos continued to chatter like a hen.

Lethe looked puzzle by the prospect of someone leaving Underworld. After all she was the Goddess of the river of forgetfulness; and most the people she met were already dead. Hades finally sighed and nodded his head as he gave in. "To Mount Olympia; if you don't mind." I told him. Nodding he opened a portal. The rip appeared in front of us showing the ivory steps that lead to the home of the Gods. Edam, Minos, Hermes, myself and my little pet all walked threw.

When we were safely on the first ivory step; the portal vanished as if it never was. Hermes had a look of dread on his face; can not say as I blamed him. He would soon know his punishment and I had a feeling it was not going to be a pleasant one. Minos was as happy as lark to be anywhere besides the Underworld. Edam was still silent and keeping his thoughts to his self. I on the other hand was looking forward into going Home. Right now that was Earthside; but in the near future I would have to make a choice on where I would rein.

That was a choice that could wait till later. I had some tasked left to do. One was making sure that Hermes got inside to his trial and the other was to make sure the last crystal was finally resting with the rest. The rest of it could wait till another day. I had proved myself worthy and more than just a Hybrid; I was asset that had a right to live.

The Gods could see that now. I did the task they were not able to do their selves and because of that I had gained respect and status of a God myself. Edam led Hermes inside, Minos and I followed closely behind. I let the events of the day slowly replay in my mind as I took in the honeycomb hallways; the art, scrolls and history of the worlds. Minos was staring at everything with eyes of a child.

Pure wonder etched across his face. I had a feeling that he would be visiting the home of his father more often now that he had seen it. The glint in his eye showed that he really didn't want to return to the Underworld. Maybe this mini vacation would be enough; maybe not.

Time would tell.

As for me, I was going home with a purpose

and a new outlook on my life. I still had to find a way to break the curse that had imprisoned my mother hopefully the Crone or the Seer would be able to assist me in that task. For now though I could go to Otherworld and let my Aunts know that I had won. That alone was enough for now.

Chapter Sixteen

~Awakening~

It's been a long journey, but at last the major part of it is behind me. I have recovered all four crystals and stored them in the Cave of Gold for safe keeping. Until the Counsel chooses to put them in their original caretakers hands; or use them to merge the worlds back as one. When the day comes to make that choice; I hope I am present.

It's been an eon since the divide. I think most of the people on Earth thought that the other three worlds were just myths. Nothing seemed real to them. I don't think it has since the division.

They had lost their faith in Gods, Demons, or any other mythical creatures. It was about time for magic to be restored to everyone and every thing again. The day would come when the pieces to the puzzle would smoothly fit back together. Today was not that day, but it would be soon.

I had dropped Hermes off on Mount Olympia

to receive his judgment. I could not bring myself to stay to see, nor hear what happened to him. I didn't have the stomach to look at him, let alone care. After everything he had done to my mother and tried to do to me; I could not be brought to care about his welfare. Edam had stayed to see the Judgment carried out; which was nice, it gave me time alone. Which I really needed after everything I had already went through.

Minos was another story. He seemed to have grown tired of being on Mount Olympia among the other Gods; and had ventured to Earth. I guess he was taking a walk down memory lane. I could only imagine how different things must seem to him now. After being in the Underworld for a couple hundred years I am sure it was like walking around in a dream world of confusion. I made a mental note to check on him from time to time. For now, I figured he would need time to adjust; so I had left him be for the moment.

Domenic and Kyle were back at the office waiting for the next supernatural case that would require their assistance; they were truly dedicated to helping people, and I was glad I could count them among my friends. I on the other hand was home just trying to cope.

Hot water from the shower seemed like salvation after being in the cold, damp, dark, neither that was Underworld it's self. I still had to go to Otherworld to give my report to both my Aunts; I was sure that Sable being the Queen of the Court of Air & Darkness had already received a report from her spies. But I needed to tell her myself what I had learned. I was looking forward to seeing Scarlet though. Even though the Seer had ways to check on me as well; I truly enjoyed her company. I also had to find away to undo the Medusa Curse on my mother. Hoping that when I did, she would be restored to her former self and not left a heaping pile of ashes. I had no clue what condition she would be in physically, let alone mentally after being trapped in stone for the last twenty odd years. Hermes was getting off light in my book; one of the very reasons I could not wait to get away from him after I dropped him off. He had made several attempts to speak with me; which I had ignored.

Edam had also tried to speak with me before I left the realm of the Gods; yet I was too tired and drained to carry on much of a conversation. I knew he wanted to change things between us. Yet, I was still not ready to think about taking our relationship to that level. I kept feeling like the whole world was getting ready to implode and take me away in a whirlwind of fire. Until that feeling passed I don't think I would be ready to discuss the future of anything.

I have just been on the job from hell. I had to save the world from my own father. The Gods of the Underworld were rolling dice to see who got to keep my soul. I had to escape the clutches of death and overcome the magic of not only Hermes; whom happens to be dear old dad, but also that of Hel the Queen of the Neither and her counter part Hades. All three of them had their own plan; none of them got what they wanted.

That alone was enough to have me smiling in the shower. Yet I was still feeling empty inside. This was supposed to feel victorious yet I kept waiting for the ball to drop. I was left with more questions than answers when I finally escaped the Underworld. Something told me that I would be seeing that place again. For now though I was going to enjoy the wonderful gift of running water and let the warmth of it wash away all the thoughts of yesterday.

For now I just wanted to soak up the quiet of my little apartment and let the water melt everything else away. I still had not read the rest of the scrolls or my mother's journal. I planned on doing so as soon as I was able to unwind from the adventure I had been on. So many thoughts were racing through my head that I felt as if the very floor I was standing on was spinning like a top out of control.

Removing the outfit I had been wearing since I had entered into the Underworld. I started to finally feel as if I was able to breathe a little. Standing in the shower allowing the beads of warmth to penetrate the cold that had gripped my body and soul since I had left to dance in the devils playground. I began to relax; laying my head back against the shower wall, I closed my eyes and let the events of the past month roll over me like waves in the ocean...

Standing in the shower with my eyes closed I was just starting to feel as if the water was working out all the kinks and providing the warmth back to my body that seemed to have been deprived from it on my recent trip. When all of a sudden the Hells Bells started blaring from the confines of my bedroom; accompanied by loud wailing. My eyes flew open, scrambling for purchase as I lost my footing. I fumbled with the faucet trying to turn off the water. Only to burn my self in the process. Ripping the towel of the hook at the back of the door; I ran from the bathroom.

Sitting on my bed with its paws stuffed into its ears was my new pet Fred. The hitch hiking gargoyle that I had picked up while I was in the Underworld. "What gives Fred?" "You don't like AC/DC?" I asked the fuzz ball as I turned off the stereo. I was answered with a moan and head shake. I couldn't do anything but laugh. So much for a relaxing shower to remove the cobwebs in my mind. I had picked up this hitch hiking cretin somewhere along the way during my stay in the Underworld. He was a gift from the Goddess of Lethe (forgetfulness) one of the many goddesses of the rivers of underworld. She felt I needed him. For what I am still not sure. Yet, here we are an unlikely pair. So far he had not been much trouble. Yet he is a curious little guy, so he was bound to get into trouble soon enough. If the Stereo situation was any indication. Looked like I would have to baby Gargoyle proof my house. Joy.

Well at least it would get my mind off everything else. Turning back to the stereo I found a cd and put it in, taking mind to make sure the volume was turned down. Bed of Roses by Hinder seeped out of the speakers. I crossed the room to go through my closet for something comfortable to wear. I had truly missed my closet full of vintage clothing. Grabbing a pair of holey jeans, and a t-shirt I wrapped the towel around my head and began to get dressed.

My shoulder bag was lying on the floor at the bottom of my closet where I had dropped it. The Scrolls the Queen had given me were glowing an odd color. Guess I wasn't going to get as much R&R as I thought. Something told me that there was something I needed to see within the odd crisp pages. Picking the roll of papers up I crossed the room to sit on the corner of my bed. Images were flashing before my eyes.

People I had never met before were randomly flipping through my minds eye. It was as if I was watching one of those old fashion black and white still life movies. Something big was taking place; and it was about to become a showdown here on earth. I could tell that much from what I was seeing. Hybrids, all of them were hybrids and something was hunting them. Something dark. The scroll tumbled from my finger tips. I sat on the bed gasping for air and blinking back tears. Children not even old enough to fight were being slaughtered. Ice shards were creeping down my spine. I had to do something. Yet what and how. I didn't know were the attacks were happening, if it was past, present, or future images I was viewing. Something told me I was getting ready to find out.

Flipping my phone open I called headquarters, Demonic and Kyle would be able to tell me if anything had gone down as of late. If not then they would have a head start in stopping this before it began.

It didn't take long before I heard Demonic's husky voice. "Supernatural Crimes" "Can I help you." Demonic sounds so professional I almost laughed. "Hey Demonic , Its Andras' I was wondering if you all had heard about anything going down with in the last say twenty four hours?" I asked. "No, nothing has gone down as far as I know." "Why do you know something I don't?" Demonic question me. He sounded as eager as dog with a bone. I think he was bored. Maybe I was the only one suffering jet lag from the recent adventures we had been on.

"I just got picked up the scrolls my aunt had given me they were glowing a rather odd color. Anyways as soon as they were in my hands, images started flashing through my mind." "I called you to check to see if it had happened yet; or if we still had time to stop it." I told him after a moments pause. "What did you see?" Demonic eagerly asked me. "Have you ever had visions before?" He asked "No, I have never had visions, but the unbinding spell could be the reason I'm having them now. Its part of my heritage after all." "I saw Hybrids like me, young ones, children, teens, and adults alike being slaughtered." "It was horrid." "I don't know if it was a past event or something yet to come." "I can tell you it was earthside, and close by." I told him.

You could hear a pen drop, it was so silent on the other end of the phone I thought I had lost the connect. "Whoa, this is serious." "Is there anyway to find out if it's a past event." "Cant you talk to the Crone, or your Aunt the Seer." Demonic Asked. "I started with you; it was so vivid that I wanted to make sure it hadn't happened." "I'll contact the Crone and see if she can tell me anything; in the meanwhile if Kyle and you aren't busy could you meet me over here? I want to go over the scrolls again, but if I have another vision I would like someone present." "Sure we could do that, just pushing papers here anyways. Would be nice to have something to do." Demonic

Replied.

I sat the phone on the nightstand, and buried my hands in my hair. Well, I guess the universe doesn't think I need a break. So be it, anything is better than sitting here feeling sorry for myself. Fred crawled into my lap and stared at me with his big red eyes. I placed my hand on his fussy head and scratched behind his ear. "Well buddy, you ready to go for a ride." "I have to talk to some people." I asked the fuzz ball as I got up with him in my arms. Fred just gargled and mumbled his reply; I took it as a yes.

 Grabbing my shoulder bag I placed Fred inside it. Swinging it over my shoulder, I grabbed my combat boots, keys and the scrolls as I headed for the door. Stopping in the kitchen, I sat down to lace up my boots. Left a quick note for Demonic or whom ever might stop by to let them know I would be back in a while. Grabbing a glass of Orange Juice, I slammed it down letting the cool liquid to slide down my throat. Taking a look around my apartment I made sure I was not forgetting anything and headed for the door.

Locking the door behind me, I started walking down the back alleyway. My motorcycle was still under its magical tarp; breathing a sigh I removed the thick canvas. My hand ran along the metal body of the bike, I closed my eyes just to take in the sensation. Wrapping my hand around the handlebar; I swung my leg over the bike and into the seat. Straddling the bike, I kicked it into gear. It came to life under me; vibrating the ground around us.

Sending shockwave after shockwave up my spine. This bike was the best therapy a girl could ask for. Patting the side of my shoulder bag. I cooed to Fred to make sure he was okay before we went roaring down the road. The cobble stone streets rippled and popped under the tires. The airs of the night was crisp and clean on my skin. I let my hair fly as I gunned the bike and headed for the outskirts of town.

A visit to the crone would hopefully provide all the answers I needed. If not then I was going to have to call Edam, and that was something I didn't want to do right now. I had zoned out so much just driving; I didn't realize that I was almost to the Crones Hut until I was less than a meter from the turn off. Coasting the bike to a stop I turned onto the gravel road and started to slowly make my way toward her home. It was not that long ago that I had met my brother in these very woods, nor was it that long ago that I found out how my mother had been turned to stone.

Now I was back here, with new images haunting my mind. More questions than answers once again. When was this going to end? When would I finally just have some peace of mind? I knew the answer but I really did not want to think about it. It was better to question the questions in my head, than it was to look at the hard truth of the matter. For now, I would just focus on what I came here for; the rest of it could wait another day.

I drove the bike through the thick canopy of trees, the red dirt road winded back toward the river. Song birds were filling the air with their song; it was peaceful out here. I enjoyed the way it felt like coming home, even though it was no where close to home. My brother was in theses woods somewhere; if he didn't show his self before I got to the Crone's house, then I would ask her where he lived. I wanted to visit with him before I left. Something told me I wouldn't have to worry about it for to much longer. He would find a way to present his self to me; I had a gut feeling on that. Fred was fussing up a storm when I finally got to the waters edge.

I pulled the bike into the same spot that the boys and I had been the last time we where here. Kicking the kickstand down, I killed the engine and dismounted the bike. "Hold on Fred." I told the fussy gargoyle as I patted the side of the shoulder bag. I guess the ride didn't set well with him. I opened the flap on the bag and peered inside. Red wild eyes stared back at me. The black tuff of fur on top of Fred's head stood on ends. I gathered the little creature up and placed him on the grassy patch in front of me.

He looked as if he was going to go crazy. I don't think he had ever smelt so many smells or see so much green grass in his whole life. He flipped and rolled threw the wildflowers that carpeted the forest floor. He was screeching with delight. I could not help by smile. I guess even gargoyles need some down time. I sat back on a stump of an old cotton wood tree and just watched him lose his self in the pure joy he was experiencing. This was what life was supposed to be like. I sighed as I looked up toward the sky, a red hawk circled over head. The peace I felt out here, soothed my soul.

Fred had finally released all his crazy energy and was cuddling up next to me. I ran my hand through his thick downy coat, and smiled. "Ok, Fred its time to go." "We can play again soon." I told him as I scooped him up and stuck him back into the shoulder bag. Tossing the strap of the bag back over my shoulder I stood. Turning to the right I headed down the path that led to the Crone's home. I needed answer to why I was having these visions, and if they were past or present. I knew she would be able to give me some answers; yet I just hoped that I could handle what was to come. Dark green foliage was littered along the forest floor, bright pink roses, and other wildflowers sprinkled here and there.

The landscape had not changed since my last visit. My soul still felt the comfort in thisuntouched place. Spites danced through the trees; sparkles of light streaked through the air. The moss covered hut that served as the Crone's home was tucked into the hillside, the mushroom rings still lined the ground around the small hut. No sounds came from the forest around me; it was as if everything was just on pause, waiting for someone to push a button and bring it all back to life.

The Crone like Scarlet can see the future and divine events, but only in the near present. She also is able to look into your heart and soul; so it is wise to speak only the truth in her presence. I stared at the front door of the cottage; my hand was posed to knock. Yet I hesitated, I looked over my shoulder back into the forest to see if anyone or anything was watching me. I found nothing just complete silence. "It's open." "I've been expecting you." Meriam's voice echoed around me.

The door swung inward, and I was able to see the light from the candle on the kitchen counter. I found Meriam in the same place as before, chopping herbs in the kitchen; the only difference was this time she was not an old woman with knobby hands. Instead she stood before me a middle aged woman full of life. Her long raven hair was braided down her back. "You knew I was coming?" I asked Meriam with a puzzled expression on my face, I had not seen a single soul in the forest except for the sprites. I didn't think they had time to tell her of my coming, yet I could be wrong. "I saw it." Meriam said as she tapped her forehead. Small smile creased her face.

"Sit, I'll get you some tea." "Oh and do tell me why you have a gargoyle in your purse." Meriam said as she turned back to the counter to grab a mug and the tea pot. "Er, He was, is a gift." "Long story short, I am kinda responsible for him now." I told her as I sat in the wooden chair by the door. "Oh I see, or is he responsible for you?" Meriam questioned with her eyebrow raised. Handing me the cup of tea she sat across from me waiting for me to talk.

I sipped my tea and pondered if Fred was my keeper or I was his. Shaking the thought from my mind, I looked up to see concern etched in the Crone's face. I had never seen a look of worry on her face before but something was troubling her. I knew it had to do with what I was about to ask. That alone was enough to have me on edge. Taking a deep breath I sat the cup on my knee, and began to tell her what had conspired since I had last saw her. "I have only been home a couple days, still haven't got the chill out of my bones." "I have been dragging my feet and not really interested in doing anything." "I know it will pass, but I want to do things on my terms." "I'm tired of feeling like a puppet." I went on and on. Pouring out my heart; Meriam just listened, she didn't try to speak or butt in.

It was as if she knew I just needed to let it all out. When I had finally told her everything I had felt or had been feeling; I told her about the visions. "I have never had a vision before; it was like watching an old movie reel and not being able to stop it." She just nodded her head. Still she didn't speak. When I had said all I was going to say she finally opened her mouth. What came out was not the most comforting thing but it was at least something.

The sigh escaped her as if it was hot air from an old balloon. I knew what was to come next was not going to be rose colored or painted with pretty bows. She would give me the straight blunt truth no matter how much it cut. It was the one thing I admired most about her. "Your vision hasn't happened yet; well at least it has not happened again." "I'll try to explain it better, just bare with me." "See the Hybrids were almost destroyed one time before. I'm sure you gathered that much from the scrolls your aunt gave you." Meriam said. I just nodded knowing there was more she still had to tell me.

Holding my breath I waited for her to continue. "There is a threat coming, its dark and unnatural; young and old alike are endanger." "Millions will be slaughtered if you are not able to find away to put an end to it." "You said you wanted things to be done when you were ready." "I am here to tell you that there are some things in life we are never ready for." "You had a destiny that is bigger than your wants, or desires." "Andras' you are special, and you need to embrace the changes that have happened and the ones still to come."

"Your brother, the other Hybrids, the worlds depend on you to make the right choice." "Some choices don't always seem right at the time dear one but they will in time." "I know I'm talking in riddles, that's because it scares me to be straight forth about the future." "When we meddle with events that have not happened we change the outcome and it is not always for the better." "I am not going to be able to give you much more to go on." "I will tell you that your brother will help you, Edam will help, and so will all those you have already touched." "When the time comes you will be in the front leading them into battle." "I have faith in you." Meriam stopped speaking; tears were rolling down her cheeks unchecked.

I could feel the crippling pain this was causing her heart. She wanted to tell me who I was fighting, why and even when but she was not able to. I understood but it was still difficult to swallow. I patted her hand, thanked her for what she was able to tell me. I stood to take leave from her beautiful, peaceful hut.

Meriam grabbed my hand, in my palm she placed a shining star attached to a chain. "Let this be your beacon." With that she closed my hand around the bright light of the star and embraced me in a hug as if it was the last time she would ever see me. I held on to her and shed a single tear. Nodding my head I gathered up Fred and walked out of her home. As soon as the door was closed, I closed my eyes and just stood still. I didn't know what I was going to face but I knew that if I didn't face it than millions would suffer. I could not have that hanging on my head. I didn't care if I never got a vacation. For now a "normal" life was not in the cards for me. A for once I was okay with it. If it meant that the pictures I had seen in my head never happened again then it was just okay.

Chapter Seventeen

When I opened my eyes, the Satyr that also happened to be my half brother; was leaning against the willow tree just outside the yard. His arms were crossed and he seem to be enjoying him self. "Taking in the sights?" I asked him. He shrugged his shoulders as if he really didn't care. I hoisted my shoulder bag higher and started walking toward him. I almost forgot that he was not completely human; the whole bottom half of his body was that of a red stag. He truly was one of the Gods creations.

Ranking right up there with Unicorns if I said so myself. "Have a lovely chat?" he questioned me. "You could say it was less than lovely, but yes." I replied. "I came here to see if she could help me with these crazy visions I seem to be having." "Seems like all I know now is that it's some sort of doomsday prophecy ability that I really don't care for." I told him. He chuckled under his breath as if I was amusing him with my theatrics. Hell maybe he was, how was I supposed to know? "So do you have a name?" "Or am I suppose to refer to you as bro." He raised his eyebrow at me as if I was pushing it with the whole bro comment. "Slater is my name." He told me.

"Well then Slater, I have to get back to town to contact a few people. I can't give you a ride, but I would like you to meet me at my apartment. I have some things I need to discuss with you." I told my brother. Nodding his head he turned to walk ahead of me down the path. I followed behind as if it was the natural thing to do. We walked in silence, I took in my surroundings it was truly peaceful here. Slater just walked through the dense tree line, until we reach my motorcycle. "So, I'll meet you at your house in an hour." He tells me as I mount the bike and get ready to leave. "Yes I'll be there." I tell him as I kick the old bike to life and take off down the dirt road. Red dust was kicking up in my wake leaving a trail behind me.

I was rattled to the core and didn't really care how fast I was going. I just needed to get back to my apartment so I could call the boys, and have this little group meeting. We would have to move fast if I was going to have any chance of stopping this mess before it began. I took a left back on to the main highway and gunned the engine. I had to get home fast. "Hold on Fred." Soon I was less than a mile from town, the street lights were starting to turn on. I slowed the bike down so I was not speeding; and kept my eyes on the road.

My mind was racing the crone may have not been able to tell me a lot of information; but what she had told me was enough to make me on edge. Images of the innocent young kids being slaughtered were lingering in my mind. Just knowing that this had already happened once before was enough to cause my skin to crawling. The cobble stone street was popping beneath my tires before I realized that I was almost home. I must have really spaced out. Shaking the cobwebs from my mind. I focused on getting to the back alley so I could make it to the safety of my apartment.

Turning off Main Street I inched my way to the alley that would lead me to the comfort of my little apartment. Killing the engine; I rolled the bike to the back corner of the cubby hole in the alley way, covering it with the magic tarp. Kicking the stand down I dismounted the bike. Turning to the door I breathed a sigh of relief; it wouldn't last long but it gave me comfort to just be home. Turning the key in the lock I laid my hip against the door and gave it a quick push. Everything looked just as it had before I left; which was great. I don't think I could handle any more at the moment. I had a head full of dread and it was only getting worse.

Closing the door behind me, I sat down in the kitchen chair; taking Fred out of my shoulder bag. I dropped to the floor; and picked up my cell phone. I had to get told of Demonic and Kyle. We were going to have to sit down and have a pow wow about what was happening. I was dreading calling Edam up but I knew I had to. I just didn't want to think about the big choices that were in front of me. I knew I would have to sooner or later. Dialing the number for the office I waited for one of the boys to answer, yet I was greeted with a voice mail. I left them a message and just hoped that they got it in time.

Ending the call, I scrolled through my contact

until I got to Edam's number; hitting send I wanted. The phone only rang one time before a husky voice greeted me. "Andras' are you okay?" The concern in Edam's voice was very apparent. I didn't know if it was do to my avoidance; or if he had knowledge of the events I was having visions about. Either way I needed him to come here so I could figure out how I was going to proceed with no real knowledge of where or whom was hurting these people. "If you're not busy; I need you to meet me at my apartment in forty five minutes." I told him. "Okay." Edam replied. It was dry to the bone; the disappointment was dripping of the word. I didn't reply I just hung up the phone. I couldn't worry about his ego. I had bigger things that were stacked up on my plate now. Getting up from the kitchen chair I made my way to my bedroom. I needed to get changed and ready for everyone to show up. I knew I was going to have to make room for Slater, I don't think he would be able to fit in my small kitchen without a tad bit of rearranging.

Stripping off the jeans and t-shirt that I had been wearing I stood in front of my wall length mirror. I was still adjusting to the new me; the silver tattoos were almost as beautiful as the transparent blue wings that were fluttering from my shoulder blades. I had a hard time remembering myself without them. Walking over to the closet I pulled out a black corset with silver and blue ribbons crisscrossing the mid-section, and a pair of black stretchy pants. Slipping into the pants, I stood and worked my way into the corset. Zipping up the side of it; I walked over to my bed and sat down. Grabbing my spiked knee high boots; I slipped them on. Slapping my knees I stood and made my way back into the kitchen. Grabbing my table I moved it to the far wall in the kitchen; sliding it firmly up against the wall. I folded up the chairs and placed them in the hall closet. There that should be enough room for Slater and the rest of the boys. I put a pot of water on the stove to boil, rummaging through my cabinets I took down the mason jar full of assorted teas. I figured it would be a nice treat.

Heading back through my bedroom; I walked into the bathroom and grabbed a pony tail. Bending over, I flipped my hair upside down and gathered it into a high ponytail. Standing up I looked in the mirror; the bright blue highlights really made my dark hair look good. Fred was snuggled up on my pillow fast asleep, soft snoring was coming from him making his black downy fur raise and fall. I didn't have to wait long and a knock sounded on my door. Rushing back into the kitchen I turned down the burner under the pot of water.

Opening the door; I was greeting with the whole gang waiting outside in the cold. Slater was standing the back behind Kyle. I couldn't help smile at the fact that he was actually here. I didn't think we would become best of friends I was happy to know that I had a brother that would help me when I needed it most. I stepped back and allowed all four boys to enter into the room. Slater got to the doorway and looked inside; I think he was judging if he was going to fit. Smiling at him I nodded and he entered slowly.

Once his hind end was threw the door way. I shut the door. Demonic had popped a squat on top of the kitchen table and everyone else was just standing around looking at my kitchen like they had never been their before. I think they were still remembering the last time they were here. Slater seemed to be really out of his element. "I'm making tea." "Does anyone want a cup?" Slater raised his eyebrow at me, which was his way of saying 'get on with it.' I took a deep breath, grabbing a mug from the cabinet and poured the hot water into.

Seeping the tea, I turned from the counter; all eyes were on me. This was the quietest I had ever seen the boys. It was if the whole world had stopped and they were waiting for me to push play again. "Demonic already knows a little of what is going on; but to fill the rest of you in I'm going to start at the beginning." "I was sitting here at home, digging through my closet for something to wear when I realized that the scrolls my aunt had given me were glowing a strange color." "I picked them up out of my bag; and saw a vision."

"It scared me the crap out of me. I never have had a vision before and what I saw was downright awful." "I saw vision of hybrids being slaughtered, young children and old alike." "It was as if I was watching an old movie that just kept repeating itself over and over." "I went to see the crone to see if she could tell me if it was a past event or something that was coming." "I was told this had already happened once before, but the events I saw were yet to come." "I don't know when, where, or why it's going on; but I am going to need each one you to help me." "We have to stop this." I told the guys. They all stared at me for a moment; no one tried to speak.

Edam was the first to break the silence. "Where are the scrolls now?" "They are in my closet where I dropped them." I replied. "I remember when this happened before and who had caused it." "The story should be in the scrolls themselves." Edam went on to say. "I too remember these events and the horrible effects they had caused for all of our kind." Slater said. "I will help you stop this any way possible." He told me. "Thank you Slater, I appreciate it." "Count us in also." Kyle and Demonic said together. Nodding my head I walked toward my bedroom; grabbing the scrolls, I braced myself for the visions that never came. I headed back into the kitchen wear all the guys were waiting on me. No one was talking; so either they were taking this as seriously as I was or they just uncomfortable being in the room together. Either way I was thankful for the peace and quiet. "Here are the scrolls; I don't know what help they will be." I said as I laid them on the table next to Edam.

He stared at me with his chocolate eyes full of hurt. I knew I was the cause of the pain I saw there but I just could not bring myself to care. I needed time he had to understand that. I could not just walk away from everything I had known for the last three years, or from the family I finally had to live on the Mount with him and the rest of the Gods. He had no right thinking I would jump aboard so readily. Edam's eyes darted to the papers I had laid on the counter and to Slater. Slater nodded.

A silent conversation was passing between these two and I again was left in the dark. Demonic and Kyle had picked up on it to and I don't think they were happy about being left out. Kyle's eyes glowed bright yellow, and Demonic was crackling with energy. Something was pissing them off and I had a feeling it had everything to do with Edam. "Mind telling the rest of us what is going on?" I said looking first to Edam and then at Slater. "Edam and I think we need to see the Seer. She has a lot to tell you." "He was asking me if I was okay going through a portal." Slater said to the whole room. Demonic, Kyle and I looked at each other. "Next time just say it out loud." "There have been enough secrets between all of us." "I for one am really tired of all of the unspoken words." I told Slater as I stared right through Edam. He knew I had directed that straight at him. He also knew that was one of the main reasons I had not spoke to him since coming back from the Underworld. He should have been honest with me from the beginning, yet he chose not to. I could forgive but I was not about to forget about it. Edam nodded and opened a portal; the bright blue bubble appeared in front of us.

"Demonic, Kyle, Slater, you three go first." I told the boys. Demonic jumped down from the table and skipped through the portals rip; Kyle followed him like a puppy being let off his leash. Slater was not as eager to walk through into the unknown. I don't think he had ever been to Otherworld; and if not he was in for a treat. Slowly he walked through the portal after giving him a few seconds I motioned for Edam to go through; I wanted to be last this time plus I still had to grab Fred.

Whistling, I called to the sleepy little gargoyle. He came bouncing out of the bedroom and straight into my arms. I gathered up the scrolls and walked through the rip into my once upon a time home.

Opening my eyes as I stepped through to my mother's homeland. I took a deep breath; the air was so much cleaner in this realm. The emerald green grass was as beautiful as ever. Slater looked as if he was in heaven. He stared at everything with a child like wonder. He looked over at me as if I had just gifted him with the most precious of gifts. I guess for a him it was. Being of the forest and of nature; to be in a place that was full of it was a dream come true to him. I smiled at my brother;

taking the lead I lead them down the cobble stone street though the hills of spun gold, and to the home of my dear aunt.

I knew that the Seer was waiting on us. I had come to realize that a surprise visit would never happen. Yet it felt good to be able to just know I was on my way to her home. This place seemed to be as untouched as it always had been. I smiled at the thought of having lived here, and the thought of coming back here for a short stay seemed like a beautiful idea. Hopefully when this was all over I could finally make a trip back that was not involved in business. Demonic and Kyle, I knew had never been here for the sheer shock on their faces. The sun was still shining high in the sky and it was not affecting Demonic in the least. He kept uncovering his had to look at his skin in the light. The sheer wonder at being able to feel the heat without it burning was wrote all across his expression.

Kyle looked as if he wanted to shift into his animal form and bound threw the fields. I chuckled to myself, and made a note to bring them back here under better conditions. We walked for a while in silence; until my aunt's cookie cutter house came into view. Clearing my throat to gain their attention I spoke. "We are almost there." Slater just nodded that he heard me, his eyes still full of wonder.

Edam had been quiet the whole time. I think he was trying to figure out a way to apologize to me. What ever was keeping him silent was a welcomed thing. I needed time to think. Walking down the purple cobblestone pathway leading to my aunt's doorway; posing to knock on Scarlet's door. It swung open before I even had a chance to; grabbing me in an embrace that screamed volumes of what she was feeling. She wept on my shoulder. Her silver hair was hanging loose down her back and she looked as if she had been up for days. Turning her heart shaped face up to me, tears brimming in her beautiful violet eyes. I could tell she had already seen more than I had. Shhing her as I pushed her back so I was able to speak. "Scarlet, I'm okay. Please stop crying." She shook her head as if she was waking from a bad dream and looked past me to the broad of guys standing behind us. "Oh, My you brought them." She said as she straightened herself from the stooped position she had been in.

Taking a step back into her home, she waved us in. Walking through the threshold I waited until the others where inside before I looked around. Scarlet had changed her décor again. Never failing to impress; she had done away with the picnic bench and the sheer curtains that had greeted me on my last visit. In its place were satin curtains of the bluest blue, and a high back chairs with the soft cushions that felt like spun silk. White and blue throw pillows littered the floor by the fireplace along with a blue and white checkered blanket. Next to it also was her rocking chair and the little dragon snuggled fast asleep on the seat. "Please make yourselves comfortable." Scarlet told us as she gathered the sleeping dragon up and sat in her usual spot.

Slater walked over to the blanket; folding his legs under him he moaned in pleasure as he rested on the mound of pillows. The rest of us took a seat in the various chairs she had provided. I let Fred out of the shoulder bag and placed him on the floor. He wobbled over to Slater and snuggled up at his side. Scarlet raised her eyebrows and stared at the red eyed creature. Her head snapped up as if she just realized it was I that had brought him. "Is he yours?" Scarlet asked me. "Yes, he was a gift from the goddess Lethe." I tell her. Scarlet's eyes went wide. It was as if there was more to it than just a gift; yet she didn't let on. "I guess you know why we are all here." I tell her. "Yes my dear niece, I have been seeing images of horrible things for the last two days." "I take it nothing has happened yet."

Shaking my head no I waited for her to go on. She petted the sleeping dragon in her lap and stared into the fire as if she was remembering what she had seen. "I never thought this would happen again." "I thought we took care of the problem, long ago." She spoke into the fire. "What problem Scarlet." I asked her. "I need to know what happened before, and why it's happening again." I tell my fragile aunt. She nodded her head as unchecked tears streamed down her heart shaped face. "It started when you were ten.

There was an uprising on Earth and millions

of Hybrids and their offspring were hunted down and killed. You have heard of the witch hunts, and the ones like it, that they had in various other parts of the country." "That was a cover up for what they were doing." "In the name of a nameless god they slaughtered innocent people for being different. That was all there was to it. Nothing else caused these deaths. It took the Gods, Fae and all other sub species pulling together to bring an end to it." The count of how many Hybrids was erased from the records to protect the remaining from harm." It's been an eon and now..." Scarlet paused in mid thought.

"An now we are getting ready to face it again." "Is that what you are telling us?" Demonic asked. Shaking her head she continued to stare into the fire. I don't know what she was remembering, but I could tell it was painful for her. "My own child was killed during the last attack; we can't allow this to happen again." She spoke to the fire. "Did you see where it was taking place, and who started it?" I asked my aunt. "I just saw images of millions being slaughtered; not who was doing it, or where it was happening."

Scarlet's head snapped up and she stared into my eyes. "You had a vision." She had a gleam of hope in her eye. It was as if that was a great thing. Maybe it was but it wasn't feeling so great at the moment. "Yes." I told her. Scarlet smiled. "I don't know who is starting this war, but I do know that we can end it if we work together." Slater tells Scarlet which causes her to smile ear to ear. "Right you are young one; right you are." Scarlet replied. "We can stop this; but we are going to need a lot more help. I have a little more to tell you all before we take leave from here." Scarlet told us.

"In the scrolls you will find the history of what happened before, and a map of words that will lead you to the keep of the records on the remaining hybrids." "We are going to have to start with the top of the list and work our way down. Each person on the list will have to be accounted for. "What and whom we are up against is still hidden from my sight, it's like it's behind a veil." "I can tell you that it is going to start Earthside and spread to the other realms if we don't stop it. Scarlet told us. It wasn't a lot to go on but at least it would give us a start. "Edam you need to go talk to the Council while I take everyone else to see Sable." I told him.

If we could get enough Gods and Fae on our side we could fight this thing. "Andras, Kyle and I have a few people we could get to work on this also." Demonic told me. "Good, if you can get a message to them now do it." I told him with a smile on my face. This was starting to feel hopeful. The feeling of dread was still sitting in the pit of my stomach but was starting to fill hope build on top of it.

We could do this; we could make sure no one ever suffered this fate. I would make sure of it. Edam didn't speak he just got up and opened a portal rip, stepped through it and into the Realm of the Gods. I knew we would hear back form him soon; I just hoped he was not the only God helping us. Scarlet had stopped staring into the fire and was finally coming back to life. Slater had not moved from his spot in front of the fireplace. He seems to be just waiting for us to give him a direction. I got a feeling that he was happy to just be a part of the group. Having a purpose that was more than just living.

"Andras; if you start to have another vision let me know." "I can help you through it." "They can be painful at first but with practice you can dull the pain down so you don't miss vital details. "We need to visit a few other people after we visit my sister." "You might not like where we have to go; but I promise it will be worth it." My beautiful Aunt told me.

"Okay then lets get started; we don't know when for sure this will happen." "I want to stop it before any blood is spilt." I told my little gang. "I could not agree more sister." Slater said as he stood and stretched. Fred ambled over to me, mumbling under his breath.

Scooping him up I stroked the top of his head. "Here he is hunger." Scarlet said as she handed me a piece of bitterroot. Fred's red eyes gleamed and expanded in size. He bounced up in down in my arms reaching his stubby little hands for the piece of bitterroot. I handed to the little gargoyle; snatching it from my grasp he munched happily on it. Raising my eyebrows I gave my aunt a questioning look. "Bitterroot and sage milk are what you need to feed him. He won't eat much of anything else right now." "He is still a baby." Nodding my head I mentally wrote down the food list, and made a note to look up other information on my new companion. "He is going to be a vital asset in the future Andras' be proud he chose you." Slater told me. I was so happy everyone knew what Fred was going to be for me, I just wanted to know why me.

"Okay if everyone is ready, we need to go address the Queen." I said as I walked toward the front door. No one made any objections; they just filed into follow. Scarlet, Kyle, Demonic, Slater, Fred and I together looked like a cartoon drawling as we stood there getting ready to set off to see the Queen of Air & Darkness. I guessed Sable was going to get the full run down since I had to inform her on what had conspired while I was in the Underworld, and now this. She was sure to be worried already; this was going to add a ton more stress to everyone. Yet we had to get to the bottom of this and stop it before it began. If we failed everything we all had worked for would be for nothing.

We left Scarlet's home looking like a convoy of misfits. Quite fitting since we were exactly that. Each one of us was something that most humans only dreamed about; they didn't think we were real anymore. Part of me preferred them continuing to think this way; the other part of me wished that no one had to hide who they truly were. Yet the strange, unknown, and powerful had always scared the crap of the common human. Trying to wrap their brains around the fact that they were not alone in this world; that creatures like us were alive at all was too much for them. Things really did go bump in the night, and that was enough to have them carrying torches and pitch forks again. That was the very thing we had to stop. Whatever was getting ready to be unleashed would yank the veil off the magical worlds and expose us in ways we didn't want to happen.

We walked along the purple flagstone road; the sprites were weaving in and out of the tall golden hay and skipping from tree to tree. Emerald green leaves hung from the branches of the willow's looking like soft silken ropes. Bright pink and yellow poppies were sprinkled along the ground. I forgot how vibrant Otherworld could be. Everything here was living and breathing; every blade of grass sighed as you walked across it. The sheer beauty of this place would take anyone's breath away. I had got so caught up in taking in my surroundings I hadn't even realized that Scarlet was talking to me. "Andras' are you listening? I blinked my eyes several times to clear my thoughts. Scarlet wore a frown and a tightlipped smile. Whatever she was saying to me must have been important. She truly looked worried about me. "I'm sorry; I got caught up in old memories." I told my sweet aunt. Smiling she nodded her head.

"After we speak to Sable and Luke; we are going to have quite a journey ahead of us. I just want you to be prepared." "Your journey to the Underworld only lead you to two cities with its walls." "Were we are going to venture are worst by far than the home of Hel could ever be." Scarlet told me. "I get it; not a picnic in the park kind a place." I responded. I already knew this was going to be one of the most frightening events I would have to face. I was prepared for almost anything; after seeing the visions of the mangled remains of hundreds of innocents. I knew that I would have to face terrors of my worst nightmares.

We walked on through the emerald green grass, the castle was in the distance, gleaming like a silver coin. The crystal columns that lead to the entrance of the court of Air & Darkness looked like a welcoming beacon as the sunlight flashed against them. A sigh escaped my lips; soon I would be in my aunt and uncles embrace, in the same room as my mother. Even if I could not hug her, or talk to her; just the thought of her being there was enough to add comfort. I still had to break the curse that Hermes had placed on her; so she no longer stood lifeless in the center of the room. Collecting dust and unable to move; a living statue was what he had resorted my mother to be. He robbed me of a childhood that every child wishes they could have. A loving mother and father to tuck them in. The children from my vision had such parents and I was going to make sure it stayed that way.

There was no way I was going to allow these monsters to take that from them. Drifting away from my thoughts; I focused on the castle steps before us. The checkerboard pattern of the throne room was just within view. Time stood still within these walls just as it always had. My lovely aunt Sable was waiting with open arms at the top of the stares. Her eyes brimming with unshed tears. Luke was by her side; arm around her dainty waist as it always had been. He would protect her with his life. I longed for a love as deep as theirs. What a beautiful gift to have witnessed such a powerful feeling in the mist of what I was going to be facing.

Embracing my family in a hug; and introducing them to my brother and two friends, we made our way inside the castle. Scarlet and Sable held hands like the must have when they were kids. The joy on their faces was truly beautiful. I was happy I was here with my family; that I had people to rely on, when darkness came a calling. They were my rock; when the world outside threatened to tear me to pieces. I felt truly blessed in that moment.

Scarlet told Sable and Luke why we had all

came; she told them of my visions. The look on Sable's face was grave to say the least. Luke squeezed her had as if it was the lifeline that kept him here. No one wanted to relive the nightmare of what had already happened; no one wanted it to happen again. They were all on board to help in whatever way was needed. I would not be facing these monsters alone. We would stop the crazy madness from happening. Nothing was going to keep us from the task we had. I lingered for a moment in the chamber of the inner throne room; after everyone else had excused their selves. I walked around the statue that was my mother, staring at the details of her wings, memorizing the curves of her face. The way her hair laid in layers down her back. I closed my eyes to seal the imagine in my mind; whispering to her that I would find away to fix all of this. I departed the room to join the others. We had a long road ahead of us and Scarlet had already told me I would not like where we were heading. We said our goodbyes to Sable and Luke; promising to update them as soon as we were able. Setting out on the road; Scarlet filled us in on where we were going next. She was right when she said I wouldn't like it. Yet, I had no choice I had to go. Doom and darkness loomed over us like a thick blanket. I felt as if the air around me was being slowly crushed from my lungs. The world spun and I felt as if I would empty the contents of my stomach at any moment.

"There are fae folk here that can help us; some of them really are not fae, but they will help none the less." Scarlet told us. "We are going to visit one of the many seas that are now apart of Otherworld in search of a couple different beings.

The first are the Undine; sea fairies that they look human but they lack souls. The are outside human law; which is why they now live here. One of their many gifts is to be able to call upon gods and goddess to help them in a crisis. We are going to see if they will help us. Many of them mingled with humans before the worlds ripped apart. Children were born to them; and those very children may be in harms way also." "While we are there we are going to call upon the Siren's they are the for bringers of the harpies which may help us since your mother and their queen were friends." Scarlet tells me. "We will then go to see Circe daughter and her consort Morpheus the god of dreams."

"Hopefully they can unlock the visions you have been having and add to them." "I have a feeling they will lead us in the direction we need to go; to put a stop to this all." Scarlet finished saying. "What happens if this turns out to be for nothing?" Slater asked. He seemed to be wondering why we needed more help.

I think being a demigod he thought we should be tough enough to stop the event from happening on our own. We probably could; but help from other sources was always welcomed. "If this fails we will go see the fates, they may not be able tell us what is happening; but they will tell us why." I told my brother.

Nodding his head he seemed satisfied with the answer I given him. Domenic and Kyle had been hard at work calling up contacts with in the sub community that may have heard something. So far nothing had been heard; but now they all knew to be on the look out. Hybrids didn't just consist of children born of fae and gods, but all species that had mingled together and created life. All of us were a form of hybrid; a mixture of two races or more. What was happening affected everyone; whether they knew it or not. Scarlet opened a small portal; it flashed a vibrant green. I arched my eyebrow at her in question; she had said we were traveling to a sea here in Otherworld so why did we need a portal? "Faster." Was the only response Scarlet gave me before she hopping threw the flimsy green bubble. The boys and I followed suit; every fiber of my being was on high alert, I could feel the magic zinging in the air. This was not a part of Otherworld I had ever traveled too. It was so different from the Court of Air & Darkness. Gray rocks emerged from the inky ocean as white foamed waves crashed into them over and over again.

The sound was deafening; I covered my ears as I looked around. Black sand lined the coast line, leaving the impression of an ink well that had been spilt. Thatch huts were built between the tree line; woman wearing togas were throwing branches into a fire circle. It was as if we had walked into a different time. I assumed the woman were the sea Fairies that Scarlet had spoke of.

They looked completely human, no wings, no glow, or tipped ears. Just beautiful woman with long flowing fair hair. Nothing about their appearance gave away that they were anything other than normal. Yet, their eyes were void as if they held no light at all. Soul less is what Scarlet had said, and you could tell in their eyes she was telling the truth. Smiles light their faces as they saw Scarlet walking their way. I followed behind my aunt taking in everything around us.

Slater by my side, and the boys walking slowly behind him. Domenic and Kyle had a look of pure lust and wonder etched into their faces. I think the shock of this place was still effecting them big time. One of Undine walked up to Slater and circled him as if they were inspecting live stock. Slater shivered under her gaze; the hair on the back of my neck stood on ends. I did not like the feeling at all. The woman's hand ran through the red fur on Slater's flank making him step sideways to avoid her touch. I was about to open my mouth to speak when I heard a rumble and snort. Turning to look at my brother I realized what was happening. He was not uncomfortable about being touched by these creatures in the way I had thought. He enjoyed it; lust was seeping off him in waves. He was trying to clear his head. Seems like these Undines had more going for them that their ability to call gods and goddess. The woman walked away from Slater; heading back in the direction she had came from, the void expression still on her face.

Scarlet was speaking to the woman in charge. She had blonde hair that flowed down her back like honey; her eyes were sea green and yet they held no warmth, or light. Her skin was sun touched; her feet where bare yet she looked comfortable walking around half naked without shoes. Smiling to us she motioned for us to follow her. Walking to the rest of the woman near the fire circle; I could see they all looked the same. The only difference was their eye color; other than that they looked like mirror images of each other. That was until they opened their mouths to speak; the blonde woman that Scarlet had been speaking to started telling her sisters what was about to take place.

She told them of the coming war it would cause; how all of our children were in danger. The undine sang out in protest; the sound was mournful like a dying bird. A woman with bright blue eyes the color of robin eggs started speaking. "How can this be; great measures were taken to prevent the hybrids and offspring from coming to harms way again."

Her voice was like silken foam of an ocean tide slowly slapping the shoreline. "Celestine; the worlds as we knew them are no more, and we will do what it takes to make sure it never happens again." The woman that led these Undine said.

Scarlet turned from the woman and looked at me. "Andras' I would like to introduce you to Shine the leader of the Undine." The seer told me. I smiled at the woman in front of me; I truly didn't know what else to do. "So what do we do now, Scarlet?" I questioned. "We are going to a cave not to far from here to talk to Morpheus the god of dreams; while shine and her girls call upon some help." Scarlet informed me. Nodding my head; I waited for her to take the lead. I didn't like not feeling of having control over the events; but at the present I didn't have a choice but to follow her directions.

Chapter Eighteen

Until we knew who was behind this plot; I had to go along with it all. The moment I knew who was responsible all bets were off. I was tired of people; whether they are Gods, Demons, Human, or other messing with lives of innocents. We walked along the coast line of these displaced sea; waves of white foam crashed over and over again into the over hanging rocks from the cliff. The inky black sand grinded softly under our feet. Salt water hung in the air, spraying us all with a fine mist.

The wind was getting stronger the further away from the Undines we got. Green vegetation was stating to show up in small patches; growing in between the rocks. Demonic, Kyle, and Slater had been quiet since we had left the campfire and stated walking toward the home of Morpheus. I knew that this place was different from what they were use to; I just didn't realize the effect it would have one them. "You guys okay?" I questioned the three boys. "Yeah I'm alright Andras'." Demonic told me. "It's just different here, I can feel the energy, and magic in the air. Like a sirens call it talks to me." "It is taking some effort to not become entranced by it." He finished saying. "What about you Kyle?" "Are you okay?" I asked my werewolf friend. "Ya, just want to run." "Have never felt the urge to do that so strongly unless it was a full moon." Kyle said. His eyes were glowing gold. It was like his animal side was fighting his human half. I made a mental note to keep an eye on him. "Slater?" I questioned my brother. "I have never felt better." "Just enjoying the sights; when this is all over I would love to come back and visit." Slater said with a far off dreamy look in his eye. "Andras' the pull of magic speaks deeply to us here. You and I are not affected by it; because we are from here." Nodding my head I listened to my aunt.

Looking up the winding path ahead of us. I saw we were coming to the edge of the tree line. Palm, date, and a few tropical bushes lined the coastline ahead. There was a hollow clearing between a group of trees. We were heading right for it; when a vision slapped me out of no where. I grabbed Scarlet's arm as I folded in half. My mind was racing; millions of images were flashing like a disco ball. I squeezed my eyes shut and tried to breathe through my nose. I had to calm myself down; or I would not be able to retain anything I was seeing.

"What do you see, Andras'?" Scarlet questioned me from my prone position on the ground. "Bodies, Dead bodies, steel table, white sheets, mans hand, ink drawings on skin, it's all going to fast." "Oh, I feel like I'm going to be sick." I told my aunt. "Breathe girl, you can do this; I'm going to step in and help." "Trust me." Nodding my head up and down; I kept my eyes closed and tried to breathe.

There was a buzzing in the back of my head; like a static from an old television. I heard a soft pop and then everything went black. I woke up on the ground with everyone around me. "What happened?" I asked from my foggy state on the cold wet sand. "I stepped in like I said I would." Scarlet told me as she sat on the ground near me rubbing her temples. "I just didn't realize the effect it would have on you."

The seer told. "You blacked out; I was left inside your head reviewing the images like a movie reel on fast forward."

"You my dear have a great gift, but it needs to be trained. I'm sorry if I caused you any pain; but we need to get to Morpheus as soon as possible." "Can you stand?" Slater asked me. Nodding my head, I allowed my brother to help me up; while Kyle and Demonic helped Scarlet. We stared walking toward the black space between the trees. I held on to Slater as we neared the clearing; my mind was still fuzzy. Everything around me was covered in a haze as if I was walking through a dream. I still didn't feel awake; shaking my head to clear the bussing sound, I looked around to see where we were headed. The bright neon green leaves of the bushes were popping out to great us; like giant green hands. Passion flowers with bright yellow and red petals poked through the bushes like tiny heads of creatures I had never seen. The sharp contrast to the pitch black of the space between them; made their colors more vibrant than they truly were. I walked slowly behind Scarlet; still unsure about where we were headed; or who would be meeting us. I only knew that this was the first time I wished I was not in Otherworld; a place that had been my home since birth. I wanted to escape all of this, the dreams, visions, nightmares, to become normal. Yet, what was truly normal about anything; or anyone.

We were all a mix of something even the non magical humans. Even the ones that were now hunting the children of the hybrids. We were all connected; this is why it touched so many that we would be facing another tragedy like the past; if we didn't stop who ever was responsible. I just hoped that we were able to do so before the first drop-off blood was shed.

Mist hung from the carpeted ground; rolling around us like puffs of smoke. Other than the bright greenery leading us into the clearing; I could see nothing. It was a pitch black space that Scarlet seem to be leading us to. "Are we close to where we are going?" I asked the Seer as I tried to catch my breath. The hairs on the back of my neck were rising and I truly didn't like the feeling I was getting. "Close; but we are no where near there yet." Scarlet said a crease forming on her brow. "What do you mean; no where there yet?" I asked my aunt with a puzzled expression. I knew I was not going to like the answer as soon as I seen her violet eyes flash nervously at the others with us.

"We have to go into the Underworld to visit Morpheus." She said as she cast a look of pity at me. "What!" I exclaimed. I had not thought I would be seeing that place again for some time; and now that I had no choice, I was angry to say the least. Hades had made it clear how he felt about me; and I did not want to deal with him, Hel, or anyone else at the moment. I just wanted to be home in my bed. Selfish feelings were bubbling over inside of me; like a pot of tea that had been left on the burner to long. I felt like I would boil right over. "Andras' I am sorry; I should have told you before we left the Undines." Scarlet said while ringing her hands. "Yes, that would have been nice; but there is no changing it now is there?" I said in a snarky tone; not really meaning to be harsh toward her, just not liking the situation at all. "On a bright note; we will be with you this time." Kyle told me as he squeezed my hand. He was right at least this time I would not be alone and trapped. Hermes was facing punishment; and I was here for a totally different reason. It would be different; and that was enough to have me smiling a little.

We walked through the inky black spot between the trees; as the mist crawled across the ground. A cave appeared just feet in front of us; Gray rocks jetted out from the pitch black space; looming over us like a giant mouth. We inched closer to the opening as if it was actually going to reach out and take a bite. I was squeezing Kyle's hand so hard, I was sure I was grinding his bones together. If I was hurting him; he was not complaining, just staring straight ahead at the entrance of the cave. "We are going in there?" Demonic asked taking a visible gulp of air. I had never seen a vampire scared of the dark before until now. "Yes we are going in there; you all need to follow behind me closely." "We are walking straight into the Underworld, there is no portal to open or close." "Things inside the Underworld are never as they seem." "Your mind and eyes will play tricks on you; don't leave the group at all." "Do you understand?" Scarlet asked the group. The boys just nodded their heads as if they had lost the ability to speak.

I didn't have to say a word; I knew what the Underworld was like; well at least two of the cities inside it. That was enough to keep me safe by the side of Scarlet. Emerging into the dark gab that was the cavern entrance; I held my breath and waited for something to happen. I could feel it deep in my gut; this was going to be a nerve rattling event to say the least.

The mist clung to out legs, coiling around us like vapor serpents before disappearing into puffs of smoke. Leaving trails of residue in its wake. Like an either slim it coated us. Cloaking us with the death of Underworld itself. The ground beneath us turned from inky black sand to solid ivory bone. The contrast of the white polished bones against the darkness of the cavern was enough to have us shielding our eyes.

"Don't take another step." A voice called out

to us. Scarlet put up her hand and motioned for us to stop were we where. Waiting in silent I looked around trying to find where the voice had stirred from. Something was here with us; I just didn't know what or whom it was at the moment. Taking a deep breath I stared out into the darkness ahead of us. That's when I seen it.

A little goat stood next to a pile of bones; looking so out of place I almost laughed. "WTF" I thought to myself as I grabbed Scarlet's arm and pointed toward the hoofed creature. "Ah so you have seen me." "Pity." The animal spoke again. I raised my eyebrow and shook my head; thinking that maybe my mind was playing tricks on me again. "You are wondering if I am real or not." The goat said again from its perch on the pile of bones.

"I'm as real as you." It said with a baa. Kyle and Demonic were snickering as it was all too funny. I on the other hand was starting to get crept out. Slater started talking as if this was a common sight for him. Maybe it was since he was part animal himself. "Phooka; I believe." Slater stated as if it was common knowledge.

"Correct two points for the big guy." The gray goat said with a chuckle.

"What the heck is a Phooka?" I asked. "Phooka, are a type of fae, a goblin of sorts, and a shape shifter. Known to be violent and vicious pranksters." Scarlet told me with a frozen expression still on her face. I got the feeling she didn't like these creatures at all; but was fearful of them to. "Two points for the little know it all." The goat said again. His tone was starting to piss me off; I had been pushed around long enough, and after my first visit to this god awful realm I was not in the mood to deal with it again. "So Goat; you got a name?" I asked the cocky creature with my hand on my hip. If he didn't stop messing with us soon; I was going to make him regret it. "Booker." 'Is what I'm called." The Phooka told me.

"Well Bookie, I have had a long day; and I'm not in the mood for games. If you want to say something; say it, so we can be on our way."

"Oh, touché' lil one. I hit a nerve I see." Booker told me from his throne of bones. "I just wanted to have a wee bit of fun; but since you're in a hurry. Please, by all means take your leave." With a sigh he turned into a little gray headed man. The three foot tall goblin with red eyes stared at me as if I was dinner. I rolled my eyes and sighed. Okay so I pissed him off a little; well it deserved him right. I mean had I not been put through enough all ready. I stared at the little man for a moment long before I turned my attention to Scarlet; I was not going to be held up any longer. This trip had already been to long for my own liking. "Lead the way; we need to get this over with." I told the seer in a point blank manner. She blinked her eyes a few times; as if she was coming back to herself, before she finally looked at me. "Yes, we do." She said in a far off voice. I raised my eyebrow and looked at the boys; something was off here, and I wanted to know if they saw it to.

They were looking passed Booker the Phooka at something behind him. Booker had a smile on his face like he already knew what was going on. I on the other hand was completely in the dark. Then I saw it; a two headed dog with a serpent tail loomed over the Phooka, a steady stream of saliva was hanging from its lower jaws.

The Phooka stood up tall and walked forward just as the giant dog took a step. I didn't know if it was a trick or if the dog was real. I had already met the Hellhounds; and they were cuddly little puppies compared to what was staring at me now. "Whoa, do you see that?" Kyle said his eyes glowing bright gold in the dark of the cave. "Yeah, man I see it." Demonic stated as his face took on an ash hue. Slater was standing there shaking like he was about to be prey; Scarlet just blinked as if she was frozen in place. I had to do something; anything to get us out of there, so we could save the innocents.

"What gives Booker, are you so lonely that you have to scare people just to have company?" I asked the little shape shifter. His red eyes gleamed, mischief smirk placed upon his lips. Curling his knobby fingers through the two head beasts' fur he looked at all of us. What I had just said seem to have grabbed my groups attention enough to snap them back to reality. The Phooka stopped in his tracks; the smirk fell from his lips. He didn't like the fact we were not scared by his pet. His forehead creased as if he was puzzled by the very thought. "Aren't you an odd bunch?" "I thought for sure you would be begging me to make Kerberos here leave you alone." "What gives?" "You must be here for an important reason; or this would have been enough to have you at my mercy." Booker stated.

"We are here for an important reason, and we are not mere mortals if you haven't noticed; so I don't understand how you thought your trickery was going to have us doing circus tricks." I told the red eyed goblin. He smiled and stated to laugh; "I do admire your spirit." He told me. "Who are you here to see; maybe I can lead you in the right direction." "We know the direction we need to travel; thank you kindly for your offer though." "We are here to see Morpheus; so if you would pardon us, we will be on our way." Scarlet told him.

Bookers eyebrows rose into his hair line at the mention of Morpheus name. Fright registered in his face. "By all means and safe travels to you and yours." Booker told Scarlet as he bowed at the waist. It was my turn to smirk; the big bad goblin and his monster dog were scared of Morpheus; he must be something else for the likes of these to be quaking at the knees. With that he vaporized as if he had never been in the little chamber to begin with. I looked around at my little group to make sure they were all still with me. After all we were at the entrance to the Underworld; and after my last trip down here I wanted to be sure.

The boys and Scarlet looked back at me with small smiles on there faces; I think they were glad I had already encountered things worse than this on my last journey. I was starting to see the silver lining and that had me smiling a little myself. "After you Seer." I told my aunt as I grabbed her hand in a reassuring squeeze. "Quite right." Scarlet said, smiling as she led the way.

This journey was going to be quit different from my last one; but not one moment of it would be dull. That I could bank on; and I was glad that I had them with me.

We walked past the throne of bones; that Booker had first appeared on, and down a tunnel. Oil lamps hung from the cavern walls; much like the ones I had seen on my last visit to the Underworld. Though this side of it did not hold a candle to what the domain of Hel had looked like. Here it was just gray rock and white ivory floors; well at least for now.

"Scarlet, can you tell us a bit about Morpheus?" "Other than being the God of Dreams we do not know what to expect." I told my aunt. "Yes, I can." "He is the Greek god of dreams, the oldest of triplets, and the attendant of Hypnos." "It is said that he is the son of Nyx (Night) and Erbus (Darkness), It's really not known if that is true. I don't think anyone has ever asked him. He is a version of the Human Sandman. His main purpose is to guide you through dreamland. He lives with two woman, one named Poppy, and the other is Circe's daughter Cassiphone his consort."

"He can appear in many forms; but here in his home he will appear in his true form, that of handsome man with dark ebony wings." "He is not prone to anger like the other deities;

and will help us for the sole reason that its part of whom he is." "Visions, Dreams, Prophecies are his essence." "We are almost there." Scarlet finishes telling us; and I look up ahead to see a field of red poppy flowers growing across the floor of the cave. It was odd to see flowers growing without a source of light; yet this was the Underworld, and strange things were known to happen here. "Wow." Was the only word I could utter as I looked around at the blood red flowers. A wilted elm tree stood to the left side of the field of flowers with phantom winged shapes hanging from its branches. Just beyond the tree was a small hut. The sheer beautiful of it all was hard to believe; if I didn't know we were in Underworld I would never have believed my eyes.

Yet, here we where walking through a field of flowers inside a cave, to a hut that looked like it had been painted by an artist. I was starting to realize why Morpheus was called the God of Dreams; he seemed to have created a dream like place for his home to rest. We walked past the Elm tree on toward the small hut; as if everything was normal, and these were things that happened everyday. I sucked in my breath; I knew I was going to have to face my visions, nightmares and all when I finally met Morpheus and that was enough to have me chasing butterflies out of my stomach.

We walked up to the hut; its shingles were a golden brown and as Scarlet knocked upon the door; little puffs of sand sprinkled down on us. I rubbed my eyes to get the grains out; a yawn escaped my lips, just as the door swung inward revealing a beautiful woman with honey colored hair down her back. She was wrapped in a sheer golden gown that seemed to move all on it's on. Her face was ivory white; but my her eyes were jet black solid pieces of obsidian. I stood there gazing at her as if I was dreaming; she looked so out of place with in the vibrant dream world that Morpheus had created. "Come in we have been expecting you." the woman told us. Scarlet looked at me and smiled right before she walked through the door.

The boys and I followed her in to the home of the God of dreams. Having no clue what awaited me; yet knowing that I had to go through this in order to help all of us, I held my breath and waited for the other shoe to drop. The inside of the hut was a drastic difference from the outside scheme of things; white pillar stood in the center of the room. Golden furs were thrown across the ivory bone floors. Several small black daises were scattered across the room we were standing in. Black and gold satin fabric draped from the ceiling pooling in piles along the floor. Bowls of fruit were standing next to each dais; and big leafy fans stood behind each. It was like walking into a romantic novel. Every aspect of the room looked as if it was pulled right out of someone's lust filled dreams.

The woman that had greeted us at the door; walked over to one of the dais and lay across it. A huge brass gong sounded from somewhere deep with in the hut. A sigh rippled through her as if it was the answer she had been waiting on. "He will be here soon; please make yourselves comfortable." I looked at the boys and my aunt to see them all rubbing sleep from their eyes.

It was as if walking through the entrance had

caused us all to feel the need to rest. Scarlet, Kyle, Demonic, and Slater all walked toward a dais; sleepy expressions across their faces as they went. I on the other hand had no intentions on sleeping; and knew if I touched the dais in front of me that is exactly what I would end up doing. I stood where I was and waited for the God of Dreams to enter. I didn't have to wait long before a raven haired beauty walked through the arch way at the back end of the room followed by the most beautiful man I had ever laid eyes on. His chestnut hair hung in curls around his ears; dark forbidden eyes stared across the distance. Black wings hung from his shoulders and seemed to sigh as he walked toward me. Rippled muscles were etched into his firm chest. He skin was golden as if he had been dipped in gold dust.

Shivering, I let my eyes return to his face to see a smirk lying across his lips. He was enjoying the way I was accessing him. I raised my eyebrow in response; which earned me a larger grin. Morpheus walked behind his consort with a look of primal lust oozing from his body. He came to stand before me as if he knew exactly who I was. I looked toward the others in my group only to see them all fast asleep on their pillowed beds.

Rolling my eyes, I looked at the God before me and waited for someone to speak. I was having trouble at the moment even forming a thought let alone a word. As if sensing that I was not going to open my mouth; the raven haired woman took her seat next to the woman who had greeted us. Morpheus stood still as a statue in front of me. Just watching me with his black eyes; as if he was trying to peer into my mind. For all I know he was trying to do just that. "You have come a long way to seek me out." "Do you even know what you are here for?" He asked me. I blinked my eyes; trying to keep the puzzled expression off my face as I fought to form a word. Either the sand that had sprinkled down on us had caused this or just the sheer beauty of the man before had me tongue tied.

Whatever the case was; I had to swallow and lick my lips to return the moisture to them so I could even bring myself to try. "The seer said you could help me; I am having visions of things so terrible that if they come to be it will be the end of us all." I told the man before me. "I am not able to make sense of them; the images come to fast, and are a mangled mess. I know the answers to who is behind the terrible acts are locked in the visions but I can't access the information on my own." "Those are the reasons I am here." I told him as I lowered my gaze to look at the spot just past his shoulder. He continued to stare at me as if I had not even spoken.

Four minutes passed before he moved at all. I was oddly relaxed in his presence which was weird; after all, everyone else I had met in the Underworld gave me the willies. He reaches his hand out and touched my forehead with his index finger; my eyes fluttered shut. Everything spun into oblivion; darkness took up residence in my mind just as Morpheus stepped into the darkness with me. The only source of light was coming from him. "Your answers wait." He said as he grabbed my hand to lead me down the dark tunnel in my mind's eye.

Chapter Nineteen

I stood there staring at him in the dark tunnel he had created within my mind; letting him lead me to where ever it was we were going. I saw ancient images of what looked like Greece; ruins of statues and old arena's. Green rolling hills and mortar homes built into sheer cliffs over looking the ocean. Mountains in the distance that seem to rise up to meet the heavens. It was rather beautiful and odd at the same time to see such sights when I had never traveled there.

On we walked through the tunnel; the scene stayed the same yet the time period did not. I watched the rise of nations; the fall of one or two different religions, men taking up arms against one another. Men taking up arms against the gods themselves. I watched the fae and other sub creatures standing along the side of man. I watched as the Gods of Old retreated to their Mount Olympia.

It was tragic to see all these things within a blink of an eye. I watched the Titans being cast out of the Heavens. I watched as they were imprisoned. Yet; the most disturbing image was that of Zeus imprisoning a Huge Monster beneath another mountain. I tapped Morpheus' arm and pointed. I didn't know if speaking would break the spell I was under. I didn't want to chance missing something by opening my mouth.

I waited for him to say something as I continued to watch the images flash slowly across the screen. "That was Typhon; he is the son of Gaia and Tartarus." I looked at him puzzled; I had been to Tartarus, it was a place how could it father a child. Gaia was name for mother earth, so again how was that even possible? "Our creation of worlds, places, and people, all come from something." Morpheus stated as he watched Zeus defeat Typhon.

"Black matter, a single spark, it all started somewhere." "But we are not here to ponder the meaning of life; pay attention Andras' the answers you seek are here." "I don't know if you will like what you see." "I am void of the emotions that effect most beings. I am just here to guide." With that he stopped speaking and just stared at the images before us. I watched as eons when by; this forgotten creature stayed buried in his prison. Then it happened, I watched as the one being I hated

more than anything at the moment released this monster from it cage.

Hermes stood in front of the Mountain; a seal in his hand that seemed to glow as he held it in front of himself. The small crack in the mountains side gave way like a door. Rolling back the entrance to the prison Zeus had created; and allowing this beast to emerge. I had never seen a being such as this.

He was a blend of so many things. He reach toward the stars, His upper half was human; his lower half was that of a gigantic viper that's coils seem to hiss as he moved. His whole body was covered in feathers; He had gray wings that stretched out like seven feet birds on either side of his shoulders. His eyes flashed with fire; his hair was snow white hanging down the middle of his back. His hands were the size of a small island each with deadly pointed nails that looked like spears. I stood there gapping at the image I was seeing.

I could not believe that my own father would release a monster such as this; just to take control over the four worlds. I shook with anger, as my stomach coiled against my rib cage; promising that it would release the contents of my last meal. This was what was hunting the children. This was what was endangering the Hybrids, and all those that had cross bred. How was I going to stop something like that? When it was clear that Zeus had trouble trapping him in the first place. I had to tell the others what I now knew. We had to warn the Gods, the Fae, Everyone. We were in dire trouble. I was shaking so bad that I was starting to have trouble breathing; when all of a sudden Morpheus snapped his fingers, and we were standing back in his room full of dais and satin sheets. Scarlet, Demonic, Kyle and Slater were just coming to; as we entered the room. I was blinking my eyes trying to get the images out of my mind. How could he do such a thing? It was unspeakable the lengths he was willing to go to take control of everything including me.

Scarlet could see I was visible sicken when she fully recovered from the sandman induced sleep she had been in. "Honey what is wrong." The seer questioned me with concern clearly on her face. She didn't know that I already had received the help we had come for. She didn't know the deeds my father had done. I couldn't speak, I was shaking so bad that all I could do was stubble toward one of the black satin dais and sit down. Morpheus stood still as a statue as the two women whom were his companions came on either side of me and started waving fans. It was as if they had been through this a thousand times. For all I knew, they probably had. I took a drink of the honey liquor that they had offered me; and let the warmth of it coat the inside of my throat. After about four drinks I had enough of my voice under control I felt I could speak.

"Scarlet, We have to get out of here." "We have to go to Mount Olympia." "It's bad... So bad..." I trailed off as I looked up and into Morpheus eyes begging him with my mind to tell them what I could not bring myself to say.

"She has seen what and whom she is up against and why." "I am afraid I really can't tell you more than that as it would disrupt the hands of fate." Morpheus spoke softly to my lovely aunt. The seer nodded her head as if she understood what he was saying; even though he had not really said anything at all.

The raven haired woman rose from her spot on the dais and moved to Morpheus side. They didn't speak; just stared at each other for a moment until the woman finally inclined her head and moved over to casting circle near the back of the room.

"She is going to open you a portal to Mount Olympia. It will be faster for you to travel through one of her's than it will for you to create one yourselves." Morpheus stated as he continued to stare at us. "Thank you for all you have done." I told the god of dreams. I meant it to; I may not have liked what I saw, but I appreciated the help and what he had showed me. It was a blessing to not have the searing pain and bright flashing images flashing so quickly through my mind. I think I would be able to walk down the vision tunnel alone the next time I needed it.

The Raven haired woman had formed a large portal of golden film. It shimmered against the floor as images of the Heavens came into view on the other side. Nodding her head she waited for us to gather around. We stepped through the portal and into the Heavens; right at the base of the big Ivory stone steps etched into the mountain. The two giant stone Angels that stood as a door were still the same as they were the last time I was here. "WOW" The boys said; as we walked up the stairs to stand at the feet of the giant Angels. "Yeah I know wait till you see the inside." I told them with a small smile on my face. It was nice to be able to see their faces light up like kids in a candy store in the midst of everything we were facing. I knocked on the stone tablets that were placed between the two statues and waited.

It took just a few seconds for those stone doors to swing inward. I was expecting to see Ares again. Since he was the one that had greeted me the last time I had showed up here. Instead Edam was standing there with his hair ruffled; looking very concerned at our sudden appearance. "What are you doing here?" The look of concern on his face had me frowning. It was as if he didn't want me to be standing on the steps of one of my own homes. I was about to speak what was on my mind when Scarlet stepped in. "We need to speak to the Counsel, and the sooner the better." She told Edam with a look in her eye that said don't test me.

Edam moved back to allow us to pass by him as he closed the doors behind him. He looked like a deer caught in the headlights and I had a feeling it had to do with Hermes. The knots in my stomach were telling me that my hunch was not that far off. We walked through the halls past the room of scrolls; toward the inner chamber with the fire pit that I had addressed the counsel on my last visit. I was shaking from the inside out; knowing that what I was about to tell everyone would send widespread panic in every direction. I just hoped there would be some way to stop this madness before innocent people were slaughtered by that monster. I had seen Typhon marking his kills with what looked like ancient runes. I didn't know if it was a spell, or just his signature. My gut said it was a spell and that the outcome would be worse than the actual murders. Crossing my fingers I held my head up and took a deep breath. We were mere feet from the chamber and I needed to get my nerves under control before I faced the room full of Gods and the one God that I was coming to hate more by the second.

Apollo, Ares, Zeus, and a few others were sitting in their chairs around the fire pit. Hermes was standing in a ring that looked like it was draining him of his powers. Zeus was staring at him with daggers in his eyes. I could tell that something big had happened; Edam went to stand beside Hermes which had me raising my eyebrow.

If I didn't know any better I would have thought that Edam was standing up for my father. Why on earth he would do that I have no clue. At the moment I was not going to worry about where Edam's loyalties laid; I had to focus on the reasons for my visit. He could be dealt with later. Zeus turned from his seat to look over at us; his eyes light with pride and love. He was happy to seem me; which was a big relief at least I had earned his trust. "Andras' What a lovely surprise." "What brings you here?" Zeus asked me; as if he was not sitting in the room to discipline my father at this very moment.

I slowly swallowed and looked over at my little make shift crew. I hadn't even told them why I was so freaked out when we left Morpheus home. "I came here. We came here; because I had a vision which led me to the home of the God of Dreams." "I went to find out if what I was seeing was a past event or one still to come." I told the white headed god before me. "An dear what did you find out?" Zeus asked me patiently as if he knew how scared I was. "I found out many things; one this has already happened before, but it will happen again if we do not do something to stop it."

"Typhon has been released" I stated. Zeus grabbed the arms of his chair and roared. I took a step back as he rose from his seat. "Lies!" He said as he took steps toward me. Scarlet and the boys placed their selves between us; like that was really going to stop him. "I assure you she is not lying." Scarlet stated. With that Zeus stopped as if the wind had been knocked out of him. "How? Who?" Zeus asked. I looked over his shoulder at Hermes; who had his head bowed. I didn't know if it was from the punishment he had already received or because of the crime he had committed.

"Hermes released him with some type of Seal. I saw the images myself when I went to see Morpheus." I told Zeus. "Innocents, along with Hybrids and any child that is created from the Gods, Fae or other races are in danger." "He will start slaughtering them soon; I saw images of him painting symbols on the dead." "We have to stop him."

The Gods just looked at each other as they were in shock. I was sure that it was a shock. No one thought that this monster would ever escape the prison Zeus had created for him. The Next thing I knew was that Hermes was dangling three feet off the ground as Zeus had his hand wrapped around his throat. "You will regret everything you have ever done; I promise you that you will regret being created when I am done with you." Zeus told the man that had fathered me.

I watched in silence as his face paled and the look of fright registered across his face. "Where is Typhon?" Zeus as my father as he held him suspending in the air. Hermes coughed and sputtered as he tried to catch enough air to speak. "He.... Is... uh..." "He... Is... At Capreae"

With that Zeus dropped him in a heap on the ground. He turned to look at Ares who had risen from his seat and had come to stand beside me. Edam was fuming as he stared at Ares from across the room. Those two had serious issues brewing between them. Whatever they were; it was not time to address them. "Take them and go." "I will meet you there." Zeus told Ares. He had a look of rage mixed with sorrow in his eyes. His eyes landed on me; and I saw a sparkle of pride, he squeezed my hand and just stared at me for a moment.

"I'm Staying here; I will be no help on the

Island of the Sirens." Scarlet and Slater both said at the same time. I looked them for a moment before nodding and turning to my guys. I knew they were going with me; I just hoped the Sirens song would not affect them. Being what they were it shouldn't but one could never tell. With that Ares had us all lock hands and we vanished from sight. Breaking the speed of sound was an understatement.

The loud boom echoed of the Ocean; causing wave after wave to crash into the small island we were now standing on. "Here this will help keep the music from affecting you." Ares said as he handed Demonic and Kyle some clear looking putty. I was a woman so I didn't have anything to worry about. I just hoped that if we came across any of the mer-people the would be willing to help us take down the monster Hermes had unleashed.

Crossing my fingers, I waited for Ares to lead the way. I took a look around at our new surroundings; this place was a lot like the sea I had just visited in Otherworld. Except the sand was a snow white, the water was sapphire blue and there was purple and red flower growing all over moss covered rocks.

The Cliff line was jagged and steep with a small pathway etched into its winding side. I could see a couple caves dotted along the coast far ahead of us; and what looked like a small village. Smoke was pouring out in a angry black cloud coming from one of the small homes.

People were screaming in the distance and I had an idea that I knew what they were screaming about. I just hoped my gut was wrong this time. I pointed in the direction of the fire; just as I watched a flash go by me at rocket speed. Ares didn't even wait for us; he charged ahead right into the screaming crowds. Kyle, Demonic and I had to run to catch up. Time we got there Ares was coming out of the home with two small children and a woman. Soot covered his face and forearms; a look of anger was on his sharp features.

He was setting the small children down just as a woman came running up to wrap her arms around them; tears steaming down her face. "Who did this?" Ares asked the woman as she clung to her children for dear life. She was shaking to bad to speak; she lifted her arm and pointed. We all turned in the direction her boney finger had jetted towards to see a symbol etched into the rock. It was a death rune; a giant black hook was etched in a cruel manner on the exposed stone.

It could only mean one thing that Typhon was truly here and he had help. Hel was in on this little scheme; I knew that the deal she made with Hermes had to have been bigger than just getting her throne back. She was the one that had giving him the seal that had opened the cage. I knew that whole heartedly now.

A roar was released from Ares mouth, that left no question who he was to anyone standing with in a hundred mile radius. I shivered as I knew the wrath that could and probably would follow if something didn't happen to calm him down soon. I reach out and gingerly placed my hand on his shoulder; the next thing I knew he had scooped me up and was kissing me.

I was struggling for air and pushing against

his body for what seemed like an eternity. When he finally released me; he had a stupid grin on his face. At least he seemed calmer now. I would have punched the crap out of him if I didn't think it would cause a war to break out. The last thing these people needed was more heartache.

"Mommy; where is Aaron?" The young girl that Ares had just rescued asked from the heap she was in on the ground. I snapped my head toward her and her mother; just as wailing sobs broke loose from a small rock in the ocean waters. A siren was screaming; Ares grabbed my hand, leaving Kyle and Demonic to find out who Aaron was and what happened. As we raced toward the little island were the mermaid sat. Her hair was the color of seaweed. A light green hue colored her skin. Blue and green scales covered her legs. She did not have a flipper; so I guess the human pictures were off a tad. She was clawing at her arms as she sat screaming in what could only be explained as pain. Ares placed his hand on her arm to get her attention; she looked up at him with sand colored eyes full of moaning. Whatever had caused her such pain was taking a toll on her in more than one way. Sirens were not seen in broad daylight; yet this one was just sitting in the sun. "He took her." was the only words she muttered before she started screaming again.

The painful wailing was starting to hurt my ears; I could only imagine what it was doing to the mortals on the little island. Ares scooped up the Siren and placed her into the water. He whispered into her ear; and I watched her head bow. Soon she was emerged beneath the ocean once more. We returned to the boys; to learn that Aaron was the woman's only son. He was also the child of Zeus. Having no magic and there for was raised as a mere mortal. She thought he was safe.

They had been gathering crabs when this winged beast with the tail of snake swooped down and grabbed him right off the sandy beach. The woman said that he had flown off toward a cave in the distance. One that have been believed to be the home of a griffin; no one in the whole village was even willing to go in it due to it.

The griffin was a giant bird that was said to understand human speech and obey whatever command was given to them by their masters. However, on they also had a habit of doing just the opposite of what they were told. The legends about them had described them as all kinds of raptors, including dragons with bird like wings and the head of a dog. Sometimes they were described as shape shifters that could turn into men. They were suppose to have sharp talons that could tear apart a grown man, fire for breath and a body of a giant dragon, that scales. Shielded it from being killed easily.

If Typhon was hiding out in the home of a griffin; there could only two reasons why. He was the master of the giant bird or knew everyone else would be scared to follow him. Either case made our situation more dire. We were going to need a lot of help to capture him. I just hoped the two children were still alive. The Siren had sounded so heart broken and helpless as she sat crying on the large rock. My own heart was breaking as I listened to her sobs.

We had to do something to stop all of this. I just wish I knew what that something was. Ares stood staring at large cave system that was in the sheer Cliffside. I couldn't help but wonder what he was thinking as he stood there quietly assessing the rocks. My mind kept lingering to the deep kiss he had delivered to me; yet I knew there was no reason for the sudden blush to be running up my neck. It was not like it meant anything.

"We are not waiting on Zeus and the others to arrive. If we do it will be too late." "I just hope they are here in time to put Typhon back under the mountain before he releases more dangerous beings than himself." Ares spoke to us. Demonic was starting to pale a bit more it was as if he was getting sick from the very thought of what we were up against. It took a couple seconds for me to realize that it was the sun that was making him sick. He was a vampire after all; even a changeling vampire had to stay out of the sun as much as possible. I forgot how the sun here was different than that of the one in Otherworld. "Demonic are you okay?" I asked my friend as we stood there waiting for Ares to lead us. "Fine as

Rain." Demonic lied as he looked at me with eyes of swirling colors. He needed to feed and soon or it would be bad. Ares seem to notice what was happening and did the most unthinkable thing. He held his hands out in front of him toward Demonic.

Go ahead I have plenty." He told Demonic as he stood there with his palms facing up. Demonic seemed to falter before he jumped forward and wrapped his mouth around Ares wrist as his hands circled around Ares wrist to hold it still. He did pierce the skin of the god before us just hovered over it and allowed the energy to recharge him. I had never seen Demonic feed off anything before; and I was expecting blood and gore. So, shocked was an understatement as I stood there with my mouth agape as I watched these two in an embrace that would have had lovers swooning. It took about four minutes before the color returned to Demonic's cheeks. The feeding didn't seem to do anything to Ares; I guess being a God had its advantages. Rubbing his wrists together Ares looked back at the cliff line. "Are you all ready?" He asked us. There was dread in his voice as he looked back at us. I don't think even the god of war was ready for the tasks we had ahead of us.

Nodding we started to follow him up the steep path that was cut into the cliff line. Past the little village; the sand grinding underfoot with each step we took. The wind was starting to kick up the closer to the cliff line we got. It was going to be a slow going trip up the side of it. Having to grab a hold of little cubby holes in the cliff its self to support our bodies as we inched forward toward the firs cave. Lightening flashed in the sky; thunder rolled across the ground causing the ground beneath us to rumble with it.

As we looked up toward the first cave we saw three of the most noted Gods standing before us. Zeus with his flowing white hair stood holding the same seal that I had seen Hermes using to release this monster. He was dressed in an ancient roman warriors outfit. It looked as if it had been hammered from fine gold. The sunlight was enhancing the outfit to the point it looked as if it was glowing and alive.

Next to Zeus was Bellona, the Roman

Goddess of war. She had long flowing red hair that seemed to be the living essence of fire; her eyes were a deep sea green. She was dressed in a silver toga with silver sandals upon her feet. She had a silver helmet on her head with a white feathery thing coming from the top of it. She was armed with a flaming sword; and looked as if she was ready to slay a dragon were she stood.

Next to her was Morrigu; the phantom queen of the Celtic people. Known as the goddess of battle, and strife. She had long black hair with tints of blue in it. Her eyes were a deep brown with honey tones; she was dressed in a black toga that seemed to be covered in crow feathers. Just when we thought we were going to have to go in alone; a miracle happens. And we are standing toe to toe with some of the most powerful beings the world has ever known. Thankfully they were on our side. We finally made it to the mouth of the cave were the trio stood waiting.

Heavy breath heaving from our lungs; we took a moment to catch our breath. We as in Kyle, Demonic and I; this little hike seemed to have no effect on Ares at all. Which was frustrating to say the least. The woman didn't speak they just stood there waiting for us to regain our composure. I was in awe at the greatness of these women; and the calm presence they seemed to carry with them. It had finally started feeling like we had a chance to correct things. Zeus clapped Ares on the back and smiled at him as a father would.

Pride coming off him in waves as he looked from him to me. I didn't know what had caused the look but it made me feel tingles from my head to my toes. "We are going to go into each of these caves until we flush him out." Zeus told us. "He is inside with two children, on is the Sirens daughter and the other is your son." Ares told Zeus. Fire lit in his eyes, as he looked at the gapping cave ahead of us. "I believe I know what he is doing with his kills.

The symbols Andras' saw were a death spell." "One that raises the dead, or forgotten." Morrigu said with a voice that sounded like a crow cawing in a field. Erie and beautiful at the same time; there was no other voice like it

I was sure. It was that quiet sound you hear as you walk through a deep forest. I didn't like the thought of the dead waking up; or whatever the forgotten ones were either. The children were the only thing I cared about. We had to stop him from harming them. Too many of us depended upon what happened right here and now. Holding my breath I waited for Zeus to say something; he had gone silent the moment the goddess had started speaking. If he was human beads of sweat would have been pouring off his forehead. I had a feeling that whom ever the forgotten ones were they were worse than the beast we were soon to face. "We will stop him Zeus." Bellona stated her fiery red hair blowing in the wind.

Her piercing green eyes had a look of determination in them. Kyle had been silent most of the trip since we had left the Undines; I looked back at my friend to see his eyes glowing gold and a look of feral need passing across his expression. He was ready for the hunt; it was calling to him. As if my thoughts had formed into a being I watched as Kyle shape shifted into a giant white wolf. He paced back and forth at my side; anticipation dripping off of him in waves.

Ares seemed to have notice the sudden change; as he turned from Zeus to look at me. Raising an eyebrow he looked down to see Kyle now in Wolf form standing head high at my waist. "We are ready." I told Zeus as I gathered my chain of justice and hooked it to my wrist band. Everyone was ready; hopefully we would get to the kids in time. I could not bare it if their blood was spilt. I had enough shame hanging off of me; from the deeds Hermes had already done I did not need two innocent children's lives to add to the pile.

We turned and entered the gapping mouth of the first cave. It was pitch black inside; it smelled of decay, and death of animals. Mildew clung to the cavern walls. Bones were scattered across the dirt covered cavern floor. Crystals and mineral deposits hung down like giant daggers. We zigzagged our way threw the huge rock formations; wading threw puddles of water that had pooled along the cavern floor in spots. Bellona's sword was a glow like a torch lighting our way through the cavern. The small chamber we were in widened and forked into two rooms.

We split into two groups and moved forward to search the two rooms. More bones were scattered along the ground; something had made this their den. I had a feeling that something was the griffin. Yet, there were no other signs of life except for the bones we were walking upon. Kyle, Ares, Demonic and I had come to the end of our room. After searching along the walls for any sign of air seeping in, we walked back toward the entrance.

Emerging from the tiny cavern room; we walked into the room that Zeus and the two Goddess were searching. It seemed like we were coming up short; when from the far end of the room Morrigu called out. "Over here." Walking with the rest of the group I let the silver chain in my hand swing loosely at my side. Kyle's nose was to the ground as we got to the backside of the room. Bellona was holding her sword up so we could see where Morrigu was. She was knelt down by a small crack in the wall. Air was blowing into the room from the crack. I figured it was just a pocketed air flow. Kind of like the ones back on earth.

It's just a crack that allows fresh air in; but I was wrong in thinking that. Bellona shoved her sword into the small grove at the top of the crack and hitting the hilt; we heard a soft pop. The crack turned out to be a doorway; stone against stone rubbed against each other as the doorway rolled back to reveal a tunneled walk way. A small lantern was hanging on the wall on an iron hook. Taking the book of matches out of my jeans pocket. I struck it against the wall; lighting the lantern. I turned up the flame; and held it out in front of us. The walls were wet from the recent rain; dampness hung in the air around us.

We walked on down through the narrow corridor letting the light from the lantern illuminate the walls around us. The tunnel seemed to go on forever; soft cries echoed off the walls around us. I stopped in the middle of the passage and listened. Zeus and the others were right behind me. I turned to look over my shoulder to see if I was the only one hearing the soft pleas for help. Morrigu nodded her head and inclined it to the side.

Kyle's ears were twitching back and forth; letting me know with his eyes aglow that he to hear the soft whimpers. That was all I needed to forge ahead. Picking up the pass I walked as fast as I was able. Squeezing sideways when the passage tightened in spots. It didn't take us long to get toward the source of the sounds. The tunnel burst open into a large cavern room; Torches light the room casting deep shadows off the walls. Making even our own look larger than they truly were.

Tied to a metal alter upon a stone slab was the two small children; head to toe they were laid out, so that they could not even look at each other. The female child was the one whom had been sobbing. Her strawberry blonde hair was matted from the dirty muck of the cave its self. Her soft sea foam green eyes sparkled in the light of the torches. Her skin was as white as the full moon; and she had the same small fish like scales on her legs as that of her mother. The pearl and pink scales were flaking off in spots from where the ropes were tied to tight around her.

The boy that happened to be one of Zeus sons had wavy light brown hair that had small streaks of gold sprinkled through out it. He was dressed in commoners clothing. His pants were tied with twine, and he wore no shoes upon his feet. He was fighting silently against his ropes; anger shown on his young face. He looked just like his father; the same glint was held in his grey blue eyes as he worked to free himself from his binding.

There was no one else in the room that we could see; yet, I knew that Typhon would not leave them alone for long. I could hear what sounded like wind coming from a corridor at the far left of the room. Either the wind was really kicking up or it was the griffin flying around outside. Either way we needed to hurry; and get these children to safety so we could capture Typhon.

Zeus and Ares had ran to the table; they were starting to take the bindings off the young ones while the rest of us hunted for any clues that would tell us were their capture was. I had been so caught up in finding these kids that I had not even realized that Edam was not with Zeus when he showed up outside the cave.

It had given me pause for a moment; after what I had seen on Mount Olympia. I made a note to find out where he was as soon as we got out of the cavern. Something told me that I was not going to be happy with the answer when I did receive them. Yet, at the moment I really couldn't bring myself to dwell on it to long.

Morrigu and Bellona standing over at the far left of the room where I had heard the wind like sound. Morrigu was drawling strange markings in the dirt as Bellona stood guard. Kyle was sniffing the ground around the edges of the walls of the cavern with Demonic at his side. Demonic had his eyes closed as if he was listening for something we couldn't hear. He probably was for all I knew. I didn't know much about changeling vampires; I was just glad that he was my friend and that he was here with me this time. Kyle started to whimper and paw at the wall; he started trying to dig beneath it. I had no clue what he had found.

 I ran over to him and Demonic; just as Zeus and Ares gathered up the children in their arms. Bellona and Morrigu were following behind them at a fast pace. Morrigu had a raven perched on her hand; I was not even going to ask where it came from. I was not sure I really wanted to know. She was powerful in her own right enough so to have men both fear and love her. I was thankful that she was on our side in this war. As she always seemed to have a say in the way any war played out. Sightings of her on many a battle field had been recorded in history books both in Otherworld and on Earth.

"What is it Kyle; I asked the large wolf as I ran my hand through his fur. Trying to settle him; it only seemed to irritate him as he nipped at my hand to get me to stop. "He has found something; I think it's another room I'm not sure." Demonic told me from the other side of Kyle's large form. I looked at the wall; holding the lantern out in front of me, I could see strange markings carved into its surface. Much like the ones that Morrigu had been drawling in the dirt. I turned to her and motioned for her to come forward. "What are these?" I asked the Goddess. Her brown eyes dilated as she sucked in her breath.

She stared at the wall for a moment before speaking. "Protection runes. Same as the ones I was marking to keep Typhon out. Only someone skilled in my arts would know about these markings. I am sure that they were not made by Typhon." She finished saying. Running her hand over two of the runes she said something to soft for me to hear. I looked at the wall and saw the runes she had just touched glow under her touch.

Raising my hand I placed my hand over the runes to see if they would do the same for me. Instead I was greeted with a vision that had me on my knees.

I saw my mother and my self as a small child. I could hear her Shhing me and telling me that everything was going to be okay as she hide me behind a wall. I opened my eyes to see Zeus face to face with me; wiping the sweat of my brow. Concern etched into his face. He just stared at me as if he didn't know what else to do. "Another Vision?" Zeus asks me softly as he lifted me off my knees. "Yes; but it doesn't make any sense. It was the past; my past." I told the old god.

The sorrow I had seen in his eyes earlier in the day had returned; he turned his head to look at the two small children that Ares now cradled. Then he looked at Morrigu. Her black toga covered in raven feathers seem to be moving on its own; her eyes were still dilated as if she was reliving something long forgotten. "I didn't realize you were the one brought to me so many years ago." The Goddess said with a far off note in her voice.

The sound of a crow cawing from the perch of her hand drew my attention away from her for a second. When I looked back up at her face; I felt it all click as if I had been punched in the gut. It was here that my mother had run to hide from Hermes; it was here that she had been turned to stone. Why didn't I remember that Morrigu had been here too?

She had tried to save my mother; after Medusa cursed her to spend the next twenty yrs as a statue collecting dust. I looked back at the wall and closed my eyes; remembering how my mother had opened the door to hide me in the small chamber behind it. I ran my hand across the wall and felt the edges of a stone that seemed to be out of place with the smooth texture of the wall itself.

Pushing the stone I held my breath. A whoosh of air sounded as the wall pushed inward revealing a small room. Medusa's head was still lying in the corner of the room facing away from all of us thankfully. I almost cried at the sight of it. Here I thought there would never be a way to release my mother from the spell. The snakes upon her severed head were still very much alive and hissing as we all walked into the room. Morrigu ripped a piece of her toga off and handed it to me. "Wrap her head in this." She told me shoving the piece of fabric into my shaking hand. I slowly walked to it; I held the fabric out in front of me as I leaned forward and through the piece of fabric over the decapitated head. Scooping it up as the snakes hissed from underneath the confines of the cloth. I tied a knot in it and stood up. Fred had been sleeping in my shoulder bag since we had left my earthside apartment; it was time for him to wake up. Removing the sleepy gargoyle; I sat him on the ground by my feet.

Placing the cloth prison that now held the head of Medusa, in my shoulder bag I stood up.

Fred was rubbing his eyes and mumbling; what I figured were curse words as he didn't like to be woken up. Handing him a piece of bitterroot that I had been carrying in my pocket; I turned to look at the group of warriors that were now standing there in silent awe watching my fuzzy little pet dance for joy over the piece of root I had just given him.

"What, haven't you seen a gargoyle before?" I asked them. "Not in a very long time." Morrigu said in a breathy voice. "You should be proud to have such a protector." She told me with a look of awe. "Well, I can see that your trip to the Underworld has bought you some strong allies." Zeus said, with a smile on his lips. He seemed to be very proud of me. For what I hadn't a clue; I was just trying to do what I was suppose to do.

What anyone with my kind of gifts should do for anyone and everyone they meet. We had spent too much time in this cave; if we didn't get these kids out of here soon, then we would be battling Typhon with them present. It was time to go.

Chapter Twenty

As if thinking the ushered words; the sound of the wind kicked up sending it howling through the cave as if it were a thousand beasts. The force of it had us fighting to stand as we tried to exit the small chamber we had been gathered in. Ares had handed Kyle and Demonic the children.

The young siren clung to the large wolfs fur for dear life. While Demonic had the boy thrown over his shoulder in a fireman hold.

"Run! Get them back to the village now." Ares told the boys as they took off the way we had come. Morrigu, Bellona, Ares, Zeus and I headed toward the entrance at the back of the cave were Morrigu had placed the protection spell. We would be ready if anything tried to break through. Hopefully it would give the guys the time they needed to get the young ones to safety. Slinging the severed head that was now in my shoulder bag over my head. I made sure that it was close to my body. I couldn't loose it after all I had been through; it was the only change I had to help my mother.

Fred hopped along behind us, snorting threw his nose. Lighting bolts were shooting out all around him; and his fuzzy coat was sticking up in all directions as he sputtered and snorted beneath my feet. He did this the last time I had faced danger. I knew what was coming; but I was no where near as prepared as I had been when I was in the Underworld. Bellona tied back her hair with a leather strap; slapping her silver helmet in place she widened her stance and raised her sword. Morrigu's black toga was now a complete suit of armor from head to toe. She looked like she was in a feathered wet suit.

Her crow perched on her shoulder as she raised her hands above her head. Zeus held his lighting bolt at his side; sparks jumped of it and arched against the ground. I held my silver chain of justice loosely at my side. Ares had a bronze sword thrust out in front of him. We were ready for whatever was coming our way. Zeus had handed me the Seal; the same one that my father had used to open the mountain that had released this beast.

"When the time comes; we will use that together. For now keep it close to you." Zeus told me as he folded his hand around mine. Nodding my head I turned my hand over so I could see the palm sized stone. It had ancient markings on it that were almost so wore that you had to feel them more than see them. Stuffing the stone into my jean pocket; I widened my stance as a gust of wind came wailing through the corridor.

It was a now or never kind of moment; we had to bring an end to this and make sure it would never happen again. A Banshee's cry sounded echoing off the walls. Shivers ran down my spine as I listened to mournful sound. He was coming; I didn't know what would happened but I was hoping we would survive this all. At first nothing but the wind came pushing into the cavern; then the rocks around the entrance that we had protected started to crack and give way. Piles of dust and rubble sprayed down around us; yet, we still did not move. A large popping sound was coming from the outside of the cave.

Cracking like a giant whip against the side of

the stone over and over again. Something was trying to break the barrier that Morrigu had put in place. A deaf defining roar pierced the already screeching wind. I felt as if my ears were going to start bleeding from the pressure of it.

"Brace yourselves." Ares said as he raised his bronze sword above his head. Fred was creating a static electrical field around all of us as he continued to hop about spitting and snorting. Little lightening bolts shot from the outside of his bubble.

Zeus aimed his Bolt of energy at the opening of the cave as we waited for impact. The screeching wind was still pouring into the cavern. The Banshee scream sounded louder as the wind started to quiet down.

We stood there listening to the mournful sound as everything around us became still. The beast slammed into the side of the wall again, causing a large crack to leak in sunlight. We had been inside the underground tunnel for a will; so the sudden burst of light had me shielding my eyes.

A warriors' scream tore through the air just as a giant vipers tail swished through the crack. Ares took aim and swung his bronze sword over his head; slicing a wide gap into the serpent tail. An eerie roar pierced the air. I snapped the silver chain at my side like a giant whip; knowing that I could not pass judgment on a being such as this; yet, I could still inflict pain. The silver chain sizzled as it hit the flesh of the giant snake's tail. Searing the same spot that Ares had just sliced open.

Causing another roar to escape the beast. Morrigu had her head thrown back, her arms high above her head as she spoke in a foreign tongue. A dark cloud gathered over head like an inky well. It slithered around the tail of the beast as if it was a giant black rope. On she screamed out her commands as the crow started to caw along with her. Bellona aimed her flaming sword and swung causing the end of the tail to catch aflame.

Zeus flung bolts of lightening over and over again out of the crack in the wall at the beast. Screeching and roars were followed by giant nails that scraped the rocks. Just when I thought it was over. That we had made the giant beast fall. The sounds of wings were heard and it slammed into the entrance once again. The crack became a gapping whole as I got my first full on look of the monster.

He looked just like he had in the dream tunnel with Morpheus; only angrier. His giant hands tore at the rocks and rubble that had at one time been a wall. His eyes were wild; looking like they were lit with fire from within. He locked eyes with Zeus and roared right into our faces.

Hate was dripping off him. Visible for everyone to see.

Zeus motioned for us all to move back; trying to lure Typhon further into the room so we could use the seal. He took the bait thinking we were running away. After all Predators love to chase prey; its common instinct for them. Backing up we gave the beast passage to enter into the small room. He would fit this we already knew. He had been living up here plotting his revenge since my father had released him.

Swiping at us with his dagger like claws he screamed some more. I don't think he could even speak the human tongue. He was a creation that should never have excited. Yet here he stood doing just that. He was wanting to make Zeus pay; but more than that he wanted to make all of us pay for his suffering. He was trying to raise the forgotten ones; which would have caused us all to be wiped out. That was something we could not allow to happen. In his angry fit he had moved closer to the metal table that we had found the children tied to. We got him as close as we could to the back wall that held the little room my mother had hide me in as a child.

Slowly we spread our group apart so that we were standing on either side of the hidden door. I placed my back against the wall; with my free hand I searched for the lock that would open it. The stone gave a soft click under my hand as I pushed it inward. The door sprung inward. I throw out the chain of justice again; this time wrapping it around his chest. Zeus and Ares on either side of me began to tug the chain as

Morrigu cast another dark cloud that pushed against Typhon from the back. Bellona swung her fire sword at his face casing him to slither on his snake like tail. It took sometime before we were able to get him in to the little room; but we managed. As soon as we had him inside I slapped the hidden stone that would shut the door and gave the chain of justice a quick tug releasing it from his body.

We had trapped him inside the small chamber but we would not be able to hold him there for long. "NOW!" Zeus said with his hand pointed at me. I grabbed the Ancient stone from my pocket and slapped it into his hand. He wrapped my free hand in his and nodded toward the others. We locked hands one by one until we had completed the circle. Leaving Zeus and Morrigu holding the stone against the wall to complete the circle.

A boom broke through the room causing the ground beneath our feet to shake. Silver liquid poured down the wall that held the hidden door. Around the Seal; covering the entire length of the wall. It hardened into a solid sheet of metal molding to the door. The metal glowed in the dim light of the cave. Sizzling as it cooled into the prison that would hold

Typhon from now till the end of time. It wasn't until the sizzling and glowing had stopped; that we broke our circle that had bonded us to this deed. Zeus removed the seal and laid it upon the metal table. Taking his lightening bolt he slammed into the ancient stone breaking it into four pieces. Gathering the pieces up he handed me one; keeping one for him self, as he handed the other two pieces to Bellona and Morrigu. "This way no one will ever be able to release him again." Zeus said as he placed the last piece in the Goddess hand. I smiled a little; it had been a long day.

We had one this battle; that was a great thing, yet I knew there would be more to come. Something told me that Hermes had done a lot more damage than just releasing Typhon from his prison. We would find out but that would be saved for another day. Turning I looked over my shoulder at the new cage we had created to lock away this beast. It would be a long time before he would ever see light again. I would make damn sure of it.

Ares patted my back to gain my attention; it was time to leave. I had Medusas' head and could finally start working on releasing my mother from her curse; the innocents were safe for now. Nothing could have been better than that. We walked back down the tunneled hallway and out into the light of day. I stood there staring out at the ocean just breathing in the salt air. It was beautiful here; peaceful and safe. The feeling of Gloom was gone leaving on a sense of contentment in its wake.

Walking back down the sandy path toward the village; Fred still sputtering at my feet as if he was trying to carry on a conversation. Maybe he was; Maybe. I reach down and scooped him up scratching the tuff of fur behind I murmured my thanks to my fuzzy little companion. He really had been a blessing. Kyle and Demonic greeted us with large smiles upon their faces. "Are you ready to go home?" They asked me.

"In a bit; we have a few stops first." I told the guys with a smile. It felt good to hunt down evil and win. It felt good to be standing along side of beings as powerful as Zeus and feel like I was just as strong. Ares, Bellona, Zeus, and Morrigu were talking a few feet behind us. I looked back to see what was going on. I guess we were parting ways with the beautiful goddess's. I ran back toward them to thank them only to be greeted with a smile as they vanished from sight. I stopped and stared at the spots were they had just been. The words of appreciation still on my lips. Well I would thank them as soon as I saw them again I thought. Zeus smiled at me. "Are you ready to collect your Aunt and Brother?" He asked me in a father like tone.

"Yes." I told him as I returned his smile. With that we were back inside the inner chamber room were Hermes had been receiving his punishment. Edam, Scarlet, and Slater were standing near the fire pit when we returned. Scarlet turned and ran into my arms hugging me for dear life. "You're safe." She whispered. "I know." I told her in reply. I had so much to tell her, but it was going to have to wait a little while.

I still had things to sort out and I didn't want to get her hopes up. "Welcome back Sister."

Slater said as he hugged me. Edam just stared at me as if he had lost his best friend. I didn't know why he was looking at me that way and right now I really didn't care. I was just happy to be surrounded by loved ones, knowing everyone was safe for now. "Hermes has been dealt with; he will not be harming anyone any time soon." Zeus told me as he took his seat by the fire. "As for Hel I will make sure that Hades knows of her deeds and that she too is punished." Nodding my head I stood there in awe. I guess you could say I was still shell shocked at the resent turn of events. "Andras." Ares said as he smiled at me before leaving the room. Edam still didn't speak just stood there watching me as I gathered my friends and loved ones so we could depart for home. It had been a long day and I was looking forward to a hot shower and some comfy clothing.

To Be Continued.....

Notes from Author:

First off thank you all for taking the time to read Andras' Journeys. I hope you enjoy reading it as much as I enjoyed creating this world of characters.

Second this story was originally four separate books; each with their own cover. If you were one of the lucky few that own a copy of the separated books; hold on to them. They are one of a kind and will never again be produced in the same manner again.

Sneak Peak At book 2 in the Andras' MoonRiver Series.

Enlightened

PROLOGUE:

Ares looked out of the stain glassed window of his room at the top of the Mount. He kept Dreaming about Andras' and the last battle they had faced. The feel of her lips was still felt on his skin. He knew he would have to fight Edam if he ever found out what happened. Yet, he could not bring himself to care. She was the most beautiful and passionate creature he had ever laid eyes on. Edam was already pin eying away after her; without any prevail. She didn't trust him; it was clearly visible in her eyes.

Watching Andras' gather up the head of Medusa made him realize what he had to do. Ares had to find a way to help her reverse the curse. Then and only then could he win her love.

www.ingramcontent.com/pod-product-compliance
Lightning Source LLC
Chambersburg PA
CBHW080750250626
47162CB00011B/3080